Who Shot Ya 3

Renta

Lock Down Publications and
Ca$h Presents
Who Shot Ya 3
A Novel by Renta

Lock Down Publications
P.O. Box 870494
Mesquite, Tx 75187

Visit our website
www.lockdownpublications.com

Copyright 2019 by Who Shot Ya 3 Renta

First Edition July 2018
Printed in the United States of America

Lock Down Publications
Like our page on Facebook: Lock Down Publications @
www.facebook.com/lockdownpublications.ldp
Cover design and layout by: **Dynasty Cover Me**
Book interior design by: **Shawn Walker**
Edited by: **Lashonda Johnson**

Stay Connected with Us!

Text **LOCKDOWN** to 22828 to stay up-to-date with new releases, sneak peeks, contests and more…

Submission Guideline.

Submit the first three chapters of your completed manuscript to ldpsubmissions@gmail.com, subject line: Your book's title. The manuscript must be in a .doc file and sent as an attachment. The document should be in Times New Roman, double-spaced and in size 12 font. Also, provide your synopsis and full contact information. If sending multiple submissions, they must each be in a separate email.

Have a story but no way to send it electronically? You can still submit to LDP/Ca$h Presents. Send in the first three chapters, written or typed, of your completed manuscript to:

LDP: Submissions Dept
Po Box 870494
Mesquite, Tx 75187

DO NOT send original manuscript. Must be a duplicate.

Provide your synopsis and a cover letter containing your full contact information.

Thanks for considering LDP and Ca$h Presents.

Dedications

This book is for the young cats out there in them trenches. The young women out there livin' fast. It's more to life than the streets. Take it from me...a dope fiend's son.

Acknowledgments

I think the mysteries of life are found within the things one chooses to believe in. Daily I find myself praying and searching for God in all that I experience. I don't know where He's at, but first, I want to give my appreciation to Him. If it wasn't for His grace, I'd be lost in the sauce or buried in the soil. Secondly, they say behind every great man is a great woman and I'm starting to agree.

Alexandria, you're my potna and I'm happy for you. We're on a different journey now. Beyond that, I truly appreciate the love and hard work that you invest. I salute you for being a Souljah and stickin' by a nigga when you coulda been in the wind. I owe you with each heartbeat, Queen. Mama Helen, Mama Leah, Aunt Debbie, Aunt San, Kim, Nisha, Terricka, Kris, Kanika, Cleo, Shae and the rest of the women in the family—me and the Queen send our love.

Cash—big homie, you gave me this opportunity to shine and I'm gonna hold it down for you and the LDP Fam. We up one, homie, and they ain't fuckin' wit' us. Jamila, wud up!

To my dawgs…my potnas…my crip niggas…Too Black, Bennie 'Papa' Price, Dunte, Yap, Kalum, Rah Rah Cody 'Lil C' Caesar, Thug, Lil K, Big J, Lele, TuTu, T, Dead-End, Clifton 'Papa' Shorter, Lil Joe, Tonio Manuel, Dino, Earl Goldsmith, Lil Herb, Uncle Herb, Tito Herman Earl, Lil Archie, Scoobi, Lil Wydell, Papa Roach, Juvie, Pablo, Ricky Govan, J-Rok Mcintosh, Lil Red, D-Ray, Scoobi, Carlos, Big Compton, Head, all you niggas and the ones I ain't name; y'all know the love's solid and I 'preciate you boys for thuggin' wit' me in the thick of shit. We here!

Lashonda Johnson, sup, ma! I know we don't see eye to eye on a lot, but that's kool. Your work is worth the headache. Lol!

Last but never least, my fans! All those that support my craft and grind. All y'all who rock with Renta and get my shit hot off the press, I do it for y'all. There's no me without y'all and as we climb to the top, I want y'all to know that it's a pleasure to thug with you. This the 'Dope Ain't The Only Way To Eat Movement. With Respect, Renta!

Renta

Chapter One

~Pain~

"Daddy, this silly ass nigga gave me his gun. Let me do him with his own shit—please?" Tessa whined like she'd climax at any moment from the anticipation of busting my head. The element of surprise was on their side, and it must have been written all over my face because Twisted stared at me with a knowing smirk as if he could read my mind. The shock of being caught with my pants down simmered, and like a computer; my mind registered my predicament. Discreetly, I analyzed my surroundings in search of an escape from the web I'd blindly walked right into. There was nothing but a few huge oak trees and a wide expanse of open country. If I'd tried to make a break for it, I'd only get whacked before I made it behind one of those trees. Not to mention before I'd taken two steps this snake bitch would have put two in my melon. Returning my gaze to Twisted, the first thing I noticed was the mini uzi he clutched at his side. When he got the drop on me the shit took me so fast I must not have noticed.

Twisted looked demonic as he said, "What you think, homie? You rather die by the hands of the nigga that's gonna erase your entire bloodline from the face of the earth or by the hands of the bitch that fucked you to your death? Literally!" he proposed as if either choice was better than the other. "Choose your poison, cuz," he hissed, inching the uzi closer to his face then pulling the lever back ensuring that the first round was ready to spit.

Something was off about homie—something deep, something mental. I watched him close his eyes as if he was about to pray. He used the short barrel of the compact gun to scratch his temple as he mumbled to himself. Even though I couldn't decipher what he was saying, I noticed the bottom parts of his eyelids were pink and his nose slightly leaked a trail of red tainted liquid. A light went off in my head, homie was as high as an astronaut. Venom bled into my pupils as my eyes studied the dope fiend, ass nigga.

At that moment, I realized that helplessness was one of the worst feelings a man that's about something can feel, yet, instead of dwelling on the shit I couldn't change, I sucked in as much saliva as I could and spit in the bitch ass nigga direction.

"Fuck you, pussy boy!" I seethed. "What you think I'ma beg you not to get your hands dirty?"

Adrenaline coursed through my veins like someone injected them with actual flames. Sweat beaded on my flesh as I growled my next words— "They say all dawgs go to Heaven, nigga. I'm ready for the family reunion! Let's get it done, pussy!"

The gangsta in me took prestige over the fear of death. Without warning, I turned my back to the sucka as a sign of disrespect. I'd rather die by the hands of a snake bitch that set me up, at least my dawgs would learn the lesson that the OG Cash and Nene Capri tried to teach in his series '*Trust No Bitch*'. Once I was face to face with Tessa's serpent ass, she tried to mask the surprise and fear of my gangsterisms, but just as any other predator, *I sensed it*. A shift in the atmosphere alerted me to the fact that Twisted had stepped closer.

"Whoa, lil' buddy, I advise you to be easy on all them sudden movements; my fingers damn near applied to much pressure on this trigger." He snickered from right behind me confirming my suspicions.

Without acknowledging the faggot, I allowed my vision to focus on the only female that's *ever* pulled the wool over my eyes. As our eyes danced, flashbacks of our every encounter leading up to this point flashed in my mental. Each scene that played caused my eyes to blink rapidly. *Every time I fucked her! The moment she set the stage by acting as if she wanted to be exclusive. The very first night I stepped to her!* It was all a part of their play, they lured me to this exact moment; *the ultimate deception*.

As I reflected, through my peripheral, I observed the lil' ese bitch that drove me to my doom circling us like a vulture. At that moment I figured if I was gonna live to chase another bag, I needed to make my next move my best move!

"Damn, bitch, you one of the most clueless females I've ever met." I confused the moment. Like a lunatic I stepped right up to the tool she aimed in my face. Once the barrel kissed my forehead, I smiled wickedly. "You're in cahoots with the same nigga that murked your *flesh and blood*—Mena, because she found out that he's the one behind Lil' Joe's murder."

Confliction showed on her face, revealing that I'd touched a tender spot, or at least added substance to what she already felt. Small beads of sweat formed on her nose. Hope sparked within me, my gut was right. I figured that Tessa's emotions were my greatest escape plan. Though *every* woman master's manipulation in one form or another, the one thing that couldn't be hidden *efficiently* is their heart and emotions. I counted on that fact at that moment, shit was crucial.

Tessa slyly glanced over my shoulder before returning her eyes to me and saying, "Nigga, miss me with the head games. You're not gonna weasel yourself outta this so save it, playboy!"

Laughter erupted from deep within. It was a nervous reaction, but to inquiring minds, it was a sign I didn't give a fuck. Dark clouds rolled in front of the sun, briefly giving the scenery a grayish tint.

I looked Tessa directly in the eyes. "Tessa, you're a smart broad, think about it. Remember that time you couldn't get in touch with this nigga for a *week*?"

I watched as she studied me to see where I was going. Curiosity kills more than cats and as the memory dawned on her, her facial expression revealed it. Twisted must have noticed it as well because before I could continue my spill, the impact of the steel contacting with the back of my head dropped me to one knee. Blood instantly poured from the gash as I tried my damnest to get my equilibrium back in check. Using my right hand, I reached behind my head to assess the damage, to my surprise, the blood flow wasn't heavy and the cut was small. My vision cleared just enough that I could focus on Tessa. Twisted whispered evilly through clenched teeth as skepticism played on Tessa's face.

"Bitch ass nigga, you're gonna die for your sins. That nigga Joe was my loc and for a drop of his blood I'ma fill a tub with yours!"

I could feel the ill intent dripping from each word as Tessa's eyes flicked back and forth between me and him. I could feel that she was wrestling between what she'd already believed, and her *want* to believe in her dude. Nervousness made her handshake; I could tell she was standing at the edge of indecision. All it would take was a bump to push her over the edge. The Hispanic girl appeared behind her. Through blurred vision I watched her wrap her arms around Tessa's waist as if that was the most natural thing between them. She placed her face in the crook of Tessa's neck and intricately ran her tongue up her flesh until her lips reached her right ear.

She stared at me from over Tessa's shoulder as she whispered just loud enough for me to hear, "Kill him, Mami! Kill him for, Twisted. Kill him for, *Mena and Joe*." Tessa's eyes glazed over as the Mexican girl continued to speak strength in her ear.

The clock was running out on me, so I said, "Who else was missing this entire week, Tess?" I stretched my arms out wide as if they were wings. My hands and face were covered with so much blood that it looked as if I had been crucified. As it leaked into my eyes, I went in for the kill. "*Mena*—you ain't seen her since this nigga popped back up, huh?" I kept my eyes focused as I awaited the bullet that would end my life. I knew Twisted wouldn't let me keep playing my hand. "Mena's dead, Tessa and after *y'all* get me out the way, *they* gonna, do you. I can bet my life on it, that this Mexican bitch is more *his* friend than yours, huh?"

A light flicked in her eyes as the pieces snapped together. Her eyes left mine and settled on Twisted's. Tears clouded her vision, she slightly shook her head as if she was trying to shake them away. In an instant, shit got ugly. Her aim diverted at the same time Twisted must have realized her plan. Through bloodshot eyes I watched the scene play like a horror movie, Tessa threw her head back as hard as she could and head-butted the Hispanic girl.

The distraction was all I needed, I threw myself to the ground in an attempt to avoid the reapers plan for me, but before I could make it out of harm's way, heat rocked the side of my head. The impact was so powerful that my head snapped back, and I blacked out for a second. I fell face first and the only thing that prevented my teeth from being knocked out was the angle my head smashed against the ground. As soon as my face made contact with the earth my consciousness returned. My eyes snapped open as a heart-wrenching headache exploded in my head and made me shut them just as they opened.

I heard a scream of anguish that turned my blood cold as bullets flew over my head, and just as fast as the gunplay started, a deadly silence took its place. The atmosphere was tense as something heavy fell on the ground. My gut told me to play dead. Any indication that was there was a sign of life in me would send me to my demise. The sound of approaching footsteps made my already weak heart pound hard against my ribs. I just *knew* that whoever the last man standing was, they were on their way to finish me off.

It took everything in my nature not to turn onto my back and face my fate like a man, but somehow, I stilled my nerves, and took *very* shallow breaths, so shallow that to the naked eye it would appear I wasn't breathing at all! My assailant approached, the dragging of their foot told me they'd been injured, and walking was a struggle for them. As the hot sun bore down, a lone shadow paused above me, I could *feel* them assessing me. Blood poured from the two head wounds I'd incurred, I knew I *looked* dead, but if the last one standing was Twisted, *looking* dead wouldn't stop him from *ensuring* I was.

However, even if the sucka didn't do me in, there was so much blood exiting my head that *if* they didn't hurry up and end it, I'd surely have died from blood loss.

"God—I swear, my nigga if you let me make it outta this one. I'll go to church every Sunday and I'll stop killin' all your children. I silently bargained with the heavens.

The shadow studied me for what seemed like forever before the silence was interrupted by a feminine voice laced with pain.

"Tw—Twisted, I'm hit, Papi, I need help!"

I recognized the Mexican girl's voice. God must have felt my plight because, after a few more seconds of deliberation, the shadow who I then knew was Twisted, moved like a wounded animal as he made his way over to the treacherous bitch. I took a gamble, I cracked my eyes open a lil' to see what was taking place, but instantly blood dripped into my eyes. I blinked rapidly in an attempt to clear my vision without drawing too much attention to myself. As soon as I accomplished my goal, I regretted it. I damn near blew my cover as I fought down a roar that clawed its way up my throat.

Not even eight inches away from me, Tessa's bloodied face was hideously swollen by the left temple. Her eyes were closed, and the skin above her right eye resembled ground beef. I ran my eyes over her. I couldn't tell how many times she'd been hit or where, but one thang was for sure—there was no way she was getting up and walking away from that shit.

"Where you hit at, Sarah?" Twisted asked.

At the sound of his voice, I diverted my attention in his direction. About ten feet away, Twisted stood with his back to me. I couldn't see the Spanish girl, but Twisted's left pants leg was soaked in blood, the uzi was at his side, and he seemed to be favoring his left leg.

"My—my side, Papi, it—burns so bad," The reply was strained.

She coughed and it sounded, gargled. I could tell blood was filling her lungs, she'd be dead if she didn't get immediate medical attention. I watched Twisted assess her in quiet contemplation. As a predator myself, I already knew what he was thinking, *see no evil, speak no evil!* Dead people can't tell no tales.

The blood loss made me dizzy, I watched Twisted come to terms with what needed to be done. Without a word, he raised the hand that clutched the tool and took aim at the lady's head,

"No!" she cried out once she saw his crooked intentions, "I did this for you—I—I'm—I'm pregnant." She coughed again, "will—will you—kill—" blood tainted her speech as it rushed up her throat. "Will you-you kill your own child?" she whispered as death danced in the air.

I knew the answer before he replied, "I like you shawty, but you'll have to give birth in heaven or hell because I can't risk allowin' you to live, and it coming back to bite me in the ass later." Twisted used his free arm to wipe his running nose, "Besides, the devil can do more for the lil' mufucka than I can," He sneered.

"Please, don't—" that's as far as she made it with her plea before fire flew from the short muzzle, and blood sprayed the air. Though her face had obliterated, Twisted squeezed the trigger until the gun clicked. Before he could turn and catch me with my eyes open, I closed them tight and listened to his slow departure.

I heard the ignition turn over, but I didn't open my eyes until I heard the squeal of his rear tires as he fishtailed away from the cemetery he left behind. As soon as my eyes opened, evil inflamed my veins. God must have been in the mood for favors because Tessa's eyes fluttered open. The sun was so bright that I could feel my skin cooking under its radiance, so I slowly pushed myself up into a sitting position. My equilibrium instantly betrayed me, I swooned in place for a few seconds before I was able to get my bearings, but the good thing was the blood dried around my wounds slowing the exit of my life from slipping through my skull.

I put my hand to the back of my head where Twisted's bitch ass had clobbered me, the knot was sticky and throbbin'. I allowed my eyes to roam my surroundings, though we were deep in the country, I didn't know if there were any nearby houses, so I needed to get the hell outta there. A whimpering sound startled me, Tessa was trying to turn over onto her back, but her limbs didn't seem to want to cooperate with her will. Struggling to my feet, I had to steady myself. I looked down at Tessa through hooded eyes, *'trust no bitch'* was the only thought as I scanned the ground for my pistol. It was three feet from the sluts outstretched hand.

So, I stumbled over to it and snatched it up before walking back over to Tessa. I used my foot to help her roll over onto her back. My breath caught in my throat, Tessa was in bad shape and it was a wonder she was still breathing. The woman wanted to live, that was for sho'. There were so many holes in lil' one that she looked like she wore a polka-dot dress. Her intestines were exposed from one of the bursts from the powerful uzi and she choked on her blood as she attempted to speak. Her lips formed words that her vocals refused to give sound to, yet, two words did escape her lips that caused me to laugh in spite of my own pain.

"Help—me!" she croaked.

Our eyes bore into each other as her treason played behind my eyelids, the words she spoke just moments, *"Daddy, this silly nigga gave me his gun, let me do him with his own shit, please."*

She'd been so eager to put me to bed. I smiled as I stepped over her and squatted down straddling her. As she looked at me with a skeptical glance, I took her limp hand in mine and wrapped it around the handle of the burna. I held it in place so that mine was on top of hers.

Glaring at her from a dark place within my mind, I allowed Satan to speak through me, "I told you that day we made it official, treason is unacceptable! I told you I'd kill you, *remember?"* I watched her facial expression change with the recollection. "Yea, you remember," I hissed.

Her eyes went wild as I pushed the barrel under her chin, her limbs still weren't cooperating with her so she was as helpless as a paralytic.

"I have a secret you can take with you," I professed through clenched teeth as visions of what I was gonna do to that fuck boy Twisted painted a picture in my mind so graphic that the thirst for his blood became so powerful I could actually *taste it.*

It took me a few moments to realize that the rust-tinted taste was my own. I was so enchanted by the thrill of whackin' that boy that I'd bitten my lip. Fear was evident on Tessa's face as I slowly applied pressure to her finger. I stared at my reflection in her eyes as I revealed to her a secret that she'd take to her grave, *literally.* "I killed lil' Joe," I whispered passionately. As I stared at the shock registering on her face, my mind transported me back to that day. The feel of the burna vibrating in my hand as I hit that boy up—Mena's shrill cries—the blood, it fed the beast in me and before I could regain control of it, I squeezed Tessa's finger down on the trigger, *Boc! Boc! Boc!* Three shots blew her top off causing blood to splash against my face. Somewhere deep inside my thoughts, I envisioned myself standing over Twisted as he pleaded for his life, the thoughts were so appealing that subconsciously my dick hardened, and I laughed as I squeezed off three more shots into Tessa's face. As I stood to leave, I steadied myself before hitting her one more time just in case God was still in the mood for favors.

****

~Freedom~

Panic raced through my veins as I stumbled through the untamed woods. It was so dark, I had a hard time seeing what was in front of me. The sounds of wildlife surrounded me and as if the woods had a warning signal, *everything* went silent. I stopped to listen, the night seemed to be alive. Maybe it was my paranoia, but I felt as if I was being watched. My fear mounted as uncertainty clouded my senses. I turned back the way I came, but it was so dark, I couldn't tell where the woods began or where they ended. Exasperated, I collapsed to the ground in an emotional heap.

I cried uncontrollably, '*How'd I get myself into this mess?*' I wondered, and just when I thought it couldn't get any worse, my naked flesh prickled as insects began to swarm me in the night.

Renta

Chapter Two
Snakes—Rats—Death

~Assata~
~*Two Days Later*~

"*Assata—Assata, Chile, wake yo' butt up!*"
I heard the soulful voice calling to me. I vaguely felt a distant pain. My body hurt, and I felt as if my arms would dislocate from their sockets, yet, I didn't know why. "*Assata, if you don't listen to me, you will die, and they will kill everything you love. I need you to wake up, baby.*"
The voice beckoned to me, recognition stirred something inside my being. I tried to force my eyes open, but they were too heavy, I was so tired.
"Lovey?" I whispered. "I—I thought you—" my voice trailed off as a heavy mist swallowed my mind.
I could feel her love filling up the empty places inside my heart as the mist cleared. Sunshine lit the meadow; beautiful Gardenias, wildflowers, and groups of passion flowers perfumed the air as I observed my surroundings. Somewhere deeper inside the clearing I heard voices having what seemed to be a debate, so I took tentative steps toward them. I rounded a huge rose bush and there, not even ten feet away was Lovey.
She was debating with a man that I would recognize even if we were in a crowded room filled with men that looked exactly like him. His hair was braided in his signature two braids. He was dressed in some blood red Versace slacks, no shirt, and the pistol tucked into the back of his waistline made me smile. They had their backs to me, and uncertainty had my feet glued in place. The only thang that made sense was a reality that rocked my world. If these two people were together, and we were all in the same place—that meant this had to be Heaven!
Heaven? Maybe this was the waiting area that we had to sit in until God made his decision where he'd send us, or maybe this

was hell. But why would Lovey be in hell? *Hell naw,* so maybe there was really a Heaven for a gangsta.

"Chile, you gonna just stand there and stare at us or come give us a hand with these weeds?" Lovey snapped me out of my thoughts.

She turned to stare at me, and as she did, my every fear and confliction melted into a puddle of peace.

Shy turned and tossed up the set. "What's poppin', Rusta?" Long time no 'P'."

Lovey smacked him in the back of his head. "What I tell you about that nonsense? You leave that devil's talk at his house, not in my place of peace." She smiled as Shy rubbed his head and flashed me a smile.

Seeing my nigga after so long touched my soul. All the bloodshed, pain and love that inflamed my heart since he'd gotten murked welled up in my eyes as I hit the set up and walked over to the only two mu'fuckas that ever understood my gangsterisms. Before I knew it, I was wrapped inside Lovey's arms allowing rain to storm from my eyes. I hugged her so tight that I thought she'd break.

"I'm sorry, mama! I shoulda been there to protect you. I—I shoulda killed—"

Lovey silenced me. "Shush, Chile." She released me and held my face in both hands like she always did whenever she wanted my undivided attention. "Chile, you couldn't change Gods plans—" she whispered with water swimming in her eyes. "A man lives his life according to his heart—some things he'll be able to control, and others he'll have to leave for God to sort out. This is just one of those things God has to deal with on his own terms." She released my face and smiled, then used her thumbs to wipe my tears.

Lovey looked at Shy, "Look who I have with me, Satta. He a sight for sore eyes ain't he, baby?"

I turned to my brotha from another mama, he had that smirk on his face that he always wore when he was 'bout to say some slick shit. "Look at you, my nigga—actin' like a lil' bitch!"

Without warning, Lovey swung a backhand, that he easily dodged, then the silly cat did the Ali Shuffle. We all laughed at his antics.

Then he said, "My fault, Lovey—you know I didn't mean no disrespect." He smiled in an attempt at disarming her and it worked like always.

"Chile, you watch your mouth, ya hear? A black man is powerful—mighty!" She balled her fist and shook it at him. "Back in the day, a man would kill you for that kinda language." She turned to me, love was real in that black woman's eyes. "I'll talk to you later, Chile, I'll give you two the space you need to catch up." She pulled me into her arms for a warm hug before walking over to the rose bush. Lovey began inspecting each rose as she hummed an old Mahalia Jackson tune, "Move on a Little Higher," a tune she always sung whenever she was deep in thought.

As soon as me and Shy were out of her earshot, our smiles dissolved and at that moment, it seemed as if there was so much to say, but neither one of us wanted to break the serenity of silence. A hare flew passed us, I jumped, Shy laughed. Out in the middle of the meadow, two tiger cubs chased each other through the brush.

Shy was the first to break the silence, "If shit was only that simple, huh, bleed?" He extended his right hand with his fingers in the shape of a 'P' for our customary gang shake.

My fingers instinctively formed the set, and we locked it up in a proper greeting, at least it was proper to us. "It's never that simple for niggas like us, Bleed. That's why we come up out that fire ready to die for what we deserve," I replied, facing him. I allowed a moment of silence to pass before I asked a question that plagued my mind. "Keep it bloody with me, Rusta—" I glanced around the huge garden before returning my hard stare to Shy. "I don't remember nothin', homie. How'd I—" I frowned in confusion before shaking my head, "I mean—" I had trouble formulating the words, but I guess Shy had anticipated me asking that very question.

He laughed as if my life was a comedy. "What—how'd you die, you mean?" He finished the sentence for me in between fits of laughter. I didn't crack a smile, and once he realized I didn't find shit amusing, he composed himself and shook his head. "Naw, Bleed, it's not your time, yet. Them Russians did a number on you, but the O.G. ain't want you yet," he told me.

Skepticism painted my facial expression all this time I'd wondered if there was a God, and here was my chance to find out. "So—God is real, fam—you've seen that nigga with your own two eyes?" I wanted clarification.

I knew if anybody would give it to me uncut, Shy was that kinda kat. For some reason, his stare became saddened. "Assata, remember when we were pups, and so naïve to life that we believed we knew everything? Think 'bout it, bro—" He squatted down and ran his hand over the grass before looking back at me. "—we didn't have to be told Santa Clause wasn't real—we never believed it anyway! We never had to be told that daddy wasn't coming back home—we already knew he wasn't—" Shy turned his eyes in Lovey's direction. "They say the first thing a medical student loses is faith in God—" Shy looked up at the Heavens. "—you know why they lose faith, bro—" Without waiting on my answer, he answered his own question. "—the anatomy, when they began to open the human body and explore every aspect of it, they learn it!" Shy stood back up and dusted his hands off. "After fixing the heart—after discovering every aspect of the body, those people search and search, but the one thing they can't seem to fix or find is the soul."

I stared at him wondering where he was going with his spiel. He chuckled when he read my facial expression. "That's us, bruh—we took life and saved a few, but life was so cold to us that we lost our faith. God came through every time though—every time our enemies caught us with our pants down. And we just so happened to beat them to the draw?" He made a gun with his fingers and mock pulled the trigger. "Every time we was locked deep in the trap with enough work and automatics that life woulda been the lowest plea them crakas came with?" He raised his arms in the air as if he was praising the sky. "That was God, my dude. Your thoughts—your instincts?" He smiled. "You've seen God too, dawg, you see him every time you look in a mirror."

I put my hands up, a thoughtful look crossed my face. If I wasn't dead, why was I there—with him in that—that place?

It must have been written all over my face because Shy read my thoughts. "This place—this is your heart. It's something deep within you, this place was created for those times you just wanna say fuck it and tap out—this place is your pride." Shy tapped my chest with the back of his hand and started walking; I followed. "Assata, have you not noticed that the only time you find Lovey is like this—" He waved his hand around the meadow. "—it's at a time when you've done some stupid shit and the results left you in a position where you were fucked up or at the times you just wanna give up?" he said as he abruptly stopped walking.

The move was so sudden that I ran right into him. "Damn, fam, say something next time!" I fumed. "Look, homie, I ain't DOA, that means you—Lovey, y'all ain't either, but—" my voice trailed off as confusion hugged my spirit.

My dawg turned to face me, I studied him—mentally willing him to understand my confliction—willing him to not give substance to a reality I *already* knew was true.

He smiled at me with a wounded smirk. "Dawg, the worst thing a man can do is become a victim to his own lies—you know its ova for me." He shrugged his shoulders as if he could care less that he'd died before he was able to live.

Impulsively my eyes found Lovey, hope toyed with my rationality as I turned my eyes back to Shy. He dropped his head in respect for my hope, but confirmed the rationality, Lovey wasn't waking up again. That shit crushed a gangsta. The taste for revenge surged through my veins as I watched her pull weeds from a group of snap-dragon flowers. They took one of the only people in life that ever loved me no matter what I did. Somebody woke up the sleeping beast and the only remedy for its thirst was blood.

The sweet sounds of Lovey's humming carried on the wind, "After the Rain," by Betty Wright.

I smiled as my thoughts transported me back to times that could never return. Moose, my moms, used to have that song turned up to the highest notch as she cleaned the house. The woman would use so much Pinesol you'd be able to smell it before you entered the house. A clicking sound snapped me back to the present time. I'd know the sound of a tool being cocked no matter what was going on around me. Me and Shy had a showdown with our eyes, there was no need to look down at his hand, the sound of him cocking the black .40 was enough confirmation.

His pupils seemed to fade to pitch black. "Dawg, you out there in them streets letting rookie boys touch you. I know losing Lovey—you and Jazz—" He tapped his heart with the burna. "—I know that shit heavy, but you know the law of the jungle just like every otha animal that's thuggin' out here. There's no innocent people during war—" He aimed the tool steady as he sighted me with the infrared. "A lion won't pass up a baby buffalo simply because it's a baby. Naw—he's gonna devour it because he understands it's just the way God made it for men like us, we gotta kill for our food. If you gonna keep letting mu'fuckas get the ups on you, I may as well put one in ya melon right now!" Shy spat. "At least you'll die by the hands of a worthy opponent!"

I stretched my arms out wide like I had wings. "What you waiting for, bruh, you tuna or something now?" I faced off with the tool. "You know I don't give a fuck about dying—what you waiting fa, huh?" That gangsta shit tumbled from my heart.

Shy's face took on the reflection of the killa I'd known him to be all our lives. The red dot danced over my face, he was on the edge of the cliff now. I knew how he killed cause we've been in the mud together since free lunch.

"You'd be doing me a favor, sucka!" I taunted him.

Shy's finger molested the trigger for a second before his body relaxed and he lowered the gun with a pained expression on his face. "When though, Bleed—when will you give a fuck?" His eyes locked with mine.

We faced off for a second or two, then my body deflated. My arms dropped to my side as his question ricocheted from my brain to my heart. *Did I care if I lived or died?* I really didn't know, and Shy read the indecision in my posture.

He shook his head in pity. "You're not getting any younger, dawg—" he paused and looked over at Lovey. "—you have too many people that depends on you, for you not to give a fuck," he murmured before he dropped a bomb on me that was so powerful it blew my heart—my mind—then my soul to so many pieces that the only pieces of myself I could salvage were the ones that caused me to react the way I did. "You not giving a fuck is what got Lovey killed, my nigga."

Rage—hurt and craziness shot through me like lava running down the slopes of a volcano, and I lunged at him with blood on my mind.

****

~Freedom~

~Three Days Later~

Assata still hadn't called me, so I feared the worst. It had been three days since I'd found my way out of those dreadful woods behind Assata's house. I'd made my way to the front of the house and as I suspected, it was destroyed. The picture windows looked like big, empty eye sockets. I could look right through to the living room. Where the once beautiful white walls were coated with gas residue and the marble floor was littered with glass. Flashbacks of the night before played inside my mind like a horror flick.

I stood there for almost ten minutes stuck in place—holding myself as the morning chill caressed my skin. *Who were those people? Where was Assata?* My mind shot off question after question until I damn near drove myself crazy. I contemplated my next move, I knew I couldn't just stand there naked as a newborn, but I feared stepping into that house. There was a million what ifs bouncing around in my head, but not enough certainties. I stood there until resolve ate away at my fear. I couldn't not go in, my clothes and keys were in Assata's room. The sound of approaching tires stole my attention, as a white Benz SUV rolled to a stop, and as the engine idled, the driver stared at me in mild shock.

That's how I met Goose. Naked—mam—mam—"

A voice brought me to the here and now. I stood at the door of my job juggling a steaming cup of Java in one hand, and a box of donuts in the other. I'd had enough wallowing, in self-pity and decided to go into work, bills weren't gonna pay themselves. Standing in front of me holding the door open was a man I assumed was there to make a withdrawal.

"Are you okay, mam? I've been trying to pass you for almost two minutes. Whatever you're on, I need some of it—you were spaced and—" I left him talking to himself at the door.

I was so embarrassed that my mind started playing tricks on me. I felt like all eyes were on me. Alarmed, I glanced back to see if the strange man was still standing at the door, but he was long gone. I turned my attention back to the tellers and at that moment my suspicious magnified.

'Could they tell what I'd been through those past few days? Did the scene at the door warrant this much attention?' I thought.

It was evident that when my colleagues realized I was alarmed they began trying to direct their attention everywhere else but on me. My heartbeat escalated, but I held it together as best as I could. It was clear there was something amiss, and I was willing to bet my life on it that *I* was that something. On my way to my office, I attempted to make eye contact with my close friend, Tonya, but like everyone else, she tried to avoid my questioning eyes.

'Well, fuck her, too!' I thought as I made it to the back of the bank.

As soon as I made it to my office door, I knew that trouble awaited me on the other side. The door was cracked open and I could hear voices speaking in hushed tones. This may not have been a problem if it wasn't for the fact that I kept my door locked and the only other person allowed in were the higher-ups.

"Are you gonna go in or keep eavesdropping?" A deep voice startled me from behind.

I jumped in surprise and spilled some of the hot coffee on my left hand. "Dammit—" I spat. "—you shouldn't be sneaking up on people like that!" I turned to face him.

He was a short man with sandy blonde hair combed back into a nice wave. He looked fresh and well-groomed as we studied each other. His presence was demanding, but his eyes were the contradiction. They were a gentle green that gave him a boyish quality. They seemed to roll over me in a very analytical assessment.

"And you shouldn't be sneaking around interfering with a federal investigation," he replied with a contemptuous smile.

I stared at him confused, with an arched brow I wondered what he meant *federal investigation?*

He read my expression correctly, flipping out his credentials he introduced himself. "Federal Agent Harrison," he announced. "You must be Freedom McDade—we've been waiting on you." He gestured to the door, he stepped around me and pushed it open the rest of the way. "Ladies first," he proposed as he stepped to the side so I could enter.

Reluctantly, I stepped through the door, I had a dreadful thought that would be my last time doing so, yet, I stepped through with my head held high. "Donuts, anyone?"

****

Swoosh!

Was the sound of me flying right through him. It felt like I'd dived inside of a cool body of water before I landed face first in a rosebush. Anger surged through me as I disentangled myself from the sharp branches. Once back on my feet, I inspected my wounds, outside of a few stinging welts and scratches, I was peace. I was more confused and humiliated to worry 'bout the physical, curiosity that got the best of me though.

"How the fuck you do that?" I demanded.

Shy laughed. "Bruh, I'm a figment of your imagination, yet, I'm real, too." He continued to laugh as if he knew a joke I didn't.

I stared at him in frustration, I didn't understand his explanation and he knew it, so he elaborated, "It's a paradox, bro, it's like that old movie Ghost with Whoopi Goldberg. Remember that shit?"

I pondered for a second, and as I recalled the movie, the rest of the pieces fell into place. In that movie, Patrick Swayze was killed but his love for his gal prevented him from crossing over. He wanted to touch her—kiss her—just make her understand how much he loved her. He could walk through walls and become solid with the right amount of will.

Shy recognized I'd figured it out and smiled sadly. "You can only touch us when it's truly in your heart, and harming me ain't in yours, Bleed."

That truth being spoken, I blew out a long breath of hot air. He was right, I loved that boy like a brotha. It could neva manifest in my heart to hurt him. The sound of the tiger cubs playing nearby stole my attention. The biggest one chased its sibling into a bush.

"So—you and Jazz finally made it happen, huh?" Shy caught me off guard.

Without looking his way, I started walking, he followed silently, yet, his aura was powerful as he anticipated my answer. "She left me, my nigga, I—I was in the hospital and she left—" I looked up at a cloud that had rolled in front of the sun. "—just up and disappeared on me. I wasn't 'pose to fall for her, Bleed, but—" my voice trailed off as the wolves bolted from the bush, and to my surprise, the smaller one was the aggressor as it nipped at the bigger one's hind legs.

Shy nodded as if he predicted to exchange of power, then he asked, "Do you love her, Satta?"

"Bruh didn't you just hear what I just told you—she left me!" I exploded.

He was picking at a scab that was best left to become a scar. "Fuck love gotta do with anything; treason murders the heart, homie."

Shy stopped walking, I turned to see if he'd pulled his strap again, if so—he'd have to do me this time. To my surprise, he did have it out, but not aimed at me, the silly mu'fucka was taking aim at the cubs.

"I didn't ask you if she left you, family, I asked do you love, my sister." The wolves wouldn't be still so he couldn't get ahead on them.

I wondered his intentions but answered his question, "Yea— you know I love her. What's your point?" Shy squinted one eye as he concentrated his aim.

"She loves you, too, Bleed. If you don't follow your heart, you'll both regret it. That's my sister, Rusta, but she's your queen. I've always known that, even before you did." He smiled to himself. "You have a lot to do before the O.G. calls you home, Bleed, but first you gotta clean your garden. It's snakes in your camp, my dude, and all 'em are poisonous!" Shy pulled the trigger, Boc! Boc!"

The shots rang off in succession. I watched the two tiger cubs explode in a red mess, this boy could never change.

****

~Freedom~

"I can't believe this shit. So, you think *I* had something to do with the bank robbery?" I asked in shock.

My boss, Mr. Jefferson sat behind my desk as Agent Harrison stood beside him. There was another agent typing away at my computer, I assumed he was downloading all my data usage onto the USB device he had hooked up to my flash drive.

"Well, Mrs. McDade, it's kinda ironic that not only did those men know the route for the truck, but also the layout of the bank. I find it kinda hard to believe that it's a coincidence that those men knew about the exit that's next door to *your* office, and it's surely not coincidental that they knew it led to the next street over. Those men had a lot of intel," Mr. Jefferson spoke with a finality that left no room for misunderstanding. He believed I was the culprit.

As I stared at him with a shocked look on my face, he busied himself with smoothing the wrinkles out of his *freshly* pressed slacks. Anger—astonishment, but most of all *fear* resonated within every molecule of my being. These people were attempting to make me the escape-goat for a federal crime. I became so enraged my hands began to shake.

"How dare *you!*" I spat. "Is it because I'm the only black woman here, huh?" My eyes turned to slits when I released my next revelation into the atmosphere. "Or is it because I turned down your every advance since I've been employed here? You prick!"

The silence that ensued was priceless. Even the agent at the computer turned to glance at my boss.

"Um-hmm," Agent Harrison cleared his throat. "Mrs. McDade this is a federal investigation, not a prejudice accusation based off your race or gender." He turned to the computer guy. "Jason, would you please?"

The man at the computer who I now know as Jason unplugged the USB stick before quickly typing in a sequence of information. He smiled and turned my computer to face me. At first, I was confused, but as I watched the screen fade from a fuzzy grey to crystal-clear footage, I had to tame my surprise. I watched in mild fascination as the robbery played out from the beginning. I watched as the president masked gunmen secured the place, their moves seemed synchronized. As soon as the man in the Ronald Reagan mask brought me from the back, I already knew what was about to happen as I recalled how roughly he handled me.

Obviously, so did Agent Harrison. "Slow it down for me right here, will ya, Jason?" he asked as he walked over to the screen now playing in slow motion.

The look in Assata's eyes—the aggression in his posture couldn't be misconstrued. He was upset at the man unprovoked treatment, and his reaction proved that.

"See, look close, the perp with the Obama mask sees you being brought from the back. He's not frustrated until the Ronald Reagan mask mishandles you. Now tell me, Mrs. McDade—"

"Mrs.—" I frowned at him. "I'm not married," I said as I wrapped my arms around myself.

It had suddenly become cold in that room, I looked like a nervous wreck sitting there bouncing my legs as if I had to pee.

Agent Harrison smiled thinly. "Ms. McDade," he corrected and pointed to the screen. "I'm trying to figure out *why* a bank robber would give two shits about a total stranger? But you know what—" he paused for effect and turned from the screen.

Harrison slowly stalked over to me as if he was a famished lion going in for the kill. Our eyes bore into each other's as he walked around my chair and stood behind me, placing both hands on my shoulders.

He whispered, "Look at the screen real good, *Ms.* McDade." He put emphasis on the Ms. Part. "As you're sitting there, your face doesn't register fear—your face doesn't even register the correct reaction that a *senior* manager should have during a bank heist that could possibly cost her, her life." He gently massaged my shoulders, but instead of enjoyment, I felt repulsed! "You know what your face registers as you and this total *stranger* make eye contact—" Harrison leaned down and put his lips inches away from my ear. *"Surprise,* Ms. McDade, that's what your facial expression shows me. You're surprised because you *recognized* the perp."

At that moment I bolted from my seat so fast the Starbucks cup toppled over, spilling luke-warm coffee onto my paperwork.

"I did not recognize that man! How—how could I recognize a man wearing a fucking mask!" I screamed. I could feel my skin flush as so many emotions blossomed inside of me. "As a matter of fact, if I'm not under arrest, I'm leaving, and if I am, I will need to notify my lawyer." The tension was so thick that the room seemed to be losing oxygen. I made eye contact with each man.

Harrison was the first to break the silence. *"Unfortunately,* you're not under arrest, Ms. McDade."

"What!" My *soon to be* ex-boss exploded. "Surely you're not about to allow this—this criminal to just walk free?" His eyes bounced back and forth between me and the agents.

When no one replied, I gathered my things. "I'll be back for the rest of my things tomorrow. I'll make sure to have my lawyer with me." My eyes rolled over Agent Harrison. "Just in case," I added. Jefferson's pale face flushed beet red when I turned my heated gaze toward him. "I'll be contacting Human Resources as well as the main office in New York to inform them of your conduct here." I made my way to the door, but before I was able to leave, Agent Harrison stepped in front of me blocking my departure.

"You know we *will* get you, right?"

In spite of my nervousness, I was able to hold his stare with an indifferent look. "You finished, Agent Harrison?"

"No, I'm not—I know that from the video you either didn't have nothing to do with this bank being held up, or you're the best actress I've ever seen." He smoothed his tie and glanced over at the video that was still playing in slow motion. "Either or, I know—two things for certain. You know those men that committed this crime, and as soon I can confirm it, I'm gonna nail their asses to a wall in a federal jail cell, and you're going down with them for obstruction!" Harrison seethed.

I winked at him as he stepped out of my way. "By the way, agent, whoever said that those were *men* wearing those mask?" I asked as I made my way out the door.

Right as it was closing, I could've sworn I heard someone say, "Son of a bitch!"

****

~Assata~

Lovey turned at the sound of the fired shots. "What in the world is wrong with you, Chile!" she demanded.

I made my way in her direction. If I wasn't dead, I wanted to be. I never wanted to be separated from these two again, and that was my sentiments exactly when I hugged Lovey for the third time that day.

She hugged me as tight as she could and whispered, "I love you so much, Chile. Ya know that don't cha?"

I pulled away so I could stand face to face with my queen. "Yes, ma'am, and you know you're my first love, too, huh?"

The corners of her lips quirked. "Chile, Moose was ya first love. You loved that woman more than life. You've always been a big ole mama's boy, Satta." Her eyes studied me. "But you know who your real true love is, baby?"

For some reason, my heartbeat quickened with that question. Confusion held me captive, but the more I searched Lovey's eyes it was as if Jazzy's face was materializing within her pupils, that shit rocked me.

Lovey smiled at my reaction. "Go get your heart, son, she's crying for you. She—"

Before she could finish her spiel, I was already shaking my head, being stubborn was just my nature. "Naw, Queen, I'll pass on that. Maybe she is crying for me, but she twisted a knife in me that's too deep to pull out." I dropped my head unintentionally. The revelation exploded in my internal like a virus on a mission.

Lovey used her fingers to lift my head up. "Chile, you'll *never* be able to figure a woman out. I'm not saying all of us are the same, but the good ones—" she paused and opened her palms, my eyes widened as a yellow caterpillar appeared on it. Lovey continued to watch it while it soaked up the sun. "—a true woman, Assata, is like the lady in that fairy tale Snow White. She's dead to the world once she finds real love. There will be numerous men that want her to belong to them because they *know* her worth."

Lovey closed her fingers around the caterpillar and looked up at me. "Many men will kiss her, they will do all things to arouse her, but loyalty—her heart won't allow her to respond. Her respect for self won't allow her to live life until that *specific* man kisses her." Lovey opened her palm and to my amazement, a beautiful yellow and black butterfly rested inside of it. "Only then, Chile, will she respond, and live to her fullest potential." The butterfly flapped its wings and hovered about Lovey's open hand, Lovey smiled down at it. "It's time that you leave this place, Satta." The hurt in my eyes must have shown through because Lovey looked up with a sad smile. "We'll meet again, Chile, but your work isn't finished yet."

Desperation was like a snake crawling through my veins. "Why though, Lovey, why can't I stay here with y'all? It's nothin' left for me out there. Please, mama let—" My plea got caught in my throat as the sky suddenly turned pitch black.

I looked up and became transfixed as a red tint blended with the darkness. I turned my attention back to Lovey, but Lovey had vanished.

Panicked, I turned and came face to face with the barrel of Shy's .40. "I never did thank you for riding for me out there, Bleed." His eyes were as black as night skies as shadows played over his face. "I love you, nigga, and good lookin' on bein' a real nigga. Take these and make sure you use 'em well!" He smiled wickedly and pulled the trigger.

Boc! Boc! Boc! Boc!

My whole body burned as my mind exploded, and my eyes opened all at once. "Well, isn't this nice." A man with electric blue eyes smiled up at me.

Chapter Three
The Game of Chess

"Check, playboy, it'll be *checkmate* in three more moves," I called to Ice-Berg.

We'd met at Lovey's spot because it was a place he already knew the location of. Lovey had stayed in that house for sixty-something years, *everybody* knew where Big Mama stayed. She wouldn't relocate for *nobody*, no matter what we said to persuade her. *"When God wants me, He'll take me no matter where I rest these old bones at, Chile,"* she'd say.

So, it wasn't a secret where niggas could get at us at. I barely knew homie, it wasn't like we were cool, but ever since shit turned sour, *we had no other choice* than to join forces. Them pussy ass Russians had my brother and the only person that could lead me to 'em was Ice-Berg's bitch, Bella. Ever since Freedom called me a few days ago informing me of what went down at my lil' brothers spot, I'd been on the hunt for that boy Russia's head.

I *begged* Freedom not to alert the authorities because that would only get my lil' nigga killed, and truth be told, some shit was just best left in the street. I'd met up with Ice-Berg to discuss our strategy and somehow ended up playing chess, *mentally and physically!*

I watched Berg study the board intently before a crooked smile formed on his lips. "Outta check," he exclaimed after taking my knight with his bishop.

'*Damn, I didn't anticipate that move,*' I thought as I rested my face in the palm of my hand and held my pointer finger against my temple in deep thought. The more I observed his setup, I understood his strategy, one false move on my part would cost me not only a pawn but also my queen.

"Say, Goose, I don't understand you sweet dick ass niggas out here. You tell me you caught the woman whispering on her phone at three in the morning, and when you pulled her coat tail she hung up acting all 'noid and shit, right?" he inquired before he took a sip of the amber liquid in his glass. "So, why not whack the bitch and eliminate the *possibilities* of the slut taking down the entire operation? Come on, cuz, you can't be *that* lame." He laughed and downed the rest of his Brandy. "Homie, that hoe is the *law*, if she moving like a snake in the middle of the night, that means either two things. The hoe got another nigga she fuckin' and she's about to set you up or she workin' for them people. My bet is the latter, you acting like *you* the folks or something, fam," He objected as if that was some cool shit to say.

Without looking up from the board, I discreetly touched the butt of the burna that was tucked in my waistband. The thought of uping it and rockin' his ass to sleep made love to my senses. But I decided to give him a pass because I understood that the young guns of this era didn't know how powerful their tongue was.

I took the tool off my waist and laid it on the table, *barrel aimed in his direction*, then looked up at lil' daddy. "Checkmate in two moves, young-gun," I concluded as I lined my queen up with my rook.

Homie looked skeptical because his knight was in position to take my bitch. The queen *seemed* free in comparison to the bishop he stood to lose. He looked up at me quizzically as I leaned back in my seat and rested my hand on the butt of the .357.

"Bruh, the problem wit' you, young niggas is when it comes to a female, you tend to focus on her assets more than her morale. Niggas focus on the bitch with the fattest ass rather than the one with the deepest mind." I toyed with the trigger as I spoke the gospel to the young brotha.

He was just one of a million cats that observed with his dick, thought with his heart, and disregarded his brain when speaking in terms of a pretty face and some wet pussy. I studied his body language as his eyes found my finger softly caressing the trigger of the pistol.

I saw his nervousness battle with his composure as he considered my intentions. "It's because boys become so focused on how good the nut will feel that they forget that just as pussy gives life, it takes life as well—" I spun the burna on the table and Ice-Berg's tension eased noticeably.

He played it off by returning his attention to the game, but I continued to psychologically beat his ass, that's the *real* objective of chess! "Yet, one never considers that the *woman* with the deepest mind could rule an empire with him. Her loyalty will transform him in ways that only a real bitch can," I jeweled him, but obviously, the cat missed the hint because just as I thought, he took my queen.

I smiled at him and took the bishop with my rook. My other rook was already one row in front of his king imprisoning it to his death. I stared at him he was still oblivious to the danger he was in. He pushed his knight directly in front of his king, but the last moment he recognized his blunder.

"Ain't that a bitch!" Ice-Berg spat.

I laughed and checkmated his ass with the other rook. I snatched the burna off the table before giving him food for thought. "My, nigga, don't *ever* disrespect me by suggesting I'm a rat. I've rocked niggas to sleep for less." He thought on it for a second then nodded in respect. "Dig, Ice-Berg, you must *always* know what typa female you're rockin' wit'. The purified truth is she's only gonna do one of two things—" I tucked the pistol back into my waistband as he began to set the board up. "Pay attention nigga, I'm giving you a life preserver—" I got his attention. He paused with one hand on a chess piece and his eyes on me, alert. I looked deep into his soul when I gave him a valuable piece of game. "She's gonna either sacrifice herself *for you,* or she's gonna sacrifice you *for herself.*"

****

~Kamika~

"Girl, this spicy tuna roll is delicious!" Johnson exclaimed.

We were at a sushi bar on the West side of Fort Worth, and she'd been stuffing her face with raw fish since we'd been seated. Not long after she'd warned me about the plots of our superiors, we'd started kicking it. Tracy Johnson was cool, but a little too chatty for my taste. The mere reason I even associated with her was because I knew she'd be a valuable asset, she'd keep me informed on the gossip at the station. I had a lot on my mind, so my appetite was almost nonexistent, but Tracy rambled on and on about how they're talkin' about trying to get Obama care eliminated as if she thought those white folks were going to leave a remembrance of a black man being in office in place.

She spoke on how bad things were since Trump been in office, but no matter how much I hated the prejudice son of a bitch, one fact stood firm in my mind, the employment rate had skyrocketed by sixty percent; that's forty percent since the eighties! Yet, I could care less about politics at the moment, I stared absently at my plate. The seaweed wrap was barely eaten. I wasn't sure if it was merely that time of the month for me or if my conscience was having a debate with my heart. Nevertheless, I felt shitty about what I was about to do to Goose. It's not like I didn't care for the man, he was just too dangerous to *not* be taken off the streets, but more so, what other choice did I have? Those fed boys had me in a corner, and I just wasn't cut out for prison.

"Kamika—girl, you're not listening to a thing I'm saying, something has your mind, or *someone* has it." Tracy startled me from my thoughts.

I was so lost in thought I must have lost track of her rants. She stared at me as if she was offended because she didn't have my undivided attention.

"Huh?" I countered with the most innocent look I could muster. "Oh—girl stop being foolish, I heard everything you said," I lied. She looked at me with her lips twisted and a, '*what the fuck ever,*' expression on her face. "What!" I laughed and picked up my fork before I glanced in her direction.

She leaned back in her seat, crossed her right leg over her left, and crossed her arms. Tracy was a plus sized woman with a pair of double D's that made the posture resemble a lecturing aunt. She narrowed her almond-shaped eyes and bounced her right leg. "You're thinking of your boyfriend, aren't you?" She assessed my reaction before reaching forward, grabbing her glass of water and taking a sip. "There is trouble in paradise, huh? Girl, let me tell you something about men, they're only loyal to two things, their mamas and home-cooked meals!" She snapped her fingers and sat her cup down on the table.

I'd never put her in my business so she couldn't have known that she was valleys away from the truth. I wonder how she'd react if she knew not only was my boyfriend a part of the infamous Kreek Circle, but I also was in alliance with the Federal Bureau of Investigations to take him down. I had to laugh at the irony of the entire situation.

Tracy must have thought she was speaking the gospel because she didn't break a stride in her sermon. "A man will only respect you as long as you don't show him the character traits of the things he's always feared in a woman in the first place."

That shut me down completely. She touched a soft spot because Goose had once told me something *almost* identical. Tracy nodded her head understanding that she'd reached something in me.

"When will I be able to meet this mystery man anyway? We've been kicking it for weeks and I've yet to meet the man that was able to steal the heart of the infamous detective with brass lower lips." She smiled at me expectantly.

Out of respect, I gave her a somber smile. "Soon!" I took a bite of my food just to buy time.

Obviously, Tracy wasn't going for it because she narrowed her eyes once again. "Baby girl, how old are you?" she inquired.

I figured that was a much safer topic than my treachery, so I humored her. "I'm twenty-nine, soon to be thirty, August thirty-first. Why do you ask?" Curiosity got the best of me.

Tracy picked up her fork and stabbed the last piece of the tuna roll she had. "That means I'm five years older than you, so cut the crap—" she replied before placing the food to her lips. "—your dude is either a street dude that you think I'll judge you for or either you're lying about having a man *period!*" She then placed the food in her mouth and winked.

****

~Ice-Berg~

I studied the board intently, but Goose had my mind racing at a hundred miles an hour. I'd just learned that even though he looked younger, the man was forty-four years of age. Yet that wasn't what had my thoughts rushing like an underwater current, the man's intellect was on some other level shit.

"What you gonna do, young gun?" he interrupted my concentration.

I glanced up at homie before looking back at the chessboard and moving my pawn up threatening his. I had him down to three pawns, a king and a rook to my queen, one pawn, and both Bishops. There was no way he'd beat me. He observed the board, he had his pawns lined up back to back, one protecting the other. There was one row between him and getting his queen, but my queen protected the back row and a bishop aimed its pistol at the row that he needed to transcend in order to be successful, and my king sat next to my queen like a lion and his lioness.

"You wanna know the unique thing 'bout a pawn, homie?" he proposed as he moved his king up to the last pawn in the line, which was also the most important in his protective strategy.

The Brandy I'd been downing had me feelin' myself as I pushed my other Bishop across the board. "I bet you're gonna tell me *after* you get yourself outta check, huh?"

I smiled, he knew he was dead, yet, his composure never slipped. I studied fam, his dreads hung wildly about his head and face hiding his eyes behind a jail cell of hair, yet, I could *feel* him staring at me. Homie had three fingers of Brandy beside him that he hadn't touched since *he'd* poured us both a shot. I was already on my third shot.

Goose noticed me staring at the glass, chuckled lightly, and positioned his king behind the last pawn. "A pawn is a child with unlimited possibilities, yet their worst attribute is their lack of intelligence, they only have a one-track mind." He finally took a sip from his cup before he anticipated my next move. "There warriors that only knows how to go forward *unless* they're killing someone, *but* if they survive beyond their predicted life expectancy, they'll grow up to save your life one day." He philosophized.

I pushed my queen all the way to the end of the board. My plan was to force his king away from the second pawn beside the first, that left them without protection. I reconsidered my angle, *'follow your first thought'* my gut spoke to my mind. I pushed my queen up. "Check." Goose nodded and pushed his king beside his pawn, I moved my queen directly behind his king. "Check," I called again, but he merely pushed his king in front of the pawn, directly behind the other two. I saw his intent and took a gamble, I pushed my queen two squares over, my intention was to push my queen back to the last row.

Goose looked up at me and shook his head with a disappointed expression on his face. "I see you *still* put *all* your trust in your bitch." He taunted before he pushed the first pawn forward. I took it with the positioned bishop, he took my bishop with the second pawn. "You work yo' bitch so much you forget you love her. When a man elevates to a certain plateau in his game, he no longer has to use his bitch to gain position—he has shootas for that," Goose spoke as if he knew something I didn't.

I pushed my queen to the row the second pawn was on. He pushed his king behind it to protect it. Frustration surged through me as I realized I'd fucked up. Goose didn't make it any better when he said, "The best way to study your foe is by observing his bitch. You know why, Berg?"

I pushed my queen to the last row preparing to take his pawn if he decided to go for the queen but instead, he pushed his third pawn up. "You observe his bitch because she's the reflection of the man and her game is *his*."

I pushed my queen in front of his pawn so he couldn't move it forward, but it was only a stalling tactic. He pushed the third pawn beside the second one threatening my queen. My Bishop was in its original place and if I took either pawn, it would be a suicide mission for my queen. But if I let him get his queen, he'd check me *and* push the other pawn down. I procrastinated as long as I could, before looking up at him in defeat. I took one pawn and allowed him to take the queen with his king.

He saluted me. "A woman has that effect on men. Once a lesser man tastes the power of a true queen, he forgets his own well-being because he's so focused on her moves. He forgets she's the most *powerful* piece in his life *merely* because of the game *he* invested in her. He can sacrifice her at will, but the power of that pussy causes him to forget the most detrimental rule of the game." Confidence exuded from his stare as he tipped my king over with his finger as if playing the rest of the game out would be pointless. "Even though she's the most *powerful*, he's the most *valuable* piece. You can play chess without a queen and win, but when the king dies, so does *everybody* else in the castle; simultaneously!" He schooled me.

At that moment shit got ugly, the door crashed open, and a bloodied mess crashed to the floor. Me and Goose dropped low, but not before pulling out our burnas. I'm guessing the universe wanted to give substance to Goose's point because we aimed our tools, *simultaneously!*"

Chapter Four

~Assata~

The very first thing that met me when I regained consciousness was excruciating pain. As soon as my eyes opened, the bright light made me feel as if my head had been cracked open.

"Arugh—" I growled in anguish.

Every portion of my nature burned—hurt—throbbed, and my shoulders and wrists felt broken. It took me a moment to think beyond the pain and assess my predicament, slowly—with strained deliberation I lifted my eyes—my arms were suspended above me, chained at the wrist. The chain was thrown over a beam in the roof and pulled tight so that my feet were suspended *at least* three feet above the ground. Blood was dried on my flesh, and as I looked down at my body, I could see what seemed like small slices canvasing my chest and abdomen. I was shoeless and naked except for a soiled pair of boxers.

I could tell that whoever worked me over focused his attention on my face because the swelling had my head feeling like a hot air balloon. Everything seemed dream-like as I attempted to numb myself to the pain. They had to have drugged me because I saw everything in a hallucination state.

"So—I finally get to meet the man of the hour, hmmm?" a deeply accented voice mused.

He wasn't an intimidating man by far, he was a small impeccably dressed cat with long, wavy, blond hair. It was hard to focus through the drugs I'd been subjected to, but even through the many colors I was seeing, the two most prominent distinguishments about the dude were his striking blue eyes and the infamous long scar that ran from his left eyebrow all the way down the middle of his jaw. He stood in front of me in a tailored Givenchy suit with his hands behind his back. Beside him stood a tall, slender bald-headed cat that resembled *Uncle Fester* of the *Addams Family*, except he wore grey attire under a long white lab coat as if he was a doctor.

"Do you know who, I am Mr. Assata? Do you know where you're at?" The accented man asked again.

I don't know why, but at that moment a white foamy liquid rushed up my throat and spewed out of my mouth. I became lightheaded and that's when shit got ugly. The room seemed to crumble before my eyes.

"What the fuck did you give—me—cock sucka?" I managed as the ceiling began to corrode as I watched.

"You've yet to answer my question, Mr. Assata. Do you know who the fuck I am?" the small man seethed. I assumed he was the cat, Russia, because of the scar, but I answered no man.

I lifted my head and roared in agony, my arms burned with an intensity so great I thought they'd rip right off my body. I turned my heated glare back to the duo. "Yea—I—I know who you are." My head felt too heavy for my neck as it dropped, and my chin fell to my chest.

It was an effort to keep my eyes focused, but somehow, I managed to glare at him as he looked up at me expectantly.

"Oh, you do hmm?" He smirked at me with an amused expression on his face. "Tell me then, Mr. Assata, who am I?" He inquired as he pushed me causing me to swing back and forth.

"Son of a bitch!" I exploded in pain. The two men shared a laugh at my expense. "Yea—you-you're the cock sucka I'ma kill when I—I—get—" suddenly, everything went black for a moment. I couldn't speak or think.

Russia chuckled. "You're gonna kill *me*?" He smiled up at me once my vision returned. "Doctor Voloarsky, please enlighten our friend here of his current predicament." He turned to the cat in the lab coat.

I observed through a heated gaze as the Uncle Fester lookin' mu'fucka reached in his coat pocket and pulled out an object that resembled a scalpel. The faggot stepped over to me and as soon as he came in my proximity, I attempted to kick his head off his shoulders, but my strength was nonexistent.

The doctor patted my stomach. "Hold still, dear boy, you're in no position to fight against these odds. If you continue to fight against it, your heart will distribute the poison deeper into our bloodstream—" he paused, and before I could react, he sliced me with the sharp blade. "You've been exposed to a Soviet-born nerve agent—it dates back to the nineteen-eighties and in Russia, it's given the name *novichoks* which in English translates *the new kid on the block!*"

The cock sucka sliced me again, the thin blade was so sharp that I didn't feel it, but the sting *afterward* was antagonizing. I watched helplessly as he walked over to a table littered with strange looking paraphernalia and packed up a syringe. He took the cap off and flicked the instrument a few times before tapping the plunger. A squirt of a yellowish liquid shot out about half a foot high as the crazed doctor stared at it adoringly before looking up at me as if he'd lived for this moment his entire existence.

"'Tis agent can be very deadly if not cared for properly—" Volodarsky headed in my direction as he spoke his insanity. "I've drained you of a few pints of blood to detoxicate you since you've been out of it. I've injected you with this serum I created, and it's working marvelously!" He chuckled as if using me for a lab rat was the most hilarious thing since comedy.

Once he stood before me, the strange man rubbed his hand up my bare inner thigh. I assumed he was on some *rainbow* shit, and though I wasn't homophobic, I wasn't a participant either. I attempted to kick him in the face, but my energy was drained.

His owlish blue eyes focused on me. "Be still, silly boy, I'm trying to find a fast way to your aorta, not grope you—" he paused once his hand stopped midthigh. "You have a main artery in your thigh which is connected to your aorta through a sequence of veins and arteries," he spoke to me as if I knew what the hell an aorta was. Even in the condition, I was in, he could read the expression on my face.

He nodded and elaborated. "An aorta is the main trunk that carries blood to the left side of your heart, and all other limbs and organs of your body, except for your lungs. Of course, you're gonna die either way, but I have a few more drugs to experiment with on you." His eyes flickered to Russia who was standing in a corner observing with an expressionless fascination. "The good man here has revived my hope in medicine by allowing me to practice it here at his humble abode." He waved his hand around the room as if he were showing me around a room at the Hilton.

Under hooded eyes I took in my surroundings, a black rat the size of a cat scurried across the stained floor. Abandoned cracked pipes, tainted condoms, and other debris littered the ground. I came to the conclusion that I was gonna die in this dilapidated building. I knew exactly where they held me because unbeknownst to them, me and Pain grew up thuggin' in this building. We used it for every extracurricular activity we could until DPD caught on and started givin' niggas trespassing tickets for entering it.

"Tis drug you've been exposed to work ruin on a person's body—it stops the normal transmission of messages between the nerves and muscles. The light-headedness you're feeling will soon morph into grogginess, that will soon become the evidence of strained breathing."

Russia interrupted my train of thought as he pushed away from the wall. "I bet you're wondering how 'tis man is so well versed in medicine?" he said as he clapped the doctor on the back. "My old friend here is from the old country. I've known him for decades now. Back when I served as an assassin for the Russian Mafia, I was poisoned by a snake of a fellow that was paid to eliminate the opposition." The two men shared a strange look before he continued. "I barely escaped with my life. Yet, as I stumbled along the putrid alleyways of the capital and largest city in Russia, Moscow—"

He stared off into the distance, transporting back to a time before the tailored suits and tons of cocaine. "—I could feel the poison swimming within my veins—like a river that empties into the ocean. The poison would pour out into the crevices of my heart until there was no more life in me. I had come to wit's end—the pain I felt at 'tis moment was so great that I crumbled to the ground ready to surrender to the hands of life, but the Angel of Death had other plans for me." He fell silent lost inside times past.

The doctor patted him on his shoulder and took it from there. "I found him gasping for air, flirting with the fate of death. I was an exiled physician from Rome. I'd been run away from my country for practicing medicines on ninety- eight people all of which died except one—the one that ruined my life and got me exiled, never to return to my home. I was named a witch doctor. In Mexico, they called me a curandero, a man who practiced folk medicine." He shook his head sadly before a bright smile lit his face. "So, you can only imagine how elated I was to find 'tis man in need. I knew if I saved him, I'd prove my expertise. I took him in and the rest is history, I've been with him ever since."

The only thought that came to mind was, '*these two sick mu'fuckas were a match made in heaven.*'

The doctor paused, and without warning, the sick son of a bitch *stabbed* me in the thigh with the needle. The pain was so great I vomited.

Volodarsky smiled up at me. "You're gonna die here, Mr. Assata, but before you do, I plan on having a lot of fun with you!"

~Goose~

My senses were in overdrive as I studied the bloody mess that lied face down on Lovey's living room floor. Instantly, recognition cooked my blood to a boiling point. I rushed over to Pain, kneeled down beside him and placed my fingers to his neck to check for a pulse.

"Say, bruh, can you hear me. Who did this shit—talk to me, fam!" I demanded.

I felt like a walking hurricane as I stared down at my lil' brothas bloodied face. The weak thump of his heart seemed to awaken demons in me that surged from a sinister place until they trespassed into the darkness of my mind. Pain hung onto life by a thread, and the thoughts of losin' him had me hanging on to my sanity by a string. While assessing my brother, I saw a blur of movement out of my peripheral.

Without a bit of hesitation, I spun on my hind legs with the tool already extended in the direction of the possible threat. I didn't know who it was, but if death had followed my brotha home, I'd take him with me wherever men like me went after the physical life.

Ice-Berg aimed his burna at me as he cautioned. "Whoa—" from the look in his eyes I could tell his intent wasn't to do any harm to me or bro, he was merely caught off guard by me drawin' down on him.

"It's me, homie, I ducked out to make sho ya boy ain't lead the devils to us." He nodded at Pain.

I lowered the pistol and turned my attention back to my brotha. I knew I needed to tame that savage in me before I ended up whackin' somebody on *accident!* I realized I was off my game because I didn't even see him leave the room in the first place. Pain was saturated in blood and traces of dirt made his dark skin look as if he had been rolling around on the ground.

Without looking at Berg, I stood up. "Help me get him to the couch, fam."

Though he could care less if my lil' nigga lived or passed on to the other side, Ice-Berg was intelligent enough to tuck his gun and grab Pain's legs to assist me as we carried him to the couch. I don't know why it came to mind, but I could hear Lovey having a fit 'bout how the old ass sofa had been in the family for generations and she was gonna blister our behinds for the mess. At the thought of the old lady, a lightning bolt of anger clashed with a typhoon of pain inside me. I missed her with the entirety of the *piece* of heart I had left. I hadn't even buried her yet, I knew she'd want all her boys present at her last stop.

"I don't ask for much, but I need you to protect my babies. I'm no saint, Father, but I do my best. My only request is that if you must—take me before you take them. My heart is too fragile to be standing over their caskets. Please, God—take me before you take them. This is my sacrifice, In Jesus name, Amen."

The prayer I overheard her sendin' to the OG replayed in my head. The shit rocked me so bad I had to shake my head vigorously to clear it of the pictures exploding behind my eyelids. I honestly don't remember closing my eyes, but after the storm calmed, I cracked my eyes open to find Ice-Berg staring at me perplexed. We stood there sizing each other up until Pain caused us to break the showdown as both of our attention diverted to him.

"Nigga, Lovey—would kick yo' ass for fuckin' up her couch," he verbalized my thoughts.

I chuckled a lil' and gave lil' bro a weak smile. "I'm more concerned with if I'm 'bout to buy you and Lovey matching caskets—" I focused on his droopin' eyes; "—you 'bout to die on me, family?" I searched his soul as if I could override God's plan and *choose* if he lived or died. My flesh laughed weakly.

"Nigga you sound like Wax and O'Dawg in that movie, Menace II Society, *"Don't die Pain—please, Pain, don't die!"* Pain whispered.

In spite, of it being the last thing I wanted to do, he got a good laugh out of me *and* Berg. At the sound of Berg's laughter, Pains eyes focused on me in surprise. Slowly, his eyes turned to Ice-Berg, and his reaction fucked up the temperature in the room. Hell could be seen in my eyes as I went for my tool at the same time Pain's energy suddenly kicked in and he went for the same thing. As we battled for the .357, Ice-Berg scrambled for his.

The words that spilt from his Pain's lips were like toxins poured into the only water supply a small village had to drink from—it affected everybody! "Nigga is you insane—this pussy ass nigga just sent Twisted to do me!" he raged.

****

~Assata~

~Three Hours Later~

It had been hours since Russia and his mad doctor left me hanging on to my life. I'd damn near gone crazy from the hallucinatory state I'd been in. I witnessed the room crash to ruble and rebuild itself three times! I'd vomited so much my stomach cramped from the lack of food and dry heaves. For a while, I couldn't get a grasp on to a coherent thought, but after the last episode of vomiting, I could feel my body and my immune system kick into overdrive. It was a dizzying—nauseous feeling that made me grit my teeth against the foreign effect. I looked up at my chained wrists—somehow—someway, I *had* to get the hell down from there. I exerted the little bit of energy I could in an attempt at trying to pull myself up the chain. Maybe—just maybe, I'd be able to unlatch the chain.

"Near the time of death, breathing is strained—intermittent. Have you made it to that stage yet, Assata?" a feminine voice spoke from behind me.

I froze—it was something about that sweet sound that struck a chord of familiarity with me and rocked my orbit.

'*Could it be,*' I thought in disbelief. The drugs had to have been working on my psyche again because there was *no way* possible for what I assumed to be a reality.

"You're feeling that as I speak to you, huh—like each breath you take is a struggle—do you know what will come next, Assata?" she asked as she stepped from the darkness.

As soon as she stood before me, the room seemed to tilt and my mental capacity swelled with so many pieces to a puzzle that *needed* completion that my system overloaded and I dry heaved. The room spun so fast I thought I'd be torn apart from the sheer speed of it.

My thoughts were on repeat. '*How is this possible—was I trippin—was this another hallucination?*'

"Soon you'll surrender to the inevitable—death!" she said as she lit a funny looking cigarette and took a long drag from it. Through a cloud of smoke, she gazed up at me with a lustful look dancing in her eyes. "Surreal, right—to see *me* after what you witnessed that day?" She laughed seductively as her eyes traveled the lengths of my battered body. Slowly—she licked her cherry red painted lips. "Absolutely delicious—" she paused before stalking over to me like a lioness that's cornered her prey.

She ran her manicured fingers up my thigh until they slid underneath the leg of my boxers. The silly bitch fondled my balls softly as she took another pull on the cancer stick. "You're just as beautiful with your life hanging in the balance as you were the first night that I met you," she whispered as she held my dick in her small hand stroking me to an erection.

I fought against her, but to no avail—my manhood betrayed me as it surged to life. The poisonous slut giggled as she pulled my nature free and gave it a long—wet—slow lick before placing it back in its confines and looking back up at me. "You have a nice dick, Assata, but I'll have enough time to taste it *after* it's all said and done," she spoke softly.

"Over my dead body—bi—bitch, you killed my flesh, you'll pay with your life," I spat dangerously.

The punk bitch laughed softly and patted my deflating dick. "Over your dead body, huh?" She seemed to think for a moment as she put her index finger against her lips. "That can be arranged, hon, rigor mortis dick?" She looked up at me before she laughed. "I've never had any, but I'd try it with you. I bet you're wondering how I pulled it off?" She smiled so big I wondered if it hurt her face. "I bet you're wondering how I freed myself from one form of slavery only to become the fuck toy of a sadistic motherfucker like Russia, huh?" she asked as if she was the original Machiavelli.

As a response, I used every ounce of energy I could muster, gathered an impressive amount of saliva and spat on her. It splashed against the right side of her face and dripped down onto her shoulder.

The silly female smiled before she spoke words into the atmosphere that couldn't be taken back. "This may have been the best thing to happen to you—but most importantly, death was the *best* thing that ever happened to your, Uncle Brains."

Murder bled into my pupils as I silently asked the atmosphere for the chance to ride on my enemies *one* more time before the hands of life took my piece off the board. Then, shawty fucked my world up.

"Assata—your uncle was a federal informant. He was working with the DEA to take you and your organization down, he just didn't anticipate the blood that would come from the Russia situation." The surprise on my face must not have been enough for the woman because she sealed the deal with one last nail. "What, you thought he got himself killed because of his love for *me?*" She laughed. "No—he could give two fucks about the prostitute he took under his wing—*he killed himself*, Assata. He ran down those stairs in the line of fire because of *guilt*, not love."

****

~Ice-Berg~

I beat those boys to the draw but honestly didn't have any intentions of rocking either of one to sleep unless that was the only solution. I held the fo'fifth steady as Goose zoned into the danger that floated in the air. It wasn't a question of *if* I'd kill—hell, I didn't even need a reason to do that. Goose latched onto Pain's wrist to prevent him from turning and upping the burna on me. I *knew* he'd peel my scalp back if he so much as sneezed too loud—his brains would be blown all over Lovey's couch right before I lit his brotha's ass up.

"Don't trip out, cuz, you survived one situation, but you won't walk away from this one, on gang!" I seethed and gave Pain pause. He slouched back onto the couch as I stood up and backpedaled toward the door. "Look, homie, I didn't have shit to do with whatever happened to you, but if my loc got at you—" I shrugged my shoulders as if to say, '*fuck it.*' "I'm just as guilty, *I'll* handle my family *myself* if he was outta pocket." I turned my eyes to Goose. "You know Pain ain't no innocent bystander, fam. Him and Twisted been at each otha's throats since the sandbox. I don't know how y'all do in San Antonio, but up here in the metroplex beef ends when death is born."

Goose snatched his pistol out of Pain's weak grasp. "In San Antonio we murda niggas! I don't give a fuck 'bout the tough shit you spittin', *yo' people touched my flesh and he didn't finish the job.*" He looked back at Pain. "We both know what typa nigga my brotha is, they'll meet up again." Goose nodded his head as if he could see the future. I nodded and made my exit, but as soon as I stepped outside my phone vibrated; without screening the call I answered. "What's crackin'?"

The silence on the other end lasted for a few seconds before an accented voice fucked my head up. "Mister, Swanson—so we meet again, hmmm?" The Russian sounded elated as if we were long lost, friends.

I paused midstride at the same time Goose rushed out the door with his phone in one hand and the .357 in the other. We stared at each other as Russia spoke his peace in my ear.

"You betrayed my trust, Mister Swanson—for 'tis grievance you will die slowly, piece—by—piece!" a painted scream punctuated his point.

My blood turned cold when recognition set in. It was Pablo, the head of the El Salva Trucha—Bella's cousin, and my boy. Russia had gotten a hold of him somehow, and I knew the outcome would be fatal.

"Tell me, Mister Swanson, when was the last time you fucked my wife—" Russia mocked me with a chuckle. "She is an animal isn't she, son? But later for that slut, you have something that belongs to the Black Mamba Mafia and we want it back. Until it's in our hands again, you will watch those you love be eliminated for your sins!" Russia taunted.

The last thing I heard before the call disconnected was Pablo swearing and screaming for me not to give him shit, and then a gunshot ended the call. I'd just lost my connections to the MS-13 organization.

I looked up at Goose, his eyes were in slits. "Say I don't know if you had anything to do with my brotha, but if I find out you did—" he left the unspoken threat hangin' in the balance and tucked his tool. "We'll deal with that at another time," he said before tossin' his phone to me. I caught it and stared at him perplexed. "Read the text, homie," Goose requested.

Reluctantly, I looked down at the screen. My thoughts were racing a hundred miles an hour. The text could lead me to Russia. It read:

//: *If you ever want to see your brother again...alive—he's at the old Morrison Mills building on the top floor. Come ready for war—*

I looked up at Goose. "What this gotta do with me?"

He smiled as he walked over to me. "That was the Russian on your phone, huh?" He surprised me and ignited suspicions all at once.

'*How the fuck would he know that?*' I wondered.

Before I could verbalize those sentiments, the screeching of tires snatched my attention causing me to spin around with the tool ready to spit. About eight SUVs pulled to a halt on the curb. Thinkin' that Russia sent a hit squad, I began backpedaling toward the house, but the doors to the first truck swung open, and a dark-skinned dude dressed in all black stepped out with a mac 90 in his grip. The red bandana that covered his face was the only indication that my assumption was wrong, but the problem was found within the fact that not only was I crip, but the possibility of me conspiring to give Pain that long nap floated in the air.

"Soowoo; what's poppin', big homie?" The man pulled the bandanna from over his mouth.

Tricky B was a solid cat whose word held some weight in the hood. I liked the nigga, but that wouldn't stop him from putting one in my head for all the blood on my hands from slaying a few of his fallen soldiers. The O.G. Hubb, Tonio Manuel, and a few other bustas stepped out of their vehicles—all were 'bout that action.

The nigga Hubb stepped forward clutchin' a chrome Desert Eagle in his paw. "Ain't that—" he began.

Goose stepped up beside me and put his arm around my shoulder. "Yea, but he good—you, niggas leave that gang bangin' shit for *after* we get my brotha back. Then y'all can kill each other's entire family for all I care." Goose looked at me, our eyes communicated a temporary peace treaty before he took his arm from around my shoulder and headed for the house. "Dig, Berg, this don't make us even—" He turned his head to look at me once again before he spoke his peace. "*Nothin'* will be sufficient compensation for the harm of my flesh. So, for your sake, let's hope your hands are clean—" he paused. "I'm going to kill your relative, Twisted, but fair exchange ain't no robbery, homie—Blood for Blood."

I still held that steel tight, so I glanced down at it before allowin' the windows to my soul to capture his. "Homie, I respected ya gangsta, but like you say—Blood is traded for blood, and for the life of my loc, you'll be standin' ova a casket or two yourself." I turned my back to the dread head and before heading for my whip, I left him with something to ponder. "The difference between a chess *game* and playing chess with *real* life is one can control the pieces on the board, but he can't control destiny. A sacrificed pawn on the board is a sacrifice for position." I tossed up the Hoova as I walked past the group of cats I'd been at odds with my entire life and spoke over my shoulder. "But a sacrificed pawn in *real* life is a heartless move for complete dominance," I jeweled him.

I heard a commotion as I hit the automatic start on the Benz that made me divert my eyes in the direction of the group of men standing beside the first SUV. Tricky B was sighting me with a compact machine gun that I'd never seen before. The infrared danced over my left eye before stopping in the middle of my forehead.

"You *know* I've been thirsty for your blood since we were lil' niggas—" he said as he placed the stock of the machinery against his right shoulder for leverage. I watched him squint one eye as his finger tickled the trigger.

"Say fam—" Goose demanded as he stepped toward me. "—fuck I tell you, Tricky? You, niggas, think this the wild-wild west where you can jus' jump out brandishing guns out 'chere?" He stepped in between me and Tricky's aim.

I took that as my opportunity to make my exit before my luck ran out. Whatever Goose was sayin' to that boy was lost on me as

I murked outta the driveway in hot pursuit of a madman I loved with a cold heart. Twisted was reckless, but I saluted him for touchin' the boy, Pain. My *only* beef wit' lil' cuz was that he didn't finish the pussy, because if I knew Pain like I thought I did—the hood was gonna rain blood soon enough.

Chapter Five
Face in The Dark

~Jazzy~

"Baby—Baby, I got it, I got the part—I got it, baby!" I screamed. "Oh my God—this is—this—I mean?" I paced the floor back and forth as I fanned myself in an attempt to calm down.

Shotta rushed into the living room with a frown on his face and pistol in his hand. He surveyed his surroundings as if he expected trouble before his Bambi's eyes landed on me. His facial expression transformed from one of battle ready to one of curiosity. "Sup, babe, you doin' all that screaming and shit like someone was trying to rape you or sumthin'. What's up?" He asked while tucking his gun.

I rushed right over to him and without warning, hopped into the air. He caught me as if it was nothin'! I instinctively wrapped my legs around his waist and my arms around his neck. His hands instantly cupped my butt as I leaned down to plant a juicy kiss on his lips. Nervousness ate at my elation as our eyes bore into each other's, his filled with anticipation—mine overflowing with the fear of his reaction.

"Baby—" I paused for the right words. "Don't be mad okay, promise me that you won't be mad or overreact?" I pleaded.

Shotta was a good dude, but his possessiveness was over the top. He was the type of man that found it hard to trust no matter what was shown. We'd be cool and I'd come to terms with my decision to give him a fair shake with my heart, then *boom!* I'd remember why I left out the gate. If I go out, I *had* to have fucked some other dude. If I went to the grocery store and was gone too long, I *had* to be out creeping. His insecurities were a sensitive bomb that could explode with the slightest shift of the wind. Sometimes, more often than not the explosion turned physical.

"Jazmina, just say what the fuck you need to say so I can go back and finish weighing this exotic. I have business to tend to. What's up?" he demanded with a slap to my behind.

I unwrapped my legs and dropped my feet to the floor with my arms still around his neck as I took a deep breath. "Well— when me and Charla were window shopping the other day, there was this sign on one of the store windows promoting a model search, and—"

The heat that bled into his eyes gave me pause. I was so familiar with his body language that I could foretell his reaction merely from the expression on his face.

"And?" he inquired.

"And—and she persuaded me to audition. They told me they'd call the girls that made the cut. I didn't think I'd make it because all the other pretty girls, but they called to tell me—I mean, I won't do it if you're not cool with it, but I really wanna do it, baby. I've always wanted to—"

My words came out in a ramble until Shotta unhooked my arms from around his neck. Without a word, he turned and headed back to his business. Just as I thought he'd just leave me standing there—maybe giving the opportunity some thought. He turned and proved to me that luck was occasional, and more often than not found in leprechauns.

"You just can't leave your hoeish ways behind, can you?" he spat with a disgusted look on his face. I visibly deflated. "What— you wanna go around the world showing niggas your ass and titties—huh? You're pitiful."

Tears welled up in my eyes, I always dreamed of modeling. I wasn't a hoe, nor did I aspire to show my assets to *anyone* but the man I was with. At that moment, I realized that the self-esteem of most woman was brittle regardless of how beautiful one was. I knew I was a bad bitch, but all it took was for a man—*my man* to reveal the things he thought about me, and I lost confidence.

"I—I've *never* been hoeish, Shotta, I just want to get us on the map. I'd never disrespect myself as a woman—I'm—my—" My face was wet with liquid heartbreak. I couldn't even finish my statement. "Forget I said anything about it—okay?" I whispered.

A look of satisfaction leaked into his expression. "That's my girl." He smiled.

****

~Face in The Dark~

"He used everybody, Assata. He was a rotten son of a bitch that deserved what he got," I hissed.

Assata was in bad shape, but he was a soldier if I must say so myself. I'd researched the Novichoks drug, and it's a wicked creation. It spoke volumes of the dangerous shit governments had at their disposal. Russia—Korea—Japan, and the United Stated created weapons that had the potential to increase global warming as well as cause national disasters. This drug Novichoks was merely *one* of the hundreds of thousands of species of chemical agents created around the world. In Italy—and Russian people are still finding chemical weapons from World War II buried in their backyards. Looking over Assata, I was surprised the man still held on to his sanity after his system was introduced to the nerve agent.

"Bitch—you-you faked your death!" Assata breathed fire down at me.

I smiled up at him, suddenly exhaustion overtook me. I was tired of all the hiding—the life. I was tired of it all, especially being a slave—a sex toy to egotistical men. "Yes, Assata, I faked my death. Yes—I switched sides. The slut, Snow, that no one expected, freed herself from the clutches of not only the grips of a mad con man turned informant, but also the clutches of the United States Government," I revealed heatedly. The look Assata gave me was contemptuous laced with a river of surprise. "Your uncle was gonna trade me for his freedom." I stared into Assata eyes as I unraveled the ball of yarn that held the missing pieces to the puzzle. "All those divine interventions you had during those times you thought you should have died—"

I allowed silence to make love to the moment as I took a pull from the leaf rolled cancer stick, I could see Assata's mind working in warp speed as the pieces snapped into place. His assumption that he had a guardian angel died as reality stood before him.

"That was *me*, hon, and I had a reason to keep you alive." My eyes descended to his cock print and I snickered naughtily. "Beyond fucking you—" I giggled. "The funny thing is –I would have never known if I wouldn't have gone to that block party in the Kreek that day. That's where I saw her, an old friend that used to work the track with me. The slut used to be one of the highest paid prostitutes hailing from the mean streets of Milwaukee. One day the bitch just up and left the stable, but the next time I saw her I got the surprise of my life—" I smiled a sad smile at the reflection. Assata seemed antsy, he seemed to be searching for a weakness in the chains that held him captive. "She was a fucking *cop!*" I spat as if the idea was the most revolting thing. "She'd somehow beat the odds, Kamika McDade, the ex-prostitute was at your block party, and I watched her infiltrate your circle. After that day, I followed her *everywhere* she went, and that's when things got interesting, Assata."

****

~Detective Harrison~

I'd been at my desk all day. In fact, I hadn't left my office at Quantico for two days. I hadn't had a lick of sleep, and the energy drinks and fast food was starting to do more harm than their intended purposes. My wife and closest friends feared for my wellbeing. They thought I was *obsessed* with cracking the bank heist case. The truth is, I was! I *dreamed* about it—I had a real hard on for those pricks that ran, off with good tax payer's money. That and the heat I was getting from the director about closing the Willow Kreek Drug Organization case had me restless. Ever since my number one link, Detective Hunter, was slain, things had become quite complicated.

I still didn't understand how things became so fucked, but I had a strong inkling that the answer to that question would be found when we found David 'Ice-Berg' Swanson. The story Detective Winslet told us that day in her boss' office blew my mind, reconstructive surgery was common in the underworld circles, but the kicker was the fact of *how* he'd gotten it. I thought Bella Dahik was the wife of a Russian.

So, *why would she help the man that her husband was undoubtedly trying to kill?* That was my thought when my desk phone jarred me to the present. "Harrison speaking," I answered.

"Harrison—this is Paul down in forensics. I think you need to come on down to the basement to have a look at this," the voice proposed in an excited tone.

I wasn't really in the mood for the scientific breakdown of a case Paul had been trying to help crack for months now. He was a good guy, but at the moment, I was foot over ass in open cases.

"Uh—Paul, I think I'm going to have to take a raincheck. I'm cock deep in unsolved cases and if I don't hurry up, and solve them, I'll be working down at the nearest IHOP." I chuckled to take the bite out of my decline, but *I* was the one that needed to soften the blow.

Paul returned the chuckle. "Well—if you don't get down here like five minutes ago, you won't even be able to get a job at the nearest crack spot," he said, pun intended. "I don't know if you know this, but there's no such thing as two people with the *same* DNA, not even identical twins. You do know that, right?"

The prick was starting to piss me off with the pokes at my intelligence. "Yes—I know that jackass. What the hell does that have to do with anything!" I demanded.

I could feel Paul's excitement exuding through the phone before he caused me to bolt from my chair. "Well—that case that you're working, the—the Russian case. The one where we found the girlfriend with her throat slit?" he stated.

"Yea—what about it, Paul? Stop busting my balls and tell me what you've found!" I demanded.

"Well, unless DNA profiling has somehow evolved or some other strange occurrence. The Jane Doe we found isn't Pandora 'Snow' Jacobs, in fact, it's her *sister.*"

****

~Snow~

"She used to meet a man that I later found out was her partner. Detective Hunter who was in alliance with the fed boys. *He* was the key to it all, my intuition told me to watch him closely, low and behold," I waved my hand in a dramatic effect. "One day I followed him to the outskirts of the city and there, in a none descript car, he and Brains traded info. Brains gave him what he wanted on *us*, but in return what neither could anticipate was a president of a fortune five-hundred company named Ashford Jordan turning us over to the cops. In an attempt to save each other, Brains sacrificed *us* in exchange for his freedom, and Hunter would become a hero for taking down the infamous Kreek Organization." I watched it all register on Assata's face, confliction battled with his rationality as he was forced to believe what his heart didn't want to. "That's neither here nor there—that's not what has your mind moving at the speed of light is it, handsome?"

A creaking sound from above caught my attention. My eyes shot skyward at the same time Assata's did. The beam that he was swinging from had splintered—if he kept up his struggle, he'd snap the old wood in half. My eyes flew to Assata's—he smiled down at me with crooked intentions swimming in his pupils. I returned his smile, the .38 special that was in my purse was my solace.

"You remember the night I met, Russia—" I paused to allow him the time to reflect before I helped jog his memory. "Yes, at the Art Gallery—I'd already had it in my mind that I'd switch sides. Your uncle was being pressed to speed up his part of the deal, and I was pressed to be free from his grasp." I took one last drag from the imported cigarette before tossing it to the floor and snubbing it with the toe of my Balenciaga boot.

"Fuuuck!" Assata screamed in agony.

I knew his arms had to have been in excruciating pain from the stretched limbs and tight chains. He swung his body until he heard the groan of the beam singing a melody that must have been the melody that aroused the beast within him because he roared and rocked harder in attempt to aid the destiny of the only thing that prevented gravity from reuniting him with the ground. I paid no mind as I revealed to him how I not only became the first angel he saw floating around in a pair of seventeen-hundred- dollar houndstooth Balenciaga Boots, but also the feminine impersonator of Machiavelli.

"After that night—after I got in the bed with the enemy, *literally*." I giggled at my own twisted sense of humor as Assata continued his pursuit for liberation. As my mind carried me back to my betrayal, I stared off into space. With each word, my pussy moistened—I could feel my nipples hardening. "Listen close, baby boy, because this is not only the tale of *how* I fooled the world, but how I got revenge on a morbid sister that introduced me to prostitution!"

Renta

Chapter Six
Reflecting

~Armani~

I laid stretched across the sleigh bed—a skimpy pair of boy shorts hugged my curves perfectly and being topless allowed my chocolate nipples to salute the Gods as my mind ran wild with thoughts of Assata's sexy ass. He was a real man and had an animalistic sex game to seal the deal. I'd slept with my share of men within my twenty-eight years of living, but none did my body the way that man did. As I allowed my thoughts to wrap around stolen moments we'd shared, my heartfelt betrayed—manipulated! Though we weren't official, we had an understanding; yet just like so many other street niggas, as soon as I gave him my pussy, he was gone in the wind.

I hadn't heard from Assata in almost a week and a half. All three of my calls and texts went unanswered. I tried not to fear the worst, but the truth was, I did. So many thoughts rushed at me from every corner of my mind.

'*Did he think I was a hoe? Did I give in to early—was it all a game?*' Thought after thought set my soul on fire.

I knew there was no way for a woman to control a man. Men looked down on women when they seemed easy. They assumed that if it was that easy for them, it was the same for the next cat. That's why I tried to protect my reputation with each step I took, but damn, Assata—he just did it for me. Somewhere along my crazed reflections, my mind detoured to the night of passion me and Assata shared. He was a different type of man, all street, but his heart was good. I'd noticed how distant he'd become after the hospital visit with his aunt Lovey.

He seemed stressed—constantly looking over his shoulder as if he expected someone to sneak up on him. Instinctively my eyes drifted closed—my body yearned to console him—to feel him taking his aggression out on my lower lips. Heat radiated from my body with the thought of each stroke he'd given me that night. I was so lost within the fantasy that my hands took on a mind of their own as I slid my finger into my warm mouth while allowing my free hand to fondle my right breast.

An intense moan slipped from my lips as my fingers made their descent—over the hill of my nipple—a slow, pleasurable trail down the flat plain of my stomach until they slipped beyond the point of no return and landed on the imprint of my hairless peach. Slowly, I teased myself by massaging my pussy through the fabric of my shorts. I could feel my juices saturating my thong as my full lips parted slightly, and my breath quickened. I went further and peeled the shorts along with my thong completely off.

I spread my legs apart as far as I could. "Assata—As-sata!" I moaned as I split my fruit open with my finger. No one knew how to touch a woman's body like she did, small circles on my clit as I pinched my nipple made me arch my back as I pictured Assata deep, strong and hard inside of me. "Fuck—me!" I demanded as I worked my clit faster and pinched my nipples harder. "Uhh!"

****

~Twisted~

I *fell* through the door of the spot—my shoulder and leg felt like they would fall off at any moment. I'd been shot before, but neither time made the experience any less painful. I had to give it to the boy Pain, the bitch ass nigga thought fast on his feet. That just goes to show you that when self-preservation kicks in, a mu'fucka will come up with some innovative ways to preserve their life.

"What the fuck—what happened to you, homie?" Crazy Loc raged as I stumbled over to the couch and fell onto it without an ounce of strength left.

My whole body burned, the homie pulled his burna, and rushed out the door—I'm assuming to ensure I hadn't been followed.

Moments later he rushed back in. "Lil Ben—B.G., you niggas put that shit down for a second and come help me with, Cuz," he yelled to the back.

My lil' homie B.G. appeared in the doorway of the kitchen, a blunt hung lazily from his lip as he assessed me. His mind must have been clouded by whatever he was smokin' because his eyes rolled over me a few times before the blunt fell from his lips, and he rushed over to me on some real active shit.

"Nigga, just say the name and I'ma go dress they mama up in that black dress—on Fo'tray, homie." He pulled out a cannon and began waving it as if the enemy was somewhere in the room.

B.G. was a lil' homie off the Noff side of Fort Worth. An eighteen-year-old Fo'tray gangsta that moved up to Denton to stay wit' his pops as a means to get him out the gutta. I guess his T-Jones didn't know much 'bout the S.E.D cause she just shipped him from the jungle to the zoo with no cages, one fucked up community to the next.

The homie crazy Loc snatched the .40 from the nigga. "Gimme this shit, cuz, fa you kill one of us or yo' self." He grilled the lil' homie before tucking the pistol in his waist beside his own.

At that moment, Lil Ben, one of my favorite lil' niggas strolled in the room like he was the coolest crip nigga since Big Took. As soon as his eyes rolled over me our eyes connected in a collision of unspoken words. He was the only one besides myself, and the two bitches that knew my plans and seeing that I got touched as well as being the only one to return to the point of no return.

"Where Tessa at, Loc?" he asked with blue flames burning in his eyes. He assessed me once more before coming to an *already* evident conclusion, "Homie, you need a doctor."

I damn near snatched one of the guns off Crazy Loc's waist and popped his ass, but instead, I did what any otha nigga woulda done in my situation—I cried!

"Nigga—fuck, Tessa!" I screamed wit' actual tears in my eyes. All eyes fell on me. "Cuz—" I looked ova at Crazy Loc, "Fuck a doctor—you know I can't go to no hospital wit' no lead in me. They'll put the laws on me before they put the IV in my arm." I thought on the decision that had to be made.

The resolve that played over my face must have revealed my thoughts before I could verbalize 'em because Crazy looked as if I'd lost my mental. "Say, homie, I hope you're not thinkin' what I think you are—" He began pacing the floor. "Twist, I ain't no doctor, homie. What if I hit an artery or crack a bone or something? Berg will whack me—hell naw, I—"

"Nigga shut the fuck up wit' all that bitchin' before *I* whack you!" I cut him off, then looked over at B.G. "Bruh, get rid of that *GTA*." Grand theft auto is what we called a stolen car. The white Lex I'd done the deed in was as hot as a grill at a fast food joint. "And don't be joy ridin', homie, ditch the mu'fucka, and get back here, asap!" I growled as I began undoing my pants. "Lil Ben, go find the sharpest knife you can find, get some sewing thread, a needle, and the strongest bottle of alcohol you got." I shot off orders as if I was in any position to do so.

I knew that regardless of the love a nigga showed, most men didn't believe in climbing their way to the top. That movie Scarface fucked a lot of boys up—so *everybody* wanted to be the boss—the chief. *Nobody* wanted to play the Indian, so I knew weakness could only be shown in small doses cause the slightest weakness could give a hungry nigga the strongest ideas.

****

~Snow~
~Reflecting~

I stared transfixed into nothing as I opened a Pandora's box that was filled with secrets—secrets that we'd both have to go to our graves with. Though my physical form was there—in that place with a man that would no doubt murder me as soon as he was pulled free from his crucifixion. My mind was miles away transported back to the night revenge and calculation gave birth to liberation. The night that I became the face in dark.

Russia's fingertips traced the outline of my curves absently in deep contemplation. His radiant eyes rolled over me as we lied naked, tangled within a web of blood red satin sheets. Sweat made our skin glow under the pale flickering orange flames dancing off the candles that surrounded us.

"So—mi friend, Ice-Berg plans to rob me, hmm?" he asked in his thick accent. "And how-how do you know all 'tis information, my dear lady? What position do you play in all 'tis? Most importantly—" *Russia ran his hand over my exposed left nipple.* "—why would you betray those that's confided something so precious to you?"

At that moment I wasted no time pushing him flat on his back and straddling him. Without inserting him inside me, I massaged his short length with my wet pussy lips. He hardened instantly, I stared down at him through a tangled mass of blonde hair as my pussy stole his rational thought process, and my words filled in the blanks.

"Yes—he's plotting with a man named Brains to rip you off. They say that your organization is weak and it's time for a new regime. They've teamed up with a ruthless street organization that deals with your competitors in the drug trade." *I began to work my hips feverishly—soaking his stiff self to enter my treasure, but I grabbed his wrists and pinned them to the bed.*

My clit was throbbing from the friction, but self-control was the key to seducing a man. No matter the animal, pussy could give birth to something, and evil intentions alike. A hard dick had overridden a man's common sense for years. One could acquire all the money, and power in the world but it wouldn't change the reality. I felt my climax swell inside my essence as Russia's hands balled into fists in antagonizing pleasure.

"I—oh shit—I'm so—so tired of being used by those people—" I moaned.

My clit was right on the pulsating vein of his dick, my nails bit into his flesh as the explosion built up inside of me. I could feel his steel jumping from the blood that raged through it. He wanted to enter me—I could feel his intensity—his weakness.

"They forced meee—" I screamed as Niagara Falls splashed from my waterfall.

The look on his face was priceless, maybe he'd never met a woman that squirted before, or maybe it was the fact that he was on the verge of an explosion of his own, but either or, I slowed my massage and began making wet circles on top of him.

"You-you're a naughty girl, Snow, but you must have a motive for telling me 'tis—fuck!" he screamed as he shot a warm load onto my stomach.

I continued to soak him with my wet kisses as I road him without allowing him to enter me. As I stared down at him with fire in my eyes, I laid all my cards on the table. "Yes—in fact, I do. I have a plan that will ensure your survival, and help you escape the clutches of the DEA and the FBI." That seemed to get his attention.

"DEA—FBI?" he inquired with a perplexed look.

"Yes—Brains has become an informant with the bureau, and the drug enforcement agency to take Ice-Berg down, and unbeknownst to him, he and you will be the surprise guest on the federal indictments," I revealed as I released his wrists, reached down and took a hold of his ready dick. I placed him at the entrance of my paradise as his hands cupped my breasts. My eyes caught fire as he began to squeeze my nipples to the point of pain.

"Tell me, hmmm—how might you know that, my lady? Let's hear your plan," he whispered dangerously, but he couldn't have known that pain was my pleasure.

I lifted up, and before he could understand that he was turning me on more than intimidating me, I dropped down onto him, burying him so deep inside of me I could feel him in my stomach. "Uhh!" I inhaled. Confusion and ecstasy lit his face with the rise and fall of my rhythm. "Yasss—" I moaned and placed my hands on his chest.

I lifted up slowly—working my pussy muscles until only the head of his strength was held by my lower lips. I squeezed and smiled down at the surprise that registered on his face. "My plan is to–shit—is–is to let them rip you off then fake my death again—" I dropped down onto him. "—allowing them to rip you off for something small, and we'll get it back after we murder them," I whispered as my fingernails dug into his chest. I could feel his body tensing—his dick swelling.

"And the D—DEA—FBI?" he asked and reached behind me to grab a handful of my ass.

"I'm—I'm fucking the agent, Russia. He's puttie in my hands." I threw my head back and popped my pussy with all I had. "After we kill Brains and fake my death—yes—spread 'em, baby!" I squealed in delight. "They'll have to come up with another plan, but by then we'll be somewhere on an exotic beach fucking under tropic sun rays and sipping drinks with—oh shit, Russia—with—oh, God—little umbrella's in them!" I screamed as we both reached the finish line simultaneously.

Wave after wave of pure power rushed through me as Russia shook underneath me. Sweat dripped from my tanned skin, and my eyes seemed to glow as I watched him look up at me amazed. A soft breeze wafted through the cracked window—as if the night blew its soft breath for that exact reason, the candles began to go out one by one until the room was bathed in pale, blue darkness.

"Fake your death—you have me confused," he whispered. "How will we be able to pull 'tis off?"

I slid off of his flaccidness and crawled out of the massive bed—ass cheeks shaking with every movement. After gathering my clothes and heading to the bathroom. I spoke over my shoulder. "It's simple—we're gonna kill my sister."

****

~Ice Berg~

I won't deny it, I'ma straight rida/ you don't wanna fuck wit' me. Got the police bustin' at me, but they can't do nothin' a G/ I won't deny it, I'ma fuckin' rida/ you don't wanna fuck wit' me—

Tupac's Ambitions of a Rida was the first thing that greeted me when I entered the trap spot we had on 525 Skinner Street. That and a strange smell lead me to the kitchen where I found a scene so mind-boggling that I paused with my jaw fallin' to the floor.

"Arugh—get that bitch, homie—fuck! I'm gonna die, huh? Cuz, my leg gonna fall off, bruh—God please don't let me have to pimp wit' one leg—" Twisted cried as Crazy Loc *dug* in his thigh with a long knife, and what looked to be a—a fork!

The look on Crazy's face was super intense as he bit down on his lip and stared down at the ghetto procedure. The nigga had on some long rubber gloves that were soaked in blood—Lil Ben stood to the side with a bottle of Coconut Ciroc that was half empty. Crazy bent the fork a little.

"Hol up, Loc, I—I think I got it!" he announced excitedly as he used the knife to open the hole that he'd cut to a slit. Twisted screamed and snatched the bottle out of Lil Ben's hand.

"Give me this shit, nigga!" he growled, then turned the bottle up and gulped thirstily as Crazy Loc surgically worked his magic.

My eyes were glued to the knife and fork. You could see the white and red meat of Twisted's thigh as the kitchen utensils slid from his leg with a smashed piece of lead clutched between them.

"I got it, homie!" he screamed.

"Good!" Twisted cried right before smashing the Ciroc bottle over Crazy's head before fainting.

****

~Snow~

Reflecting

"Hey sis, whatcha been up to?" I asked my sister merrily as soon as she picked up the phone.

There was a long pause before the voice on the other end hesitantly responded. "Pandora—is that you?"

74

The sound of her voice enraged me so deeply that my hands began to shake. "Yes—yes, it's me, Sarah. Long time no see—no hear, right?"

"You could hear the pain in my voice as memories that I'd buried long ago began to unearth themselves as if they were zombies. Memories so inhumane that I broke out in a full-fledged cry. See, Assata, I was such an innocent girl back then, beautiful intelligent child that *everybody* adored. I was the youngest of two children, and the apple of my parent's eye. My eldest sister, Sarah hated me for that—for something I had no control of. The crazy part was, I loved my sister deeply—looked up to her! She was wild and so—so free!

"I looked up to her so much in fact, one day as she was leaving, I begged her to allow me to tag along with her and her friends to what was supposed to be a frat party. But turned out to be a trip to a busy strip that I learned later on in life was Harry Hines—a strip known for prostitution. Long story short; we hung out at a bar filled with rough looking men that look at me with this strange look in their eyes. Even at seventeen-years-old, Assata, I had a full figure, but I was lame to the ways of a predator. I was a sheltered suburban girl that vowed to save my virginity until marriage, but that night—there was this guy, very handsome in a college jock type of way.

"He'd approached my sister, and her friends, he spoke to Sarah, and nodded in my direction. I couldn't hear what was being said, but I saw him hand my sister something, then her and her friends smiled at me assuredly, but inside—inside I regretted leaving my computer and the safety of my room. Sarah walked over to me with a strange smile on her face—

"Pandora, do you love me, little sister?" she asked sweetly. All sorts of alarms went off in my head, but hey—this was Sarah my eldest sister. She wouldn't do anything to hurt me—right? So, I smiled and said yes. Sarah turned and beckoned to the cute dude, and once he was standing in front of me, Sarah introduced us—

"Pandora—this is Brad—Brad, this is Dora, my sister. Dora—" She turned her piercing eyes to me with that look that she'd always

gave me when she wanted me to do what she asked of me. *"—Brad is about to take you to his car so you two can get to know each other."*

"She looked at Brad but spoke to me. "We'll be right there Dora, but whatever Brad asks you-you do, and you can hang with the big girls from now on." She played on my adolescent mind. I was stupid—that night, Brad took me to his car and fucked—fucked my virgin snatch as if I was a grown woman that had been fucking my whole life. That night gave birth to hate for my sister that would last a lifetime. I hated myself for consenting to the deed—I hated him, but I *loved* the feeling of his dick going in and out of me. That night a slut was born, the crazy part is—he paid a gram of cocaine for my virginity. Hence the name I chose later in life when I met my first pimp.

"Dora—Dora, are you okay!" My darling sister brought me out of the painful recollection.

"Yes—I'm—I'm here," I said through the shower of hate that fell from my baby blues. "I—I just miss you so much, I want to see you, Sarah—there's so much I want to tell you," I cried.

"Anytime, Dora, you just name the time, and place I'll be there. There's so much I need to mend with you, sweetie," she instantly responded.

I sniffled. "How about tonight?" I asked hopefully.

The pause was long, I began to think I'd overplayed my hand until— "Text me the place and time—I wouldn't miss it for the world.

****

~Agent Harrison~

As Paul explained how we'd missed the obvious, my mind was in overdrive. Something big was going down, I just couldn't wrap my mind around it.

'What type of sick bitch would kill her sister, and saturate her corpse with her own blood,' I thought.

The two women looked *almost* identical for sure, so I understood how we made the slip-up.

"Step over here, would ya?" Paul proposed.

He led me to a machine that looked like an upside-down movie projector, he looked over at me with suppressed eagerness.

He couldn't wait to show me how his toy worked and add to my irritation. "This is digital analog's newest toy. It converts a digital signal into an analog signal that transforms into an electrical signal whose voltage reflects the digital values. It's like an election microscope built *inside* a high-tech spectrographic machine," he explained.

I gave him a bored, and irritated look. He knew I didn't have the slightest idea what the hell he was speaking of, so he chuckled to himself and reached over to pick up an object that looked like a ball of play-doe shaped in the form of a molecule. He held it up so I could see it, and after he was sure I wås dumbfounded—he smiled and placed it on a clear slate that was attached to the machine. He turned to the keyboard and his fingers began to stroke the keys in what seemed to be hyperspeed.

Without looking up, he educated me on recombinant analysis. "Once I ran the test that the ME asked of me, something strange occurred. The molecule profiling didn't match up with the DNA barcoding," he spoke over his shoulder.

My ignorance to his fancy explanation boiled into hot lava inside of me until it overflowed. "What the fuck does this mean, Paul? This isn't a fucking pissing contest, it's a federal investigation that has the director busting my balls." I slammed a closed fist into my open palm. "You're the wise guy with the degrees in forensics, and criminal science—you're the chief science tech here at Quantico. I'm just the fucking agent in charge—" I was ranting before the scruffy haired bloke interrupted me with his usual charm.

"And a damn good agent in charge," he conceded.

He turned his attention to the mold he'd set on the tray. "This mold is made from a replica of the stiffs genetic makeup. Everyone that's born has to be logged into a database as a number which becomes your security number that you'll be identified by the rest of your life." He walked over to a set of tubes and after a brief moment of deliberation, he found the one he was looking for.

Using gloved hands, he uncorked it and walked over to the mold. "Take a look at this shit, Harrison, it's some neat shit!" he said and nodded to the mold before using his free hand and typing something into the digital system.

Before my eyes, the claylike mold lifted and began to evolve. It became transparent as it molded itself into a human form. The figure began as what looked to me as thousands of fireflies, slowly they merged into one big ball of light that exploded into a clue— slowly revolving image of Pandora Jacobs. Well, at least that was my first impression, but hazel eyes and raven hair was the only distinction that made my assumption faulty. It was a miniature prototype of Sarah Jacobs. Paul smiled gleefully as a computer automated voice spoke from the surround sound system.

"Sarah Jacobs
Social Security: 436-91...
Birth Place: Dallas, Tx
Date and Time of Birth: 12/16/1986 at 8:40 am
Race: Caucasian
Gender: Female
Height: 5'7
Age: 32
Last known address: 2205... Dr. Huntsville Tx 77320!"

Paul held his smile and stepped up to the image, he tilted the glass valve, and a few drops of a red liquid I assumed was blood dribbled onto the image. Astonishment rocketed through my veins as the image melted and reformed into a grotesque image of the same woman, but with two of every limb, and a deformed head.

The automatic voice went haywire, *"Incorrect DNASE—Incorrect DNASE—Incorrect DNASE."*

Paul pulled the mold off the tray and replaced it with only a dribble of the blood. the computer responded immediately,

"DNASE—DNA profiling accepted
Subject: Pandora Jacobs

Social Security: 435-86-2302
Birthplace: Dallas Tx
Date and Time of Birth: 01/05/1989 at 12:30 am
Race: Caucasian
Height: 5'9
Age: 29
Last known address: Unknown!"

Paul looked back at me with a knowing smirk. "Do you know what *Parricide* is, Agent Harrison?" he asked thinking he'd got one over on me again.

I returned his smile before turning and heading for the door— "It's a crime is what it is, smart ass. It's the murder of one's father, mother or *any* near relative. In this case—it's the murder of one's sister."

****

~Snow~

"That night I lured my only sister to that beautiful house, and she sat and cried, she told me how sorry she was. She told me how much she'd changed—how she'd started a family with a nice man that loved her, and her two children. I cried with her, but for a different reason. As she dabbed at her tear-streaked face with the napkin, I'd given her, a lone killer snuck up behind her and slit her neck from ear to ear. Russia's evil doctor friend licked her blood from the blade of his knife as he smiled at me.

"Now, we must take a pint of your blood and saturate her with it in a way the medical examiner will think she died in bed. Crime scene photographers will study the position of the body—the spray of blood—" he'd said.

I crawled my way back to the present just in time to see Assata staring at something or *someone* behind me. Before I could turn around, Russia's voice caused my blood to freeze. "Chu forgot to mention the part of us fucking on the bed next to your dead sister, hmmm. Now—can someone enlighten me on *why* you're *here*, and most importantly—" I turned to face him.

His two bodyguards stood like frozen statutes clutching massive assault rifles, but the knife that was in the doctor's hands is what let me know their intentions.

"*Ho*w did you find him here when I'm vedy sure 'tis information was withheld from you?" Russia finished in his Russian accent.

My heart pounded hard against my chest as I gave him a sad smile and shrugged my shoulders. "A girl can't prepare for everything," I said in defeat, I knew I was a goner.

"It's fine my dear, Pandora, you were a nice fok—" Russia sneered as he took a step toward me, I took a step back. "But the fun is over—you mus die with the secret, and tis—tis—"

"Suwoooo!" A shrill—strange sound echoed throughout the building.

Russia and his entourage spun on their heels. Bewildered, Russia began to speak in his native tongue to his shooters. They sprang into action and headed for the door as Russia pulled out a pistol and hand-held radio I hadn't noticed until then. He spoke fluent Russian into the device and listened to the response as a nervous look etched into his facial features. He looked to me, then up at Assata. My eyes followed his—Assata laughed lightly before taking a deep breath and making the same strange noise that had caused the panic to taint the atmosphere. I knew that it was the sound the Blood Street Gang used to communicate to each other to alert one another of danger or recognition.

At that moment, things seemed to freeze in place, no one moved until Assata stared at Russia with death in his cold eyes. "Death is here, pussy boy, and I can't wait to cook your cabbage!" he hissed through clenched teeth.

Russia smiled a smile I couldn't place before he raised his pistol and aimed in *my* direction. "You will pay for your treachery!"

At that moment, evil enveloped the room. The sounds of dawgs barking could be heard, the light went out, and what seemed to be hundreds of infrareds lit the room. Then—Assata made an animalistic roar and before anyone could react, he swung his body dramatically and though the room was too dark to see what had transpired, the sound, and feel of shattered wood was all the evidence needed to know Satan had fallen from Heaven. I dropped to the floor in that instant, and that instinct may have saved my life as who I assumed to be Russia began firing blindly. The scariest part about the whole scene was the sound of Assata singing the song those kids on that movie *'Nightmare on Elm Street'* used to sing.

I heard him over the roar of gunfire. *"One, two, Assata's comin' for you—three, four, better lock your doors—five, six, grab a crucifix!*

Renta

Chapter Seven
Blood on The Floor

~Pain~

"Damn, boy, be still!" Kristasia huffed in frustration.

After having a thirty-minute fall out with the homies for pointing out the fact, I was in no condition to ride out for my brotha. I finally conceded and called Kristasia's fine ass ova to render her services. It was whispered round our way that she was an RN, so I figured she'd be my best option for medical attention. It was just my luck that Armani's sexy ass tagged along, and maybe the worst luck that Marcella came with the package.

"Bitch, you need to hurry up, mayne—my brotha's life is hangin' in the balance, and he needs me!" I spat heatedly. The prick of the needle made me wince in pain.

"Nigga, quit cryin' like a lil' girl, I'm on the last stitch," she mumbled and told Armani to hand her the pair of scissors from the first-aid box. "Ain't nobody told yo' ruggish ass to do *whatever* it was that got you havin' to get eight stitches in ya head. I can't believe you niggas *still* doing this childish stuff, and Assata—!" she exclaimed as she tied the last stitch closed. "I can't wait to see his ass—he knows betta!" After she applied some type of ointment to the back of my head, she walked around to look at the damage done to my forehead that I incurred.

As she assessed me, my eyes rolled over her five-eight frame, the lady was one of the baddest nurses I'd ever seen. The white running tights hugged her frame so thoroughly that her lower lips smiled at me as the strapless halter top gave me a peek at her chocolate twins that were enough to make my mouth water. Shawty had the darkest—healthiest skin I'd ever seen, long hair tied back into a ponytail, and her full lips set flame to erotic thoughts that made my lil' nigga stand up.

"Do you know if, Assata, will be okay?" A soft voice pulled me out of my fantasy of havin' Kriss's lips wrapped around my dick.

"Huh—oh, yeah my nigga a Souljah," I stuttered as my eyes made contact with Armani's.

The knowing smirk she gave me let me know I'd been caught lustin' for her sister. I hoped that didn't ruin my chances with *her* cause I'd been wantin' to know what that bidness was like since I'd first laid eyes on her.

"How *you* know my fam anyway? You just came to the city, and already know all the mova's and shaka's, huh?" I inquired.

She rolled her eyes at me. "No—I don't know the movers or the shakers. Me and Assata are just good friends—that's all," she clarified.

The looks Marcella, *and* Kristasia gave her were laced with amusement, and what could be described as the *'bitch please'* look. I didn't push it though, even if Assata had cut lil' baby, we'd been fuckin' the same hoes our whole lives, so I knew bruh wouldn't mind.

Turning my attention back to Kristasia, I said, "Sup, you, through?"

She stuck out her hand. "Yea, now break me off so I can get back to my husband. You know how that nigga is."

An instant frown fell over my face as I dug in my pocket and pulled out a bankroll. "Yea, I know how the nigga is, he's a lil' Bi—"

"Boy—watch out now!" she interrupted me with a frown on her face. "Don't get disrespectful, Pain. Art ain't did nothin' to yo' ass. Miss me with the extras and give me my money so I can go, boy."

I smiled at shawty, I didn't just admire her physical, I also respected her mind. She wasn't one of those hoes that lead niggas on and allowed them to spit on her dude's name. Most females were so dodo brained that they allowed the next man to speak foul of their dudes, never realizing *they* were reflections of the men they chose. Without acknowledging her outburst, I peeled five big faces off the knot and handed them to her. I knew I coulda paid for less, but *maybe* she was the typa bitch that did something strange for a lil' piece of change. So, I watched her count it in front of me with a look on her face as if I'd shortened her!

"That's what's up, daddy, but you may wanna be careful out there in them streets. Five hundred dollars may be enough to compensate me for my services, but it won't get you *none* of this pussy, and it's surely not enough for a topnotch casket." She smiled at me deading my fantasies but touchin' a gangsta's heart with concern.

"Umph—that's like telling a rabid dog not to bite you," Marcella's trick ass interjected without being acknowledged.

I looked at her on the verge of sarcasm, but I was interrupted by kisses of death crashing through the windows and walls. Hot lead shredded Lovey's couch in seconds, and luckily, I tackled Kristasia to the floor just in time before a burst of bullets cut the couch in half. Armani had dropped to the floor beside us with a terrified look on her face. In that instant, as shredded glass and sheetrock rained down on us, I realized the reaper seemed to have that typa effect on *everybody!*

****

~Assata~

Pain ricocheted through my body as soon as I landed on that hard ass floor, but I didn't let that deter me from rolling away from the spot Russia would assume I'd fallen. My suspicions proved to be my savior because as soon as I rolled away—sparks lit the spot I'd just rolled from. The dick sucka was wasting bullets as he shot in the blind. The good thing about it was he'd be easy prey when death came for him—the bad thing was he could get lucky and hit his target. I wondered if he'd hit Snow, but that was a fleeting thought as I rolled into something solid and couldn't move any further.

Pain shot through my limbs and I wanted to cry out in agony, but self-preservation gave me the will to smother that natural reaction. Suddenly, the shooting stopped, and the room became funeral home silently, yet, I could still taste the danger in the air. I pulled myself to a crouch—my eyes adjusting to the darkness when a movement to my left alerted me to the danger lurking close by. They must have *felt* my presence as well because their footsteps faltered before coming to a complete stop. Adrenaline surged through me as I prepared to charge the darkness, but just as I braced myself—the hunter's radio revealed their change in direction.

I silently exhaled as I felt around in an attempt to familiarize myself with my surroundings. Despair hung in the air when the sound of footsteps sounded nearby, but Shy or Lovey musta had me in their sights because as the steps came closer, my hand hit a flat surface—a table of some sort. Recognition surged through me, it was the table where the crazed doctor had all those strange objects! Elation gave me company as I felt around for the scalpel I'd seen him lay down on it. It took me a few seconds, but I found it and did my best to position the blade between my wrist and the rope without slicing myself. A walkie talkie static sounded somewhere near—too near.

'Come on—come on, Lovey, I need you, baby,' I thought as I worked.

"He's here—I've found him!" Someone called out, and just as the blade sliced through the rope and freed my wrist; I flung the blade at the darkness—hoping I could do like those cats in the movies and hit my target, but the sound of the blade hitting the floor let me know it wasn't a movie.

Just when resolve began to set in the lights roared to life and took us all by surprise. A few feet away from me stood a short brute of a man with sun-kissed skin, a buzz cut, and a strong jaw. He stared at me wide-eyed as he aimed an AR15 in my direction, seemingly unsure of what his next course of action should be.

"Kill him—kill him, *now,* Dimitri! Russia raged from across the room.

Buz Kut's facial expression melted into one of deadly intent as his finger twitched on the trigger. "You're a dead man!" he spat in his thick Russian accent.

He smiled wickedly and at that moment, for reasons I couldn't rationalize, a serene feeling poured over me. I was ready to die.

'*Fuck it,*' I thought as I returned the grin and stared the reaper in his eyes. "What you waitin' fa pussy!" I tempted fate through clenched teeth.

The Russian braced the weapon against his shoulder and as his finger applied pressure to the trigger, a deadly whisper hissed from the barrel of a suppressed weapon. Surprise was evident in my eyes as a small ball of fire raced through the air. In slow motion, I could actually see a trail of steam trailing behind it right before it snapped Buz Kut's head back as if an invisible force had punched him. The ball of lead disappeared inside a small hole it made in the middle of his forehead, and a thick burst of blood squirt from it before making a trail down the middle of his face. I stared in fascination as the bullet exploded out the back of his cranium in a mess of blood cartilage, and brain matter. Homie's body rocked backward but stayed upright for a moment as his soul wrestled from his body in a woosh of soft breath.

I stared transfixed as his dead eyes focused on me before gravity pulled him to the floor. The room seemed frozen in place for all of six seconds before pandemonium erupted! I dove for the dead man's discarded weapon at the same time as volleys of lead spat in opposite directions. The entry door exploded into thousands of pieces as a figure with a red bandanna tied around the bottom part of his face dove through it relentlessly squeezing the trigger of a mini 14. In that same instant, the huge window blew to shreds as two black-clad men fired wildly as if they could care less who they hit.

My dawgs poured into the room as Russia's people emerged out of thin air. Confusion blindfolded me until I remembered the fire escape that was next to the big generator. It led to the side of the building so I figured Russia must have known the layout of the old building just as much as I did. Bullets and blood flew from both sides, and just as I had a grip on the AR, I spun around just in time to spot the opposition takin' aim at someone to my left. My eyes followed in aim and my blood froze in my veins as I squeezed the trigger. The red that spread across his chest gave me a moment's satisfaction, but like roaches, just as I took one down—another one took his place.

"Hub—watch out, bleed—" I attempted to yell over the roar of gunfire, but it was no use.

The O.G.'s body shook from the impact of the slugs hitting him in rapid succession. My eyes clouded as the big homie fell to his demise—his blood merged with the river of blood already on the floor. I wasted no time swinging the burna on the pussy that had just slain my dawg, but a strange whopping sound roared over the war cries and malice in the room. The wash from a helicopter's blades gave the room pause and we all turned our attention to the orifice that was once stained with glass. Not even ten feet away, a uniquely designed Eurocopter panther's hatch slid open to reveal a fatigue-clad Russian aiming an impressive .50 Cal machine gun at us, and the stand that it was supported by would make it easy to swing in all directions.

In the heat of our shock, Russia appeared from behind the generator aiming his heat in my direction, but that wasn't what prevented me from whacking his clown ass—besides the .50 having the potential to demolish the entire room, the masked gunman that crashed through the window stood beside Russia, and in his clutches he held someone dear to me and my niggas. Tricky B had an expression on his face as if he couldn't believe he'd got caught slippin'. Blood leaked from a cut on his forehead as his captor held him tight in a choke hold.

Russia took that moment to yell over the roar of the chopper's rotors. "No more death 'tis day—we shall meet again, mi friend, and next time you'll die!" he shook with his pistol aimed at me to punctuate his point. "But today, you shall rejoice another day amongst de living—and me—" he smiled and gestured to the window. "—*I* mas catch de ride—if anyone fires another round, mi friends will eradicate the entire room." His eyes turned cold as he backed toward the window, and his escape from the hands of death.

In his native tongue, he spoke to his soldiers, and they rushed out the same way they came, except for Russia and the two devils that made the grand entrance. As soon as Russia reached the window, a roped ladder was thrown to him. He wasted no time grabbing it and saying something to his henchmen that I couldn't hear over the roar of the propellers. Hatred for the man burned like a wildfire deep inside my gut as I watched him, and one of the masked men climb the ladder leaving the man that was holding my family's life in the balance. His eyes bore into mine as he released Tricky and whispered something in his ear that made Tricky walk toward us.

Me and the stranger never broke eye contact as he removed his mask and though we never met, I recognized him without an introduction. The tribal designs that covered his head, and face were tiger stripes, and as our eyes clashed, my mind carried me back to that day at the hospital when Lovey first laid eyes on the tattoo of the lion's head on my neck.

Lovey smiled at me. "No, no—don't be silly; it's just that I've been having this reoccurring dream about a lion squaring off with this giant tiger, it always ends with the tiger defeating the lion."

My eyes locked on his as my mind brought me back to the present, something was off with the smile that the fuck boy gave me, and before he raised his gloved hand, I *knew* his crooked intentions.

Without giving it much thought—I raised the tool and tried to warn Tricky, "Get down—get down, he's—" but I was drowned out by the wash of the blades cutting through the air.

Bewilderment was the last look that registered on Tricky's face before his chest opened up. He fell to his knees as I rushed forward firing at the fleeing figure. The helicopter was long gone as he turned and disappeared off the ledge of the window, so I fired the tool until the click alerted me that the banana was spent. The room stank of death—loss—and gun powder as I stepped to the window seal and gazed around. I knew the sucka had gotten away, but hope gave me the *right* to inspect the ground. Empty! Disappointment swan in my stomach as I turned to face reality, but just as I was turning away, something caught my eye and made me smile.

A splash of blood was still warm on the window seal, maybe the fuck boy wasn't so lucky after all. I ran my fingers over the small puddle, and once they were wet with my enemy's blood, I rubbed them together and vowed my revenge.

"Naw, Trick, you gotta hold on, bruh, yo kids need you, fam," the homie Spyda's heartbroken melody caused me to turn my attention to him.

He knelt over Tricky B with blood staining his clothes and flesh. Tricky was a gangsta through and through as he smiled up at his younger brotha and lifted a bloodied hand in the shape of the set.

"Take—take care of my se—seeds, bro, let—tell my story. N—n no tears, fam, real niggas don't die," he rasped as him and Spyda's bloody hands locked in the villain handshake.

Spyda wiped his eyes with bloody hands, yet, the tears couldn't be contained. They merged with the blood on his face and rolled down red tinted and slow as Tricky B's body went slack, and his eyes went blank. Spyda's eyes closed for a moment but reopened suddenly as if he was surprised. He stared off into space, and a smile creased his lips. He hit the set up and saluted the air as if he was seeing something we weren't. My heart throbbed for my niggas as the sound of sirens tainted the night.

"We gotta burn, you, niggas get Hub and Tricky—we need to smash out!" Goose shouted as he turned to me. "Nice to see you amongst the living, Junior."

I was on the verge of replying until the sound of guns cocking diverted my attention to a petrified white woman. The blood and dirt that stained her skin made her look like an orphaned prostitute. Snow had an uncertain look on her face, but the rage that rushed through my veins closed my heart to understanding. I raised the tool with murda in my soul, but before I could snatch the slut's spirit from her.

Goose stepped in my line of fire, I glared at him. "Bruh—fuck you doing, this bitch—"

"Saved your life," my brotha whispered as he pushed the barrel of the rifle toward the ground.

I stared at the woman, then laughed—I forgot the clip was empty.

Part Two
A Rotten Apple

~The Prisoner~

Judas Iscariot betrayed Jesus for thirty pieces of silver, the same thirty pieces that he returned before hanging himself for crossing the same man that he sat at the table, and broke bread with. These past few months, I've lived with the same guilt that Judas took to his grave with him, treason! My mind is more of a prison than my surroundings and my thoughts are the jailers. Lately, I've tried to find peace with a God that I can only hope exist. I siphon my prayers through a blue-eyed man that is said to have died so I could be purged of sin, yet the war within reveals the core of a rotten apple.

In my life, I've witnessed people's actions and intentions place the wrong definitions behind words that held totally different meanings. Love is supposed to mean devotion—sacrifice—protection—happiness—truth! Yet, love in my world was demonstrated by women who left their men when shit got ugly. By mothers who used their seeds as a way to hold on to what they'd soon lose— Loyalty! Loyalty was 'pose to mean by all means—honor—love— til' death—Through the good and bad. But it was taught to me by niggas that fucked each other's wives. Men that allowed pennies to cloud their senses—men that sliced the throat of the cats they came out the sandbox wit.

So, my core holds no ill intentions, but my survival is dependent on deception—self-preservation! I've observed that the truth is like a reflection. The reflection of an ugly and scarred woman. No man or woman wants to feel insecure, so they use cosmetics—

preen themselves for their flaws. Truth is a curse to the ears of a person that believes in fairytales, even though our hearts yearn for the truth—truth is, we can't handle it.

The first Miranda Right, "What you say will be held against you in the court of law! The truth may set you free mentally, but in reality—the truth will get you five to ninety-nine in a cold prison cell for the things you considered justified, but the world viewed unjustly. Adulation is beautiful—even when it's fabricated. The illusion of an apple is visual, at first sight, the fruit seems ripe for the picking—its exterior appears to be mouthwatering, but it's all a façade. Once you take a bite, you'll fall onto the realization of its interior being rotten. Then—as you gaze into its core, you'll see the worm smiling at you!

Chapter Eight
Death and Revelation

~Goose~
Two Days Later

Jigga Man's Blueprint album kept us company as we swept and cleaned Lovey's living room. It was the first day we'd been back at the house since the showdown with the Russians. That night was filled with crazy shit! After we got Assata, he wanted to go to the emergency room to be checked out—the wounds he'd sustained were minimal, but he'd spoken of poisons and nerve agents, some real Adolf Hitler shit. The hospital wanted to keep him overnight even though they didn't find any traces of poison or nerve agents. They'd fed homie antitoxins and laughed at his claim of being exposed to some shit called *Novichoks*.

The doctor pulled me to the side and explained how impossible that was, the man of medicine explained that *Novichoks* was a 1980s nerve agent that is nearly impossible to obtain.

The dick sucka told me, *"Mr. Price, this stuff your brother claims to have been exposed to would have driven him crazy before killing him. The stuff is so powerful that in the eighties a lab engineer in Moscow named, Andrei Zheleznyakov whose job was to test the toxicity of this nascent weapon for the Soviet boys, accidentally inhaled some of it. The man recovered, but later said he'd lost his mind! So, you see how crazy this sounds?"* The man had me questioning my brother's sanity until Assata snapped and snatched off the shirt he'd taken off one of the deceased at the warehouse.

The doctor's mouth dropped in horror as Assata explained how he'd been fed antitoxins and drained of his blood to detoxicate his body, he showed the man cuts *his* experience with the drug. Though he *still* seemed skeptical, they admitted homie for his tests. That was only a portion of the craziness—when I made it home, the police had been there! Someone had hit Lovey's spot up. Shit was ugly, so, me and Pain ducked off at Pain's crib until things cooled down.

"Say, bro, why the fuck would you put yo' tool *behind* the TV? How you gonna get to it *before* the enemy put one in your head—or was Lovey a secret assassin?" Pain interrupted my thoughts.

Mine and Assata's eyes shot to him, Assata's stare was inquisitive, mine was blank as my mind instantly transported me back to the night the gun must have been *planted* there.

"Don't lie, Bennie—" she said as she walked up to me and peeled my fingers from around the burna. She took it by the barrel and walked over to her purse. I watched as she placed it inside and found her way back in front of me. We don't start a relationship with lies," she said.

Disappointment was like a pit of serpents swimming in my stomach, the venomous bitch had soothed my soul and put the blade in my back at the same time. As my pride snapped, I realized that no matter how much game a man possessed, a woman would *always* have the upper hand. Charm had nothin' on seduction, and a hard dick was a dangerous weapon for a woman with the knowledge of her lower lips and ill intent in her heart. I heard snappin' sounds before I felt the sting of pain, but I was too far into my thoughts to comprehend the sources as I reflected.

Kamika eased down from the bed as soon as she thought I had slipped off into a sex seduced slumber. She must have forgotten that I was a madman with blood on my hands because the sneaky bitch neva glanced back to see if I'd awaken. A man that lived the life I did, had to be aware at all times—even when he's asleep! I gave her the benefit of the doubt, but after enough time had passed that was needed for one to use the restroom or get a late-night snack. I slipped from the warmth of the bed as silently as a panther in stalk and pursued my prey. She must have done the deed in record time because, by the time I made my presence known, she'd been standing in the dark—anxiously awaiting the other end of her call to pick up.

"Goose!" Assata shouted. "What the hell is wrong with you, bruh?"

Hearing the confusion in his voice, I had to crawl my way back from the pits of my thoughts only to find my brothas staring at me as if I'd lost my marbles. Assata's eyes fell to my hands and stared at them bewilderedly. Curious, I followed his gaze—the broom I held resembled two chopsticks. Somehow, I'd snapped it in half and the evidence of my broken pride dripped red from my left palm where the wood had sliced into the soft flesh.

"Fam, you know Lovey ain't had no gun, and I damn sure ain't put no tool behind the TV!" I growled as my eyes found those of my ridas.

Both men had confused looks on their faces as I dropped the broom pieces and strode over to Pain. "If this shit ain't Lovey's and you ain't put it there—" he begun before I took the tool from him and opened their eyes to the power of a treacherous woman that possessed a sex appeal and some good pussy.

As I explained, I had to smile at the realization—those were the same two attributes that Cleopatra used in seducing Julius Caesar when she appeared before him rolled up in a bundle of red carpet. Once it was unfurled—a goddess stood before him laced with seduction and an ulterior motive. As I studied the black Glock nine, the only thought that registered was – *Even before Christ, women had more game than men.*

****

~Twisted~

My wounds were healing properly—after I'd allowed Crazy to get the lead out my leg and shoulder, I'd had to be rushed to the hospital. Homie was able to open the wounds, but had the slightest idea how to close them, so it was imperative that I got medical attention. While there, the physician had to be threatened *and* paid under the table not to report me to them, folks. I sat for hours as he stitched me up and blabbered about how I coulda ruptured arteries or severed nerves. I ignored homie, paid him, and got the hell up outta there. It had been a fucked-up day, so as soon as I made it to the crib, I headed straight for my smoke stash, I was out!

Frustrated—I crumbled to the couch and rested my head against the soft leather. I *needed* something to take my thoughts away from my losses, but more conflicting, Tessa's blood wasn't even dry on my hands yet, and I already missed the dumb bitch. I couldn't believe shit had turned so sour. I had never intended to whack my bitch and run off with that Mexican slut, but I had to give it to the nigga, Pain—he thought quick on his toes. Tessa should have been smarter than that, but that goes to show how feeble a female's mind could be when the man she was dedicated to didn't mold her and cultivate the proper morale within their bond.

Anotha nigga should neva be able to play on the next man's woman psyche, but if a man failed to jewel his gal, he deserved to lose to a better man's game. I lifted my head—my eyes absently scanning my plush living room until something caught my attention. A perfectly rolled blunt rested on the tiled floor by the door, one of my potnas must have dropped it when they helped me to the house. I struggled to my feet—I now regretted refusing the crutches the hospital tried to offer.

'*Pride is a man's worst enemy,*' I thought as I retrieved the blunt and dragged myself back to the couch.

I took a lighter out of my pocket and smiled at my luck—the universe must have known, I needed to escape. I put the flame to the tip and inhaled deeply! I held the funny tasting smoke before exhaling—that shit had no potency. I took another deep pull from the stick, then repeated the process over and over again until a quarter of the blunt was gone, but somewhere between my yearn to get lifted, and thinking that whoever bought that shit shoulda shot the mu'fucka that sold it to 'em, something fucked up transpired.

"What the fuck?" I mumbled as the blunt fell from my lips and my brain exploded.

****

~Ice Berg~

I'd been out of bounds for days tryin' to get my business back on track. After getting Twisted's stupid ass to the hospital, I'd chose to duck off for a while at one of my lil' freaks spots to let the heat die off. I knew my choice of not aiding them Blood niggas in their rescue of Assata's pussy ass had relit the fuse to our beef, but fuck 'em! I couldn't reveal myself to Russia, even though he knew I was still amongst the living, he *couldn't* have known I'd gotten a new face, and I wasn't 'bout to give him the only leverage I had in exchange for the life of a nigga that's been the opposition all my life. The only thing that plagued my thoughts was *who* opened Russia's eyes to me? The only two people that had a connection to Russia was Belle and Pueblo.

Someone had led him to Pueblo, and Belle wanted him dead too bad, so *who* was a powerful question. *Could it be Belle?* I wondered as I followed the curving fish tank through my domain. It was dark in my house, but familiarity and the aqua waters were the only things I needed to lead me to my room. As I walked, I couldn't shake the feeling that nagged at me. I'd been calling Belle all day since she texted to tell me she'd made it back in town, but she'd ignored every text and call.

'Could she be the culprit? Was Russia stupid enough to accept her back into his fold after such betrayal?' Those were my thoughts as I pulled my phone off my hip and speed dialed Belle's number for the tenth time that day.

Though she didn't pick up, the strangest thing happened, and I drew the heat from my waist as I eased to the doorway of my bedroom. A phone rang and I knew the ringtone belonged to Belle. As I disconnected the phone, the ringing cut off as I swiftly stepped into the room—gun first! My fingers were firm on the trigger as I anticipated a gunfight, but all I found was a pitch-black room bathed in a soft blue glow from the bulbs in the tank. Belle slept peacefully with her face to the door. Her pretty face was pale from the glow of the still waters, and in an attempt at not waking her, I headed for the shower with timid steps.

As soon as I'd showered, I was gonna fuck the shit outta her for ignoring my calls. I laughed to myself as I slipped into the huge bathroom—I was 'noid as fuck to assume that she had crossed the squad, but then a thought caused the hairs on the back of my neck to stand up and it hit me.

'How the fuck Bella get a key to my house?'

****

~Twisted~

My head swiveled with every voice I heard, "Kill yourself—you can join lil' Joe and O.G. Capp, they need you!" An evil voice whispered in my left ear.

"No—don't do it, Cuz, the lil' homies need you!" someone screamed in my right.

"Fuck the lil' homies, they planted that blunt there—strap up and go find them, niggas, they're tryin' to kill you!" the demon hissed.

"He's lying—just get—"

"She the fuck up!" I roared as I bolted up from the couch. I was losin' it. *'What the fuck was that I'd smoked?'* I wondered as my TV exploded and transformed into a transformer. It became a robotic villain that was trying to do me in. "Shoot it, Cuz, shoot it!" The demonic voice screamed as I took my tool off my waist and aimed at the TV.

The evil mu'fucka aimed the remote at me and pressed a button—the green laser beam that emitted from it missed but told me it was do or die as I squeezed off two shots and dove over the couch. That was the worst thing I could do cause as soon as I landed, I spotted lil' small people hiding back there. One of them looked at me and put his finger to his lips as if to tell me to stay quiet. He peeked around the couch, and hurriedly ducked back down as a knock at the door alerted us to company.

"He's called reinforcements!" the lil' guy whispered in a shrill voice.

My heartbeat was outta this world as I clutched the tool.

"Get yo' bitch ass up and fight like a man—shoot through the door, dumb ass!" the evil voice hissed."

"No—stay hidden, your life depends on it!" said the angelic voice.

"You sound like a lil' bitch, right now," replied the other voice.

****

~Ice Berg~

As soon as I stepped out the shower, my horn vibrated on the counter. I dried my hands and looked at the screen before I answered.

"Sup, homie?"

"Say big homie, did I leave a blunt in your car?" Lil Ben asked.

I shook my head at the careless lil' nigga as if he could see me. "Groove, I don't know, I'll check tomorrow—right now I'm 'bout to call it a night, fam. I'm on my last leg. Why you ask, though?"

Lil Ben inhaled something before speaking through a cloud of smoke. "It's nothin', big homie, I had a toon stick before we left the spot, but when I got home it was gone. I assume it's either one or two places—either in yo' whip or I dropped it at Twisted's. I'm 'bout to go check on the homie anyway, get you some rest, Loco."

"Groove, homie," I replied before disconnecting the call.

As I made my way to my bed, I wondered *how* these young boys smoked toon like that. I know toon was another name for K2—synthetic marijuana, potpourri sprayed with chemicals that I didn't know the name of. Belle was still in the same position when

I walked to my side of the bed and patted myself dry with the towel I had around my waist. I slid under the blanket and scooted over to her sexy ass, but as soon as I wrapped my arm around her, I knew something was terribly wrong! I jerked my arm back in repulsion—Belle's body was as cold and stiff as a frozen piece of meat. I jumped from the bed and rushed to turn the lights on and as soon as the pale light washed over the room, the blood smeared word let me know shit had gotten real.

'*VOR*' was spelled out in blood across the wall. I remembered hearing the terminology used by Russia's workers when I used to meet 'em for pick up, VOR was a Russian slang for Drug Lord. I slowly made my way over to Belle. My instincts told me to get the hell out of there, but curiosity got the best of me. I pulled the blanket away from her still frame. Rigor mortis hadn't sat in *completely* which told me she hadn't been dead more than twenty-four hours. She clutched something in her hands that I couldn't see, but what I could see is she'd died from a slit throat, and no telling what other horrors she'd been subjected to.

I had to pry her hand open, and what I discovered confused me for only a moment before the device began to beep rapidly. I bolted for the nearest window, there was no time to think before the explosive detonated. I crashed through the glass at an odd angle with flames at my back—the blow propelled me about fifteen feet into the air before I fell to the ground in a heap of burned and smoking flesh.

The last thing I remembered thinking was, "At least I'm alive!"

Then everything went black.

****

~Twisted~

"Say, homie, it's me—open the door, fam, its cold as a bitch out here," someone called from the other side of the door.

"Me, who?" I screamed from behind the couch.

"Twist, fuck wrong with you, my nig, it's Lil Ben. Now open the door before I freeze out this bitch."

Somewhere beyond the surface of my insanity, recognition was spiked. I climbed back over the couch and dropped to the floor like bullets were flying over my head. I army crawled to the door then climbed to my feet. I spun to the side of the door frame and held the tool away from my body like the police do before they busted into a room.

I counted to ten before snatching the door open and thrusting the burna forward. "You tryna murk me—huh, pussy!" I raged wit' my finger molesting the trigger.

Lil Ben's face held a shocked expression. "Wha—what the fuck you talmbout, homie, I—hold up." He paused in midsentence and studied me, then the nigga busted out laughing as if my 'G' was comical or something.

I was on the verge of squeezing on him until he did the most fucked up shit I couldn't have anticipated in my life. Lil Ben slapped the gun sideways before kicking me in the nuts! The tool fired as I doubled over and tried to catch my breath.

Lil Ben snatched the gun out my grasp and said, "My fault, homie, but this was for your own good." Then he fell to the ground laughing.

Renta

Chapter Nine
Talk with Lovey

~Detective Winslet~

"We're gathered here to celebrate the homecoming of a woman that touched the hearts of everyone she met. A mother—an Aunt—a Queen!" Reverend Hamilton shouted to the congregation.

The Church of Christ was packed to capacity, and if I didn't *know* that Lovey had been a pillar of her community, I'd think she was a hood superstar. As soon as the thoughts crossed my mind, I saw the truth within the epiphany, to the Kreek she was! The woman was loved by the young, and the old alike, the church was evidence to that. Young and the old came to see her off, she was truly loved.

"I'd like to present something to the congregation," the preacher announced as he opened a folder of some sort.

After he found what he was looking for, his eyes scanned the room as if he were looking for someone in particular. Nervousness raced through me as his eyes paused in a studious manner, but before I could pray he didn't single me out, his eyes rolled to Goose, and Pain who was seated on the pew beside me. His eyes lingered there for a while before they drifted to the empty spot where Assata would have sat, and something like understanding swept across the man of the cloth's face. It was a known fact that Assata hated funerals, but this one particularly would tear him to shreds. He wouldn't show to see the cold face of the only woman besides his deceased mother he'd ever loved completely, confined to a pine box. I understood that sometimes even the heart of a warrior isn't strong enough for certain things.

"Bennie—" Rev. Hamilton addressed Goose by his government name. "Dunte—" he acknowledged Pain. "Lovey loved you boys more than herself and she'd prepared for this day. She used to tell me that you boys were the only reason God kept her here on earth. She *knew* God would take her before he took one of y'all—" the preacher paused and pulled out a silk handkerchief to dab his eyes. "She said God loved her too much to make her suffer like that." He then held up the folder and semi waved it around to ensure it was seen by all. "This is her words that she wrote for you boys and *made* me promise to read them to y'all on this day." He laughed presumingly remembering that particular conversation between him and the old lady.

He then placed his glasses on, and began reading the words that touched the hearts of every man and woman in attendance,

Hey Boys,

I know today is a day you two wasn't expecting. I say you two because I knew Assata wouldn't show up to see me off. That knucklehead is as stubborn as a horse being broken, and he'll need you two in the days to come because out of you three, he's always had the most powerful emotions. He got that from his mama, sho did. I don't need no back talk when you hear this, don't make me— what's that term you young people use, trip out? I don't wanna see no tears for me—not a one!

You see, life is only a creation of purpose, everything under the sun has its purpose, Chile. The sun provides heat and light to the earth. The trees help provide oxygen to the atmosphere. Animals provide food for each other, and the moon is the earth's natural satellite and holds the waters in place. Me—my purpose was to love and teach, and I fulfilled that purpose. I lived for you boys to know that God wasn't only Jesus in flesh, but also love in the flesh!

Without love, there's no reason to breathe because the birth of love gives reason to things. I want you boys to make something of yourselves and leave them streets behind you. There's no promise there, and when one dedicates his life to something or someone that can't love them back, they're only making an investment in heartache. Life is beautiful, Chile, so enjoy it while you're here. I won't preach to you boys but remember this: Don't cry for me, Chile— I lived my days after being born by the river. Survived times when white people called us niggers and we had to chop wood for the winter.

So, don't cry for me, Chile. Know that I'm still there, even though you can't see me. The love I left you with will guide you if only you trust in it when you need me. Remember me for who I am rather than the past tense. God just needed me for better things, so I had to pass through the last fence. Don't cry for me, Chile. If you do, it means you're sad that I made it to Heaven, and Heaven is exactly where I lived my whole life to reach. So, why would you be sad about that? Don't cry for me, Chile.

****

~The Hit~

On the twentieth floor of Dubai's most opulent hotel, a lone figure lounged in one of two overstuffed armchairs. His eyes gazed into a crystal tumbler, seemingly transfixed with the three symmetrical ice cubes spinning within the chilled scotch as he gently swirled the glass. Russia lifted his eyes and gazed out the tinted windows of the fifty-six story BURJ Arab Jumeirah—a beautiful, but expensive hotel. Russia marveled at the blue waters of the Persian Gulf as he thought of how ironic it was that the hotel was created in the shape of a sail swelling on the wide expanse of water.

He was all the way across the globe, quite a safe distance from the eye of the Bureau, yet—he knew the United States had no qualms tempting to extradite him back, even the UAE wouldn't protect him from state dogs if they caught a whiff of his whereabouts. The vibration of his phone disturbed the serenity of his thoughts, but the old Russian understood that in his business there was no peace for the weary.

"Speak," he spoke into the receiver.

"It's done—what do we do with de girl?" an accented voice inquired.

Russia thought on it for a second before replying, "All means to achieve de goal."

There was a pause on the other end of the line before the other voice replied, "There's a child?"

A knock at the room's door pulled Russia's eyes in that direction. "As I said, all means to achieve de goal—de child?" Russia stood and headed for the door before completing his sentence, "De child is collateral damage."

****

~Assata~

'For a nigga out of the gutta, it's hard to have faith in something unseen,' that's what I thought as I held a single white rose in my left hand and strolled slowly through the gates of the dead's bedroom.

My whole life has been one big horror movie where I prayed to a savior that never saved me. At times I wondered why the people that didn't deserve to die, died early, and there were so many evil mu'fuckas that observed to take that eternal rest but thrived in life. I guess life really had no conscience, and if God was really up there sitting on a mu'fuckin' throne watching real niggas and good women get bammed, neither did He! The chill that blew through the cemetery carried a strange smell—*maybe* that's what loneliness smelt like.

To be trapped six feet under—locked in a pine box, I wondered how that kinda loneliness could come with an inscription of rest in peace? The temperature had dropped from the days predicted fifty degrees and the Heavens cast a dark shadow upon the city. All the mourners had departed, and the only ones left on the silent ground were me, the dead, and the groundskeeper tendin' to another plot, the *reaper never slept.* I was dressed to the nines for that specific moment—to bid farewell to Lovey. A charcoal black three-piece Valentino suit covered my skin, as the ostrich skin, Salvatore Ferragamo Boots that adorned my feet carried me to my destination.

A forty-two-inch gold cable designed by TV Johnny hung from my neck supporting the weight of the six-ounce diamond encrusted medusa head medallion that hung from it. The pain that resided in my eyes hid behind a pair of gold tented eyewear that lavished the Maybach monogram on each lens. I inhaled deeply from the pineapple Kush stick that hung from my lips and held the powerful smoke in my lungs until they felt like they'd explode, with a strained deliberation, I exhaled. I paused once I reached the large mound of dirt that separated me from my Queen.

As I stood there staring at the moist earth, it felt as if icy fingers were squeezing my heart. I wondered if there was even a reason to have worn the glasses as a slow river streaked from my left eye. The animal in me cried for what the gangsta in me knew I'd neva get back—The love of an old woman that took her last breath for my sins. I didn't attempt to wipe the salty water from my face as I pulled the first petal from the rose, and let it flutter to the pile of dirt.

I dropped the blunt to the ground before I spoke, "Lovey, I know you want me to hold my head up, but this shit is too heavy of a burden. I—I don't know what to do, baby. I don't know *how* to hold my head when missing you is what's weighing it down." I pulled another pedal from the flower and watched it drift lazily to the earth.

Tears wet my dark face as I searched for the words to express what it felt like to *feel* your soul trying to separate from your physical. "See, mama, I told you God wasn't real why-why would He let this happen if He was—huh?" A gust of cold wind blew through the graveyard as if Lovey was trying to check me for questioning God, but the beast in me was beyond the point of containment.

I peeled another pedal away and released it to the wind. "I'm sorry I—I didn't show up to see you off, Queen, but this—" I got choked up and wave my hand around the plot as if she could understand my implication. "—this shit right here—baby how do I say goodbye to *you*, Lovey? How can I stop my heart from bleeding when the wound is so deep, mama? Huh! Tell me—talk to me,

Goddamnit!" I crashed to my knees in despair and pulled the glasses from my face before flinging them through the air.

My eyes were baptized in my tears as soft kisses from heaven slowly attacked me, the drizzle was soft—wet –and cold. I wondered was it true that it rained every time someone died? I dismissed the thought—that shit *had* to be coincidental because if it was fact, it would be the great flood of Noah all over again. Mu'fuckas died so consistently, we'd been drowned by now. Yeah, I reached down, took up a handful of the moist dirt and let it slip through my fingers, and before I knew what I was doing, I found myself digging and tossing dirt in every direction. I *needed* to hug her one more time before the earth hardened on top of her.

"Hey, come on buddy, you can't do that. What the hell is wrong with you, you some typa psycho?" Someone called and attempted to prevent my animalistic urge.

He grabbed the sleeve of my suit jacket, and before he could wrap his mind around the fact that monsters truly existed. I'd drawn the Heckler and Koch mp7 and was seconds away from relocating his thoughts to the massive tombstone behind him, but Heaven sent an angel that intervened—

"No Assata— he's not worth it!" a feminine voice screamed.

Without diverting my aim, my watery eyes flicked to a small figure running toward me. Armani rushed between me and the clown—out of breath, but beautiful. She stared at me through wet eyes, and I could tell the moisture wasn't from the rain. Her heart bled in her stare as she reached over and took the still extended gun by the barrel, and gently took it from my hands.

"It's okay, baby, it's okay!" She soothed me.

"Naw—it's not okay, ma, it *can't* be!" I exclaimed before turning back to the hole I'd dug in the pile of dirt. I resumed my task as I looked back at her. "Help me, Armani, I need to hug her, baby, just-just—" I couldn't finish my sentence due to the fact that to formulate the words *one more time* meant that it was true. If I'd only get *one* more time to hug the woman that raised me. It would give substance to finality.

A confused look tainted Armani's face as she tried to understand my implications. I turned my back to her and began to dig with all I had, realization must have dawned on lady because she fell to her knees and wrapped her arms around me.

"She's gone, baby, she's—"

"No!" I raged and pushed her away from me. "She ain't gone nowhere, Mani. She—she can't be! Can't you see, ma—she can't be—she wouldn't leave me like this, baby! I—I just wanna hug her one more time," I cried and resumed digging.

Armani grabbed my wrists—using her soft hands with a firm grip. I turned my bloodshot eyes to her, streams of hurt poured from her eyes as the Heavens opened up into an all-out downpour. Armani took my muddy hands in hers and did the only thing she could to give me peace she released me and with manicured hands, began digging and tossing dirt away from the pile. We began the task in silence as the groundskeeper stormed off, but not before giving us fair warning.

"I'm calling the police!"

We paid him no mind as heaven cried, and what was left of the white rose drowned in the muddy waters.

Renta

Chapter Ten
The Deal

~Agent Harrison~

I watched the numbers light up on the side panel as the elevator took me to the fifteenth floor. I'd just received the best news of my life! I hadn't been home in days and I'd practically lived out of my office out in Quantico when I received a phone call that made all my efforts worth it. *It was a wet Tuesday morning when the vibration of my cell snatched me out of a doze, so intense I had to peel my face from the pool of drool I'd made on my desk. Disoriented and exhausted, I snatched the cell off my hip and was jolted fully awake by the animated voice on the other end of the line.*

"We got him—we got the son of a bitch, Harrison! Can you believe it?"

My heart hammered against my chest in anticipation. "Got who—what the hell are you talkin' about, Forrest?" I snapped at the ecstatic DEA agent.

"The drug lord, David 'Ice-Berg' Swanson—we got the cock sucker. My informant clued me in earlier this morning. So, get your head out your ass and get down to Denton Reginal Trauma Unit."

I was already out of my seat and heading for the door. I wouldn't take more than an hour and a half to get from Virginia to Texas on one of the Bureau's jets.

"Trauma Unit?" I asked as I headed out to the hanger.

Forrest laughed heartily. "Yea, someone tried to fry the motherfucker, now stop asking so many questions, and get down there and take the case from the state boys before they let the elusive son of a bitch elude us again."

Now, after all the leadless anonymous calls—the false sightings—after all the bullshit that had dulled my confidence in finding the drug czar. Here he was—a wounded fish to a starved bear. The elevator dinged open on my designated floor and the cool air filled the area. I stepped off and took a left at the reception's desk, and another one at the sign that read: *Burn Trauma Unit.* The sights and smells of the hospital were antiseptic. It had been months since I'd been to a medical facility and I hadn't missed the clamor and phantom feel of death that clung to the atmosphere.

"Agent Harrison, I suppose?" the ranking officer guarding the door extended his hand.

He was a tall, athletic man with sandy, blonde hair slicked back to give him a polished look. I took his hand and shook it exuberantly unable to contain my excitement for who laid on the other side of that door. After the pleasantries were over with, I handed my identification to the good man.

He inspected it thoroughly but still gave me an apologetic expression. "Thompson, stay here with, Mr. Harrison, while I go check this with the captain, would ya?" He leaned into the room and spoke.

Moments later, a short, pot-bellied man stepped out of the room that my obsession was being held in. The sergeant turned his attention back to me.

"I don't mean to be an ass, Agent Harrison, but as you know, this is a high profile case and with the stunts the perp has pulled in the past—" He left the rest hanging in the air and shrugged his shoulders as if to say this was something he *had* to do.

I saluted him, I fully understood the precautionary measures the brass had to take with Mr. Swanson. After the sergeant went about his business, I turned to officer Thompson.

"Has he made an official statement—you guys did Miranda him, right? Is he coherent?" I shot off questions in succession. I didn't want any mistakes to be made this time around.

"I'm not at liberty to speak about—" the pudgy officer began before his partner returned and interrupted him as he handed me my badge back.

"Yes, we've read him his rights, we had to wait two days for him to wake up, and another day for his noggin' to clear from being knocked around in the blast. He hasn't said one word to anybody, that includes the doctors, but his status has upgraded from critical to stable condition."

I took my identification. "Am I cleared?" I asked as I put it back in my pocket.

The officer nodded. "Yea; you're clear, but let me brief you," he said before pulling out a small notepad and flipping it open. "Our bomb experts said they found a small device charred beyond recognition, but they summarized that it was some sort of explosive element. The tech found traces of magnesium on it so that explains the combustible element." He looked up at me inquiringly.

I nodded to let him know I was following him, I knew that magnesium was an explosive element that is obtained from magnesite and dolomite and is usually used in structural alloys and incendiary bombs.

"The tech assessment coincides with the medical examiner's thesis—they say whoever planted the device had been meticulous. The perp placed the device in the deceased hand and *held* it in place until rigor mortis set in and her hand locked onto the pressure sensor that would trigger with the slightest sense of deprivation."

I nodded as the sergeant went on to tell me how incoherent Swanson had been in the wake of emergency surgeries to clear the shrapnel. After being debriefed, my long wait was over—I stepped inside the room and merely the sight of the burned and wounded man was a relief. Ice-Berg looked like he'd had a head-on collision with an eighteen-wheeler. Though he lay adrift in a morphine-induced subconsciousness, I could tell he was in pain. His head was mummified in gauze, an IV was taped to his right arm and a catheter had been inserted.

Three of his ribs had been broken and one had ruptured one of his lungs. To keep fluids from Drowning him internally, a translucent tube was inserted through his nose and pulled down into his stomach. He was in bad shape.

As I watched him struggle for his life, a strange thought bottle through my mind. *'Who the hell was Agent Forrest's informant?'*

****

~The Visitor~

Russia stopped at the door with a pistol clutched in his left hand. "Who's there?" he demanded in his heavy Russian accent.

"Guess!" the voice replied.

A smile quirked at the corners of Russia's lips in excitement; he knew his lover loved kinky games and *guess who* questions, but he wasn't in the mood for games.

"Who de fuck is 'tis!" he growled, but the visitor wasn't moved by the aggression in his voice.

Instead, the visitor reacted in a totally different manner. "You open this fuckin' door, right this minute, you, Soviet prick!" They demanded in a deep—sultry voice.

A slight chill ran down Russia's spine, he hurriedly unbolted the door and as soon as it swung open, a fair skin lady with a slightly muscular build reached back as far as she could and slapped him so hard that spit flew from his mouth. Dressed in skin-tight black leather, she stormed into the room and slammed the door behind her, her long brunette hair tossed over her right shoulder as she stood glaring at Russia.

Unable to resist not having her in his arms for another minute, Russia rushed to wrap her in his embrace, but she wasn't trying to hear none of it. Using a stiff kick, she planted a size thirteen heel in his chest and knocked him to the floor.

"Did I fucking tell you to touch me, you-you scum!" she spat, her radiant eyes narrowed into slits. "Crawl to me; on your hands and knees like the dog you are!"

Fire ignited in Russia's gaze as he hurriedly complied, thinking, '*This is so arousing—I'm glad I eliminated that piece of trash wife of mine. Now I am free to partake of all de forbidden fruits.*' Once at his lover's feet, he looked at her through a mess of long blonde hair. "May I?" he pleaded.

His lover smiled down at him happily, before doing a complete transformation. She first peeled the itching wig from her head to reveal a short crew cut. She then shimmied out of the leather get up she wore and discarded her foam stuffed bra. She continued the transformation until she was no longer a she but a *he!* Drug enforcement Agent Forrest stood tall in all his glory.

Russia rushed to his feet and took him into his arms. *The two had met years earlier, during an international sting operation that was conducted on the Russia Black Mamba Cartel. Agent Forrest had been a part of the Rainbow Coalition for years and had instantly recognized traits in Russia. So, one cold afternoon Forrest decided to throw caution to the wind and reveal not only himself and the plans of the US Drug Enforcement Agency, but also, he opened dark doors that no man could come back from once they entered them.*

In the heat of a strong kiss, Russia contained himself. "Later—later for 'tis, my love, tell me what's happened," he requested in his deep Russian accent before he took Forrest's hand and led him to one of the two overstuffed chairs.

As he took the over chilled glasses of Scotch, Agent Forrest explained how after they'd tracked down Pablo and murdered him, they'd found Bella's number in his phone and began texting her under the pretense of it being him. She trusted her cousin and never questioned his reasons for wanting to meet at Ice-Berg's house for an emergency meeting, but her trust proved to be her undoing once she arrived and was abducted by him and the few members of the *BMC*.

The Tiger had gone to the extreme in torturing info out of her, and in the end—she'd broken and told them about Ice-Berg's surgeries and what she knew about, Assata. After The Tiger squeezed as much as he needed out of her, he slit her throat and handed her over to the crazed Doctor V. The demonic doctor drained all her blood before slicing her open and removing her internal organs. The sick son of a bitch seemed as happy as a punk in a dick factory as he sewed her closed and explained why he'd done what he'd done.

He said it was imperative that they minimize the stench of rotten flesh because if Ice-Berg caught a whiff of death he'd know something was amiss and run for the hills before their plans could be carried out to completion. So, they placed Bella in the bed as if she was sleeping and embalmed her in that position before placing a pressure sensor impregnated with magnesium in her hand. The Tiger had held her hand closed over the device until her muscles contracted and held it in place, the next time her hand opened, it would be a deadly Fourth of July.

The plan seemed foolproof, but somehow Ice-Berg had survived the blast and was now a hazard to them all. Russia smiled in spite, of the botched hit, he was already a wanted man, so Berg could do little else to him. Within the midst of hearing the sordid details, lust danced in Russia's eyes. No one knew of his dark secrets of strange fetishes—so he thought, but little did he know, someone was on to his Sodom and Gomorrah ways and had hired a private investigator to track him.

The PI had been following him, capturing his every move on film before making a call. "They're in the room and things seem to be quite—" he paused to find the words adequate enough to elaborate on the strange erotica he'd just witnessed. "—quite unnatural." He winced, recalling the strange behavior of the two.

Across the globe in America, Snow smiled at the disgust heard in her private investigator's tone. Being a pansexual herself, she recognized the traits in Russia. When his dick stopped rising for her, she knew there was something imbalanced within him, so she hired the PI to investigate.

The results proved to be very interesting, to say the least. "Nice work, e-mail me the photos and your money will be sent to the account the same as always."

****

~Goose~
~A Week Later~

I'd been following Kamika for the past few days. The woman truly had no life: work, gym, and more work were her daily activities. A creature of habit was a danger to themselves because it gave the hunter an easy job. Yet, there was one change to Kamika's activities, and that one change would be used to my advantage. There was a juicy big breasted woman that Kamika seemed to be quite close to. They went shopping and out to eat on the regular, I could tell they had a bond forged by *gossiping*. The other woman seemed to never shut up, and I planned to use that to my advantage.

I watched her enter the Walmart after getting a food basket. *'Good—she plans on being there for a while,'* I thought.

I gave her a few minutes head start and pursued my prey. From my observation those few days, I could tell the detective needed some excitement in her life, and I was the cat to give it to her. In fact—she'd thank Jesus for this shit I was 'bout to expose her to.

****

~Detective Tonya Johnson~

I studied the strawberries to make sure they weren't rotten or bruised. Satisfied, I placed them in the basket and turned to push my cart but was blindsided by a clash of metal against metal.

My heart leaped up into my throat. "What the hell?" The words slipped from my lip as my eyes found those of a handsome young man with dreadlocks braided into an intricate design.

I could tell they'd been freshly oil and well-manicured. His handsome face held a look of surprise as he wrapped up his call.

He raised his hand in a just a moment gesture. "J, let me give you a call later—I just had a head-on collision with one of the most gorgeous sistas I've ever seen," his words made me smile as I watched him disconnect and turn to me. "I don't know if I should be apologizing or thanking God for fate, but either or—" He pushed his basket to the side and walked over to me with an extended hand. "My name is Mark Miners and I am so sorry for being so reckless."

I took his hand as our eyes played the game of who would look away first. His stare was seductively predatorial and it became a task keeping my composure as my panties became sticky. I lost the stare down and allowed my eyes to fall to his ring finger—empty! Not even a shadow of pale skin that the consistency of wearing a ring created. I blushed when my eyes met his smiling face, he'd caught my assessment.

"I know I didn't cause that much damage?" he said with a quirk of his left eyebrow.

The statement confused me. "Huh? I don't understand."

Mark's eyes were aglow with humor. "I mean, we're still holding hands, but you haven't given me a name."

Embarrassment surged through me as I hurriedly tried to separate my hand from his, but he held fast. I was on the verge of informing him that I was a cop and it wasn't a good idea to tick me off, but he boggled my mind even more than it already was by bringing my hand to his lips and planting the softest kiss I've ever felt on each—and—every—knuckle.

The jester stole my breath and instinctively my mind wondered how his lips would feel on my— "Well, maybe fate wasn't truly on my side, sweet lady. So, I'll let you get back to your shopping." He released my hand and prepared to leave.

My heart fluttered—I missed the man's touch already, and we'd never been intimate. "No—" I said a little too urgently. "I—I mean, my name is Tonya Johnson."

Mark turned to face me again and I swear—life felt whole again. Walking back over to me, he reached in my basket and took out the strawberries. He looked at me and open the package before plucking one from it.

"Tonya, huh?" he whispered and studied the strawberries before placing it in his pocket. "That's a beautiful name, and when we meet again, I'll give you this fruit back."

Confused, I studied him. "And what makes you think we'll meet again?" I inquired.

Mark took his phone off his hip and dropped it in my shopping cart. "Because I'm gonna call you tomorrow at seven-thirty to tell you where we have reservations for dinner, so be ready," he replied before turning and leaving me and *his* cart standing there dumbfounded.

****

~The Prisoner~

They pushed my wheelchair through the highly polished corridor of the Florence Supermax Federal Prison. My thoughts were congested, and my pride was broken for what I'd subjected myself to, but I couldn't spend the rest of my life trapped inside that underground cell. Not only imprisoned to myself, but also to the wheelchair that was now my legs. I was paralyzed from the waist down and I hated it! I hated myself, I hated my past and most passionately, I hated my—

"Thank you, officers, that will be all," a short, blue-eyed, white man ended my thoughts.

I'd *finally* been summoned by the same mu'fuckas that buried me in that concrete basket.

"We can't leave the prisoner, Mr. Harrison, he's too dangerous and—" the guard began before the smaller man gave him an arctic glare.

"I am a federal agent under strict orders for the director of the Federal Bureau. This meeting is protected under the United States Seal and mandated under the guidelines of the federal agency's protective custody program. That means you two good men *must* excuse yourselves," he spat at the two prison officers. They had a brief stare-down, but finally, the leading officer conceded.

"Pick your poison, Sir." He and his flunkey chained me to the table and left me alone with the man I'd had nightmares about ever since we met almost a year ago.

"Agent Harrison—it's a pleasure to see you again, dick sucka!" I seethed.

The man took his seat and steepled his fingers as he stared at me. "I don't have time for your sick mind games, asshole, you sent for me, so talk," he retorted.

I studied him. "Yea, I sent for you bitch—but that's not how it works. I'm not saying shit til' you give me some guarantees!" I whispered heatedly.

Agent Harrison stood and with agonizing slow steps strolled over to me, one finger tracing the surface of the table as he walked. Once he stood before me, he glared down at my insecurity.

"Nice wheels!" He laughed at the steam in my eyes, I was defenseless! "You listen here, you paralytic piece of shit—you don't know how shit works!" He kicked the middle of my chair causing it to tilt and me to scramble for something—anything to hold on to.

Yet, the chain that secured me to the table prevented the fall. My body shook with danger—I wanted to blow the white boys brains out but we both knew it was an empty fantasy.

"As we speak, we have David 'Ice-Berg' Swanson chained to a hospital bed awaiting transportation to the most secured prison we have." He smiled sinisterly.

The look of shock on my face must have contented him cause the pussy leaned back against the table, crossed his legs at the ankles, and crossed his arms over his chest with a smug look on his face.

"So, *this* is how it works cock sucker—you called me down here because you want to turn informant on all those small-time street punks, but how about giving us what you have on *Ice-Berg*. You remember him, don't you?"

A pained look twisted my face. What he was asking me was more blasphemous then my intended purpose. "What if I give you something else worthier?" I proposed I didn't want to sink that low. "It depends—but if you can help us nail this scumbag to the floor, you may see daylight in twenty years."

The flash of anger that played behind my eyes told him that wasn't enough. I may sell my soul to the devil, but it won't be cheap. "That's not gonna cut it," I said and stopped to give my next words some thought, my heart cracked before betrayal slipped from my lips. "What if I could give you, Ice-Berg *and* the blow by blow of the slayings at the Russian's house?"

The agent bolted up off the table. "No fucking way—there is no way you can do that!" He began pacing the floor and mumbling to himself, I guess I'd hit a nerve. He stopped in midstride. "How?"

Eye to eye with the man that held my get out of jail free card in his hand, I revealed a secret that I shoulda taken to my grave. "I was there!"

Renta

Chapter Eleven
Goodbyes

~Jazzy~

It was three days away from my big day. It seemed like forever had passed since the day that Shotta proposed. Forever since my heart numbed itself to who it long for. I guess, in some way things turned out for the best. Shotta had been on his best behavior and I rationalized that it was only his fear of me leaving him like his mom did his father that had him losing his temper. As my people say, *'God is love!'*

"Gurrl, you're gonna kill 'em in that Marchesa Gown and those Zanotti Pumps are fierce!" Charla complimented, I smiled a smile that didn't quite reach my eyes, and like always—Charla caught it. "Spill it!" she demanded with a stern look on her face.

"What?"

"Uhhuh—don't even try it, Jazmina. I've known you too long, and that look in your eyes is one that's all too familiar. So, cut the bullshit and tell me what's on your mind."

I turned to the mirror, as I brushed my long wavy hair. I thought back on the day I decided to grow it back out. I had gone out for drinks with Charla and some friends of hers and as we sipped margaritas one of her friends complimented me on the texture of my hair—asked me what I used to keep it that way. They insisted that I must have used chemical, but Charla and I fought tooth and nails to convince them that it was all natural. One of the girls made a comment about how beautiful it would be if I let it grow out and for some reason, it triggered buried memories. Memories so far back that it was hard remembering the exact time and place, but I did—

"Stop boy—why you keep pulling my hair, Assata!" I screamed at him.

He laughed, I could never understand why he'd do that.

"That shit ain't real anyway—you need to give that horseback his shit!" he taunted.

"Boy—my hair is real, ask Shy, he'll tell you." I wanted so bad for Assata to believe me.

I had noticed how all the girls I saw him with had long hair, so maybe if he knew for sure that mine was real, he'd look at me differently.

"Girl, whateva—I ain't gotta ask, Shy nothin'. I know real hair when I see it," he replied.

Days passed and I still wanted him to believe me. My moms and pops were together back then, and moms was one of the most beautiful women I'd ever seen. I came in heartbroken one day after school because I had worn makeup and the tightest dress I had to get his attention, but instead— he scolded me like he was my big brother and I wasn't only one year younger than him. Shy laughed at me— he knew I was in love with Assata and thought that it was so comical for me to be getting dissed by him.

So that day, I sulked my way passed my mom vacuuming the floor and headed to my room. I closed the door and buried my face in my old quilt that my grandma Ellen had made for me years ago and cried like a big ole baby.

I heard the door open and assumed it was my brother coming to meddle me some more, so I turned and spazzed on him. "Leave me the hell alone, Shy, it's not—"

"Whoa!" Assata held his hand up in surrender. "Just me, don't shoot." He got a smile out of me.

We were only twelve and thirteen, but Assata had been in the streets his whole life. Moose made him grow up fast, so he was mature for his age. Closing the door, he sat down on the edge of the bed. "What are you crying for, Jazzy?"

I used the balls of my palms to wipe my face. I was so embarrassed—he would surely think I was a big baby now. "Leave me alone Assata—won't your girlfriend be mad at you for being in my room? What's her name?" I acted as if I was thinking hard before I snapped my fingers. "Yea—that's it, Drea!" I rolled my eyes at the mere mention of the winches name.

An adolescent heart is one of the purest in terms of love. At those younger ages, we love deep and untamed. We believe we'll love forever, but that's because we honestly had the slightest clue what love was. Assata ignored me, got up and walked over to my dresser, I saw him pick up something but I couldn't tell what it was.

"Come here, Jazmina," he requested as he watched me from the reflection in my mirror.

My eyes were red and puffy as I stared back, but I complied. "What, Assata," I huffed my way over to him.

He again ignored me and pulled me in front of him and the mirror. As he stood behind me, we stared at each other from our reflections. Slowly, Assata began to unbraid one of the two long braids I'd had my hair in.

"I'm not good for you, Jazzy. I know you think so, but I'm not. We're family, mayne, and family don't hurt family—" The first braid was undone and he began on the other one. "And that's exactly what I'll do if you was my girlfriend."

Tears welled up in my eyes. "Why Assata—why do you like Drea but not me? My hair is longer than hers," I argued.

Freeing the other braid, Assata laughed hard at my comment, but I didn't share in his humor—I was dead serious. Composing himself, I finally saw what he'd picked up off the dresser—it was my comb. He began to run it through my kinky hair, at first the shit hurt as it kept getting stuck in my thick mane, but I toughed it out and after a while, it raked through easily.

"You're prettier than, Drea too," he whispered so softly that I thought I had dreamed it.

"Wha—what did you just say?" I stuttered.

Assata smiled. "I love your hair, Jazzy, this that—"

"Boy, what are you doing in here—get ya mannish ass out this room, right now, Assata Lamar!" my mama interrupted us.

Assata left the comb stuck in my hair as he rushed for the door. "I—I wasn't doing nothin', Mama Leah, I—I'm—"

Smack!

My mama popped him upside his head as he exited the room. "You, betta keep ya tail out of here, yuh hear?" her Trinidadian accent was strong when she was mad.

"Jazzy—Jazmina!" I heard my name being called repeatedly. I had to shake my head to clear it of the past and focus my eyes on Charla.

"Wha—what's wrong?" I looked at her as if she'd lost her mind.

She stared back at me like I had two heads. "Where the hell was you—girl, you just spaced out on me as you combed your hair." She looked royally pissed off. She huffed, grabbed my arm and turned me to face her. "You still love him, don't you?"

Her question caught me off guard. Here was my fiancé's sister and my best friend asking me did I love another man, three days before my wedding day. Our eyes studied each others.

'*Did I love, Assata?*' The answer swelled inside my heart until the absurdity of it threatened to erupt inside me. Hot tears blinded me—though I didn't admit it to Charla, the answer echoed within my internal like a loud sound inside a tunnel. '*Yes—I was madly in love with, Assata, and I'd die that way.*'

****

~Assata~

I pulled the SS up to the curb of Freedom's spot. It was a chilly afternoon, and I'd finally decided it was time to check in with the Queen, she proly thought I was dead and stankin' by now. As I observed the mover's truck and the men carrying furniture out of the house, my heart sank, seemed like the good things always had an expiration date, while the fucked-up shit seemed to last *forever*! I watched Free step outside, the woman was as beautiful as the first day I met her. She spoke to one of the guys as I studied her—she wore a cotton forest green jumpsuit with a simple dark brown leather coat, but the brown snow boots she wore was what brought life to her ensemble.

Her hair was wild but pulled back in a scarf, and I wondered for the millionth time why I couldn't love her? I watched her smile at something that the cat said, and for reasons unknown, a spike of envy was born. I think all the men are selfish in that aspect. We're afraid of committing but don't want the next man to obtain what we didn't deserve. Finally noticing my whip, Freedom's eyes became the size of dinner plates as she walked away from the man in mid-sentence but paused about three feet away from the Chevy.

Taking that as my cue, I climbed out of the driver's seat. The chill hit me instantly and made me pull the hood of my black hoodie over my head. After adjusting the twin .40s on my waist. I gazed at Free from over the top of my car, for a moment she just stood there with her arms crossed over her chest and stared at the God. I wasn't a mind reader, so I walked around to her and faced off with her like a man.

"Peace, Earth, what the bidness is?" I broke the silence.

Freedom's eyes revealed a storm as she studied me as if I was Lazarus from the biblical days, but still—she stood in her comfort zone, a safe distance from what seemed to be a dream. My patience was getting thin, but just when it began to snap, *something* changed in Queen's posture and before I knew it, she'd ran up to me, and was wrapped in my gangsterisms.

I wrapped my arms tight around her shoulders in an attempt to absorb her pain, her face was in my chest as she cried, "I—I thought you were—" her words trailed off, but it didn't take rocket science to complete the sentence. Queen pulled away and looked up at me. "I thought I'd never see you again."

I placed the soft kiss on lil' one's juicy lips and allowed my hands to flow down her back, and past her waist until they rested on the plushness of her ass cheeks. She smiled up at me with a blush rushing to her cheeks, her love for a real nigga radiated from her aura. At that moment, I knew life had a different story for lady—shawty wanted more out of life. She deserved a good man that held a steady job, a man that could love her to no limit, Queen deserved security!

As I held Free, my eyes traveled to the mover's truck—her eyes followed mine and reality set in as she disentangled herself from my embrace. Even before she opened her mouth, I understood her decision. A lot of cats smother their female's growth—*knowing* they weren't the right nigga for 'em but refusing to let 'em spread their wings and reach their full potential. Men are so fucked up that they worry more about the next man running dick in the girl than her deserving the shit *he* can't or won't give.

That shit always ends up poisonous, so I flashed a diamond smile at Ms. Lady and got the bullshit out the way. "So—you was just gonna up and vanish?" I never dropped my smile to ensure her it was Gucci wit' me.

Freedom reached over and took my hand in hers. "Let's step in the house out of the cold and talk." She had a look in her eyes as if I'd reject her. I stepped into her space, stepped behind her and led her toward the house.

****

~Armani~
Days Later

I could feel his eyes on me—following the sway of my hips. Lust was like a burning flame in his stare as my ass cheeks jiggled like warm jello with each step I took. He'd been observing me ever since he'd entered the club and took up a booth in the back corner. Playboy was a different type of customer than the ones that usually frequented the establishment, but he looked and smell like money, so the ladies were in raw form for his attention. Surprisingly, he turned down every advance from even the choice bitches so he had my direct attention.

That night I had pep to my step—the evidence of some thug loving and the feeling of loving a real nigga. Assata had dicked me down real good that morning, and we'd been spending a lot of time together. I hated to say it, but for the first time in my life, I was willing to place a man before my hustle. Though Assata hadn't mentioned it, I didn't want him to view me as anything less than the woman I'd presented myself as. I'd been tired of the nightlife anyway, and my day job paid well enough for me to make the sacrifice. So, for what I wanted with Assata I was gonna make the sacrifice and make that my last night at the club.

That night I was topless—a transparent G-string rested perfectly between my chocolate crevices, and I made sure that it was pulled up as far as it would go so my lower lips protruded, and blew a nice—wet—juicy kiss at anyone that was sneaking a peek at my paradise. I knew I was a bad bitch as I sashayed through the room with a twist to my hips that gave a new meaning to the term: *a slutty walk.* My feet had a fresh pedi with clear polish accented by the black tips to match mani. My long tresses hung past my glittered backside—two-toned, beginning as a bright white at my roots, fading into a charcoal black in the middle. I had it twisted into two long braids that gave me the appearance of a Hershey chocolate Indian girl.

As I headed to the back to freshen up after a lap dance, my mind carried me on a mental expedition. The night the police had shown up and *forced* me and Assata to leave the cemetery. We'd went back to my apartment and showered. Afterward, we laid up and I held that man as liquid pain drip from his eyes. The experience was one of the most intimate I've ever had with a man, and in that instant, I realized the realism within the cliché, *'a mental love is deeper than the physical.'* When a man gave a female *more* than his dick, allowed her beyond the act of blowing a few grand on her and making her a side bitch. He saw something inside that women that he respected.

That night, after a storm of emotions, Assata made passionate love to me. He took his time with each stroke, then after I had a peek at heaven—the animal inside the man clawed its way to the surface as he fucked me from the back and taught me that even the devil could take you to paradise.

"Say—let me get that dance, lil' mama!" someone shouted and grabbed me by the wrist.

Anger instantly ignited in my posture as I was forced out of my daydream, I hated thirsty niggas, but I despised men that felt a *conversation* was part physical, with a dramatic roll of my eyes and fire on the tip of my tongue, I turned to give the violator a piece of my mind, but before I could release the beast on him, the owner of the club caught my eye. Gucci was sitting at the bar nursing a shot glass, observing his money. Our eyes met, and I had to tame myself, though it was my last night, one never knew what the future would bring.

Gucci didn't play about his chips and his policy of keepin' the customers happy was instrumental to my employment. I didn't want to cause bad blood and not be able to fall back on the hustle if things got hard.

"My ears work perfectly fine, handsome, there is no need for the physical." I leaned over and spoke in his ear so he could hear me over the music.

My nipples instantly hardened as they grazed his right shoulder. He released my wrist as I stood back to appraise him. He had pretty boy features framed by silky curls. To some, he'd be a prize, but me personally, I like my men dark, gangsta, and a little rough around the edges. Pretty boy smiled up at me, probably used to women fawning over him, and being the seductress that I am, I used his ego to my benefit. I could tell that he was a youngsta, and shorty next to him added to my assumption as be goaded his boy to try his shot.

"My—my fault, Mami, it's just my B-day and you—I just—" he was flustered as I stared at him through long lashes and chinky eyes.

He was intimidated by me, and I used it against his young ass. In between the DJ changing songs I jeweled him, "That doesn't give you the right to be groping women that didn't invite you to do so. What if my man was up in here, youngin?" I replied and placed my hand on my left hip and anticipated his answer.

I could feel the eyes of the stranger from earlier boring into my backside as the youngster responded, "I ain't scared of ya dude, ma, I can handle my own. Feel me?" He patted the bulge on his waist and smiled revealing a dimple in his left cheek that was so deep it looked as if I could hide something inside of it. He was adorable.

I laughed at his adolescent bravado as the DJ spun *Lil Keke's 'Show Me What It's Made For.'* I made up my mind and straddled the birthday boy reverse cowgirl so that I was facing the stranger as he sat in the shadows of the back of the club. Since the lights were dim, it was hard to see him clearly, but I knew his eyes were on me.

I'm here to spend this money /so take it off for me/ Girl, I want you to show me what that Pussy made fa /Work the edge of the stage, I see it in your face/ Girl you wanna show me what that pussy made for/ At the end of the night, I'm gonna do you right/but you gotta show me what that pussy made fa—what that pussy made fa.

I check ya forecast, they tell me when it rains, it pours/that pussy all mine, this money all yours/don't get it twisted, I'm a G, but I paid her—she took me to school then showed me what it's made fa.

Lil Keke energized the room as I paced my hands on my knees and leaned forward, staring into the shadows where I knew he was staring back watching my performance. I wound my waist in time with the beat, youngin' slapped my ass and I put an arch in my back, his lil' ass was too excited. Using my special technique, I popped each ass cheek, isolating one, as the other vibrated like it was spasming. I knew I had more than just the youngsta's attention because I peeped how a dude at the table to my left elbowed his potna to get his attention. The potna was in the process of turning the ace of spade bottle up when I bent all the way over and placed my palms flat on the floor.

I lifted myself into a headstand before wrapping my legs around the yougin's waist. My ass cheeks began to vibrate as if they were boiling water in a scalding pot. The brotha spat a mouthful of spade onto the table and his man's arm in astonishment. I could feel youngsta's manhood throb against me as Keke gave him the incentive to stuff different denominations of bills under my garter.

Super thick but being sexy wasn't the same thing/ between ya legs can get ya chedda and a betta name/ I love ya stage show, get low so I can see/ I gotta couple stacks for you girl believe me/ I'm on patron with them Kush squares and feelin' lovely/ work ya goal mind—say boo, you so lucky/ up and down, bust it open, then take it slow/ I'm here to spend this money, you gon' have to show me tho.

****

~The Back of the Club~

The observer sat hidden in the shadows nursing a three-finger glass of rum, neat. His eyes never left the beautiful dancer as she put on a spectacular show. A show he knew was meant for his eyes to see. As he took a small sip of the brown liquor, a gentle smile quirked at the corners of his lip if only she knew that not only was she making his *business* his pleasure, but also easy, she wouldn't be so eager to entice his thirst for blood.

He knew she was the key to finding where the man Assata was hiding at, the observer had been staking out Assata's house for the past three days, but knew he'd never show. What smart man would after his eyes have been opened to the enemy being privy of where he rested his head? The observer had only found out about Armani after following her from the Cemetery where she and Assata shared their insane moment. The observer knew he'd be able to find Assata at his aunt's funeral. Through his investigations he learned that the man loved the woman deeper than life and concluded that he wouldn't miss the burial for nothing in the world, but when Assata didn't show up for the funeral, the observer was ready to search elsewhere, but figured he'd see the burial site, and lo and behold.

"Tonight, my last night, handsome, and I'd truly enjoy being your entertainment for the rest of the evening," a soft—honey laced voice disturbed his thoughts.

The observer cursed himself for being so careless as to allow the pretty girl to sneak up on him. He took a slight sip from his drink to cover up his natural reaction. *"Tat' depends,"* he continued

"On?" The pretty little woman smiled seductively with a curious expression and flirting with death came to life in that instant.

****

~Armani~

The man was a strange character—I always been attracted to the art of tattoos, but this man had not only went overboard with the ink but obviously, he had a fetish for exotic animals. I loved Tigers as well, but this man was obviously obsessed! As far as I could tell, his arm, face, and head were covered in a strange Tiger stripe pattern. His features were Middle Eastern if I wasn't mistaken, but I couldn't be sure. What I was sure about was the Bezel Audemars that glistened on his wrist despite the dimness of the light, and the dark YSL bubble shades he wore cost five-hundred or more. Without the gaudy jewelry that most of the youngsters wore to express their level of success, his were more conservative—silent money.

"Depending on your intentions, and how entertaining you can be," he replied with a thick accent.

At that moment, the DJ put on *Yo Gotti* and *Nicki Minaj's 'Rake it Up,'* with a mischievous grin, the strange man sat his glass on the table and patted his lap. I couldn't explain why, but it was something about the dude that set off alarms. I glanced back to the bar where Gucci and his bouncer Bear sat and made eye contact with Gucci. The man had always had a thing for me, but I never mixed business with pleasure and he respected me for that. He gave me a slight nod of confirmation before I turned back to my prey—my eyes turn to slits as I licked my lips as if I was anticipating devouring him for dinner.

I climbed in his lap, and he instantly cupped my ass. "Your boyfriend?" He nodded in Gucci's direction.

I glanced down at him as I placed my hands on his shoulders and gyrated my hips to the beat. "And if he was?" I smiled.

The man reached up and took off his glasses. He sat them down and locked eyes with me. My breath got caught in my throat, his pupils were an inky blackness that told a story of cemeteries and bullets.

My heartbeat against my chest as he reached behind me and spread my cheeks open. "Let him watch—by de way, I'm de Tiger," he whispered.

****

~Agent Harrison~

I had been back in Quantico for merely hours and already I was immersed in paperwork. If what I was told was correct, I may have been able to close not only the slaughter at the Russian's house but also the capture of the infamous drug Lord, David 'Ice-Berg' Swanson, had made headlines the day after he'd been identified. The ironic part was that they were connected. Mr. Swanson had been very busy since his infamous elude of justice.

I shook my head in amazement when my phone rung. "Yello!" There was a pungent silence on the other end of the line. "Hello— is anyone there?" I inquired, irritation lurking just beyond the surface.

Someone had been playing phone tag with me all day. A few times they'd just sit there silently, soft breathing the only confirmation that they were on the other end.

I mentally vowed not to answer the blocked number again and was seconds away from hanging up when— "May I speak to Harrison—Agent Harrison?" a soft voice sparked my senses.

For reasons unknown, the hairs on the back of my neck stood up. "This—this is he. Who am I speaking with?"

She giggled seductively as a deep moan escaped her lips. "It— shit, it matters not *who* I am, *pig*, but what—oh God, faster, mutherfucker!" She growled.

Confusion quickly registered on my face. *'Was someone playing a sick game? Were they toying with me?'* I wondered.

"You have to—shit—to excuse me, *pig*. I'm getting my pussy ate as we speak, but that's not—wait—*fuck*," she sounded as if she'd just reached her climax. I was on the verge of giving the psycho the dial tone when she rocked my world. "I'm calling to tell you that you have a dirty cop in your midst, and if you want to catch the Russian, you have to catch the compromised officer first," she spoke matter of factly.

My knuckles were white from the grip I had on the edge of my desk. *'Was this some typa sick prank?'* Are you there—hello?" she sang into the receiver.

My mood was in high gear. "Yea—yea, I'm here," I replied skeptically. There was no way any of my fellow officers had gone rogue—sure, it happened, but not on *my* watch.

"Listen close, Mr. Harrison, because I'm about to give you enough information to push you to the highest position it is in the office, but only under *one* condition—"

The silence was thick as I weighed the possibilities of what she could ask for. "What condition is that?" I asked hesitantly.

"You have to eat my pussy for three days!" She giggled with the request.

Blood rushed to my face. "Listen here, you—"

"No, you listen!" she screamed. "I'm doing you this favor because I need you just as much as you need me. So—enough of the games—" At that moment my laptop chirped to alert me that I had an e-mail. "I just sent you a few surprises, *Pig*, make sure you make it count," she said before disconnecting the call.

I had nothing to lose, so I signed into my e-mail, and as soon as I gained access. My heart almost exploded in my chest, about a hundred and fifty pictures flashed across the screen. Two men in very compromising images—some of those two men out for drinks, but many were insidious and very graphic captures of the two men in sexual trysts.

Disgusted, I forced myself to look at each picture. "I'll be damned!" I murmured to myself upon recognizing Agent Forrest and the Russian mob boss.

I continued my observation until I came upon a picture of a very majestic image of a glass structure erected from a vast body of blue water. I frowned as I studied it closer—something about the image struck a chord with me, but I couldn't place it. Sweat beaded on the bridge of my nose, as I studied the other pictures.

A knock at my office door startled me so much that I jumped. "Come in!" I shouted after I composed myself.

The door opened and a woman that I'd never seen stepped in. "Hi, Mr. Harrison, my name is Janice, and I'm covering for Angela. She's caught a bug and couldn't come in, so I'm your temp replacement." She extended her hand.

I wiped my hands on my pant legs before standing and taking her hand. My eyes took in her features, her resemblance to Pandora Jacobs was uncanny. The only contrast to the two was this woman's pixie cut hairstyle and slightly pudgy build was a major difference in comparison to Pandora's long blonde hair and exotic curves.

"That's peculiar, Angela is like a sister to me—I'd thought that she'd at least call and inform me that she was ill," I murmured with a mock hurt look on my face.

That got a smile out of her. "Well, I'm just dropping this package someone left for you at the front desk. It was certified so I had to—" She shrugged her shoulders as if to say it was no big deal to forge my signature.

Janice held the small box out to me, and without taking my eyes off her, I accepted it. I couldn't shake the nagging feeling that I'd met her somewhere before. "Not to sound typical, but have we met before?" I threw caution to the wind.

She gave me a studious gaze as if she was attempting to place me. I could tell if she'd lost a couple of pounds, she'd be quite a looker. "No, I'm sure if I'd met you or even seen a face as handsome as yours, I'd have remembered." She smiled brilliantly.

I returned the gesture before walking behind my desk and observing the picture again—a light bulb clicked on in my head. "Uh—before you leave, do you mind taking a look at this?" I stopped her before she reached the door.

Janice had a strange look on her face that I couldn't describe but strolled over. "Sure," she said and looked down at the picture. "Have you ever seen this place before?" I inquired.

She studied the image for a moment before that contagious smile erupted onto her face again. "Oh my, God, yes—I've always dreamed about going there—they say it's the *most luxurious hotel in the world!*" she stated. My blood surged in my veins as I awaited her to continue and she did. "It's over in the United Arab Emirates—that's the *BURJ AL Jumeirah Hotel!*

****

~The Tiger~

I parked a few spaces down from where she'd parked. I'd followed de girl Armani to her home from de club and gave her enough time to get situated before I grabbed my famous friend and slipped from mi car with serpentine silence. I'd watched her stop to retrieve her daughter before coming here, so I knew she wasn't alone. I hated harming children, so my attitude was quite fucked up when I knocked at the door I'd watched her enter.

Second, passed before hurried footsteps spattered a stop at de door. "Mama—mama, there's somebody at the door!" An angelic voice broke mi heart.

The sounds of locks being turned sped mi heartbeat before it was flung open to reveal a tiny beautiful child clutching a black doll to her chest. "Lili, you better not open that door or I'ma whoop yo' lil' ass!" A woman's voice raged from the back room, but she had to have realized how late the warning was as she rounded the corner and our eyes connected in a battle of hunger and fear.

"Hello, Armani—I'm afraid I wasn't all the way truthful with you."

****

~Agent Harrison~

As soon as Janice left, I'd called the director to inform him of my findings, and he'd informed me that not only did we have people on the Emirates soil, but also, I couldn't go after Forrest without clearance from the boys up high *and* the DEA! I'd argued that it was my case and *I* deserved the bust, but he stood firm on us giving the DEA first rights to their own man. He'd ask me how'd I come to a conclusion so outlandish, and out of spite, I twisted the truth. I informed him of the anonymous call and e-mailed him the pictures *except* for the one that would lead them to the treasure.

The one good thing that has come out of the conversation was the director's vow to not reveal our findings until Agent Forrest led us to the Russian. He didn't know I didn't need Forrest for that, but this was the biggest bust of my life. There would be a cold day in hell before I allowed anyone to steal my glory.

Minutes after we'd hung up, my phone had rung again—frustrated, I answered, "Yeah!"

"Well, who pissed in your cheerios?" a completely healthy sounding Angela inquired.

My mind carried me back to Janice. "Well, for one, you could have told me you were sick—I thought we were better than that and—"

"Wait, what the hell are you talking about, Harrison, sick?" my receptionist interrupted my rant. The tone and surprise in her voice told me that something was off.

"Well—didn't you call in sick—that's what the new girl told me."

Angela was silent for a moment before she said something that made me race to the door in hot pursuit. "Uh—Harrison, I think we have a problem—" She seemed to ponder her next words, "I was in a wreck this morning on my way into work, and when I got out to assess the damage, someone robbed me! Funny thing is, the only things they wanted was my phone and car keys. I *just* arrived here minutes ago.

Renta

Chapter Twelve
The Reversal

~Goose~
~Two Weeks Later~

Boc! Boc! Boc! Boc! Boc!

Shots sounded off as a bullet hit their mark, I stared at Kamika Winslet in awe. The woman was a nice shot, and I knew she was hip to that fact. I was counting on her pride to help me bring my plans into fruition. It had been weeks since Pain had stumbled across the burner that was meant to bury me under the prison, and I'd laid down my plans to return the favor brick by brick. For the past few days, me and Tonya had been building a nice relationship. The day after we'd met, I'd taken her out to, '*Olive Garden.*'

That night after we'd eaten, I took her to the pier by Lake Dallas. We sat on the edge of the deck and watched the moon reflect off the frigid water.

"I had a splendid night, Mark, it's been a while since I was able to just unwind," she'd broken the silence.

I was so busy sneaking a peek at them big ass titties that her words caught me off guard. "Oh—that's—that's what's up, lady. I'm glad you enjoyed yourself," I replied before reaching in my pocket and pulling out a gold wrapped object with a red ribbon tied in a bow. I handed it to her, and Tonya stared at it as if it was a wedding proposal that came too early. I laughed. "Well—are you gonna open it or stare at it like it's a disease?" I asked with humor in my voice.

Her eyes lifted from the gift and found mine before she reached over and took it from my hand. A slow smile spread across her face as she unwrapped it to reveal white chocolate dipped strawberry.

"I had it dipped this morning and frozen; it may be soft to the touch, but—" my words trailed off as I plucked the fruit from her hands and held it up to her succulent lips.

Her round eyes found mine as her lips parted and closed around the tip of the strawberry. She moaned as she partook of the fruit—and as her eyes closed at half mass, I understood why it was so easy for the serpent to push Eve to violate the Garden. Women had a tendency to trust a man no matter how many times she'd been burnt for the act. She just wants to trust the man that builds and molds her. The man that opens her mind to the shit she was once blind to. As I came to terms with that truth, I realized that men had that same desire.

At times, we want to love and trust a mu'fucka so bad that we never take time to see beyond the hand that's feeding us the forbidden fruit that's used to open our eyes to the bullshit we shoulda already had 'em peeled to. If we did, Eve woulda recognized that the serpent's intent was never pure, and if Adam had been a thinker, he woulda recognized the serpent in his bitch by feeding him the fruit that a snake gave her.

Tonya's eyes opened and it was if she'd read my thoughts. "What's your intentions with me, Mark?"

I gazed out at the dark waters before popping the rest of the half-eaten delicacy in my mouth. "I intend to take you on a journey that you'll never forget. It's dark 'round my way, mama," I replied. She looked at me as if she didn't understand, so I stood and offered her my hand to help her to her feet. "It's dark and I need you to be the light to guide my steps." I smiled at the smile my words gave birth to.

"Goose! Are you alright, baby? You just zoned out on me," Kamika brought me back to the present.

I smiled at her before planting a quick kiss on her lips. "Yea…I was just so amazed by your shooting that I came up with an idea—a challenge." I eased the confusion on her face.

She stared at me for a few more seconds and then she accepted my excuse. "Okay—what do you have in mind?" she asked as she reloaded her service weapon.

I held up my hand and ran off to take the bullet-riddled paper off the tree and replaced it with a fresh diagram of a man with a red target where his heart should be. I glanced around out of habit, it was good we were out in the country—far away from the ears of anyone that would botch my plans. I jogged back over to Kamika and reached in the duffle bag I'd brought a few snacks and toys in.

I pulled out a blindfold and turned to show it to her. "*Any* cop can hit a target so close up. That's part of y'all's training, but let's see how you do blindfolded with an unfamiliar gun!" he challenged.

****

~Freedom~

Assata thought I was long gone—back in New York, but the truth was—I was still there in Denton, Texas. I hated to lie to him because as a woman, I didn't believe in fabrications, but sometimes lies just had a way of finding residence in relations that wasn't built to house them. That day that he showed up to my house, he'd caught me by surprise. I truly assumed he'd been killed by those crazy people, but his return not only contradicted my belief but also changed my plans. My body still relished in his touch—his kiss—*him!* If this was another lifetime, maybe our love would have been boundless, but we have to wait until that next lifetime to find out. I shivered in pleasure as I reflected on our last night together.

After hot tea, we'd talked about everything under the sun. we'd laughed, and I cried when he reminded me his aunt that was taken due to a good man that chose the worst road to travel. I opened up to him a little about my family. My family back home, and my younger brother that was stolen from me by heartless hands, men that lived the same life he lived. Somewhere in between the laughter and tears, our clothes were discarded, and I found myself standing in the middle of an empty living room facing a naked gangsta with images of the life he lived etched into his dark skin.

We faced off for what seemed like forever trapped within seconds—a lioness and the lion. When he pulled me into his warm body, my heart and soul seemed to hate him for the type of man he turned out to be but yearn for him for that exact reality. It was a beautiful contradiction, lost inside an out of control intimacy as our lips met under the moonlight pouring in from a bare picture window. If anyone was to walk close enough, they'd witness passion in its rarest form.

A growl escaped from somewhere deep inside him as his hands found my backside. Assata lifted me off my feet and took off walking with me until my back was plastered against the wall. I instinctively wrapped my legs around his waist, and my arms around his sculpted shoulders. Our tongues danced a slow—passionate dance, and with our eyes open—a queen gazed into the orbs that held a warrior's deepest secrets. Assata plunged inside of my oasis with a delicious urgency. I inhaled deeply before burying my face in the crook of his neck, with each stroke the man seemed to be searching for Atlantis inside of me.

"Assata!" I moaned as I sunk my teeth into his shoulder. Heaven and earth ceased to exist as his pace became fervid. "Deeper—God!"

****

~Detective Winslet~

My eyes were covered by the black cloth, the feel of the pistol was familiar in a sense of my being used to handling guns, but it wasn't *mine*! I didn't know the make—the color—nothing, but I adjusted to the size and balanced it in preparation.

"Let's see how good you are now, badass," Goose taunted.

I focused and squared my shoulders off—I loved a good challenge.

Boc! Boc! Boc!

I squeezed the trigger three times—confident I'd hit my mark, but Goose wasn't satisfied. He took the pistol out of my hand and placed another one in it.

"Now try!" he challenged.

Though the grip was different, and the weight was off, my confidence was heightened. Without hesitation, I squeezed the trigger until the slider jammed back indicating that the clip was empty.

Goose untied the blindfold and smiled at me. "Baby, where the fuck did you learn to shoot like that?" he exclaimed and pointed to the target.

A triumphant smile exploded across my face—the red spot on the target was completely gone. In fact, the entire chest and head area were shredded and as holy as the church. I couldn't contain my excitement. "I told you I was bad, boy, keep that in mind while you're running around here sticking your dick in those hot tail girls out there!" I kidded him.

Goose nodded with a funny smirk on his face that made me wonder if he was concealing a secret or if he knew I was dead serious!

****

~Detective Johnson~

I sat at my desk at the station—I'd decided to attempt to catch up on a few things, but my mind and intentions wouldn't coincide with one another. While my intentions were to do what I loved the most, *investigate,* my mind was burglarized with thoughts of Mark. The man was a piece of work—though he wasn't the caliber of man I'd usually be attracted to, every day that we spent getting to know each other contradicted everything I thought I knew about a street dude. Mark had allowed me a peek at his life, and it took my breath away to hear of his experiences in San Antonio.

I was surprised he didn't grow up to be a killer like so many of the men that raised him. Instead, the man chose to come here for college to pursue a better life. That was admirable, but like they say—*you can take the man out the streets, but you can't take the streets out of the man.* There was something-something different about him that I couldn't quite put my finger on, but I knew in time all would be revealed. We'd been seeing each other for weeks, and as unlike me as it was. I'd already given him my goodies. I was in love with the *idea* of him coming home to me every day. *I was in love—already? Was it the sex?*

I was deep in thought when a nearby phone tore through my reverie. I glanced around to see if anyone would answer the annoying jingle of the outdated device, but the station was all but deserted. Out of myself, and a few other lonely souls—people had lives outside of work and relished in their escape from the madness of detective work. To my relief, the caller hung up, but just when I was on the edge of slipping back into my thoughts, the irritating jingle started again. My eyes followed the sound to Winslet's desk where with every ring—a red button glowed on the phone base. Sista girl was one of the ones that had a life outside of there, and she was probably out with her mystery guy that she was so secretive about.

'*What's the big deal anyway?*' I wondered as I huffed my juiciness out of the chair, and over to the phone. '*Kamicka acted as if the man was one of Americas most wanted or something.*' That was a thought that made me giggle to myself before answering the phone. "Division One Precinct—Johnson speaking."

There was a brief pause ensued before a hushed voice came through the earpiece. *"I know what you did last summer!"* it sang in a sickeningly sweet tone before hanging up.

I was baffled as I placed the phone back on its base, and turned to go back to my desk, but before I could take a step in the opposite direction, the notification alert on Winslet's computer stopped me in my tracks. I assumed she was in a hurry to leave the day before, and not only left her computer on but her e-mail as well. An attachment blinked red on the screen—I just *knew* that whomever the caller had been had sent it. I glanced around to make sure no one was paying me any mind before taking a seat in Winslet's chair. I knew I was violating my girl's space, but the detective in me overrode my respect for human privacy.

The screen was one of those smart ones where I could touch the icons—so I did. I instantly wished I'd never stuck my nose where it didn't belong. What flashed on the screen stirred an earthquake of emotions inside me that was an iota away from driving me crazy.

****

~Assata~

I took the dozen roses off the passenger seat and stepped out the car as if I owned the entire apartment complex. The sun was out and reflected off my jewels, but the day was blinding with an arctic chill to the breeze. Like always, I scanned my surroundings for predators lurking in wait, but everything seemed peaceful. I shook my head in shame—the constant need to look ova my shoulda had become old. At a time in every street nigga's life, he should come to the realization that the streets were a dead-end road. I was already at that point, and that was the mere reason I'd showed up to Armani's spot unannounced. I'd read and reread the letter Jazzy had left, and I was certain that I was missing something.

Though I didn't know what that *somethin'* was, I was following my heart and giving it what it craved the most. Every animal had its weakness, and mine was Jazmina. The mountains she'd mentioned in her letter struck a chord with me cause I used to tell her that she'd gotten too big for the hood, and to run for the mountains, *California*. So, on a whim I called up to the college she used to go to—it was a long shot, but it paid off. I was able to bribe her last known residence out of a sweet flirtatious lady that worked in administrations. It was listed to a three-bedroom stucco in Long Beach, and me and the pound already scheduled a round trip.

Pain and a few of the homies had already driven our arsenal of heat out there so we'd be able to set the temperature if shit got ugly. I paused at Armani's door—there were two things that pushed my instincts into overdrive and made me up the tool. One: it was too quiet, Armani had kids, and on weekends her son would come down to visit from his old man's spot. Two: the door was ajar, and it wasn't like Armani to be so careless. I hid the MP behind the bouquet of roses and glanced around to see if her truck was parked in its usual spot—it was.

'*That's not a good sign!*' I thought as I used my foot to silently push the door open and slip into the living room.

The curtains were drawn closed, so it was dark—I stood still with the roses held out in front of me—my finger tight around the trigga, and ready to molest that bitch if trouble awaited me in the darkness. Everythang seemed cool, but I knew death wore many disguises, so I stayed on my toes as I crept through the apartment as silently as the plague of death that God sent through Egypt to force Pharaoh to let his people go. I had to pause again once I made it to the doorway to Armani's room. An almost inaudible whimpering sound froze my heart in my chest.

I'd grown to love Lili like she was my own daughter, and there was no doubt in my mind that I'd paint the city red if *any* harm had been done to the child. I reached through the door and fumbled for the switch on the wall until I felt it, then flooded the room with light. It took me a minute to register what my eyes were capturing, but after the confusion wore off—my blood turned black in my veins. Lili's tear-streaked face was facing me as she laid on top of Armani with her face against her mother's bare chest. Armani stared at me wide-eyed as if she was shocked to see me, but the glazed over tint to her eyes was a clear indication that her soul had departed from that room long ago.

There was a lazy movement underneath the sheets that confused me because Lili was lying still—watching me as if she were in a trance. Either Armani had gotten a pet I didn't know 'bout, or her soul was trapped under that sheet searching for a way to heaven.

"Mr. Assata, please tell my mommy to wake up—the bad man left his special friend, and he bites my mommy," Lili cried softly before raising slightly and placing gentle kisses all over her mama's face. "Wake up, mommy, Mr. Assata is here to help us now. Wake up, mommy, *please?*" The child's plea cracked my soul. She turned her innocent eyes to me. "Won't you, Mr. Assata—won't you help us?" she asked. Impulsively, I rushed over to her. I had to pry her hands away from Armani's cold body. "No—no, Mr. Assata, my mommy's cold, I was warming her up!" she cried.

An urgent hissing sound caused me to stumble back a few steps with the child safely in my arms. My eyes darted to the now still lump under the sheet, but a warm feeling caused me to look down to where I cradled the child behind her knees. Blood seeped from small puncture wounds that resembled a vampire's bite.

"I—I'm tired," Lili whined.

I rushed her through the hallway and laid her on the floor as gently as possible. "Stay here, baby, don't move, okay?" I stared down at the beautiful little girl as I snatched my phone off my hip and dialed 911.

She was weak, and hot with fever when I rushed back into the room with the tool clutched tightly—I snatched the sheet off the bed. *"What the fuck!"* the words exploded out my mouth as a man's worse enemy rose like a genie does from its bottle.

A long, black mamba snake swayed back and forth. Its black tongue flickering out of its mouth as it tasted the air. I knew that snakes were blind, and they use their tongue to sense their prey. "Nine-one-one, emergency center, state your emergency," the operator came on the line. The giant snake seemed to smile at me as it flashed its fangs in a menacing hiss. "Nine-one-one—are you there?" The operator was persistent as I slowly backpedaled toward the door.

My mind had transported me back to a convo me and the boy Ice-Berg had before shit got funky. *"We have a problem, homie, the Russian has sent his assassins to the states to do his dirty work,"* he said in a panic.

I was unbothered with his revelation. "Naw, bruh, you have a problem. I don't give a fuck 'bout that Russian or his henchmen."

I looked into his eyes to give him a glimpse of the 'G' that resided there. "Besides—you're the one that's sticking dick to the man's bitch." I laughed and stood to leave.

Berg didn't find no humor in my truths, whoever these people were that the Russian had sent had the man off balance. I knew Berg was a gangsta, so that was enough to get my attention. He looked at me with an amused expression. "See, that's where you got shit fucked up. Yea the dick sucka know that I fucked his bitch, but he thinks I'm dead—" He let his words sink in before continuing. "—and even if he knows I'm amongst the living, this new face of mine will surely be my ace in the hole!" He patted the side of his face to punctuate his statement.

I lifted my arms in an 'and what' gesture. "So, what you sayin', homie? I should be shakin' in my boots or somthin'?"

Ice-Berg's smile disappeared. "Naw, fam, you know I know how you get down, but it pays to know ya, enemy. These fools that the fuck boy sent is 'bout their work, one of 'em especially. They call him The Tiger—some looney ass Russian with tiger striped tattoos all over his skin. My folks tell me that the sucka's specialty is to use the black mamba's as his callin' card!"

I frowned when he said that. "Mambas—as in the dance?" I asked.

Ice-Berg was dead serious when he placed his hands on my shoulders and looked me in the eyes. "Naw, fam, Black Mamba as in the snake!"

"Hello—Mr. Lamar, help is on the way. Talk to me, sir! Is everything alright?" The emergency operator brought me back to the present.

I was almost to the door when the serpent uncoiled itself from Armani's arm and struck at me.

****

~Detective Johnson~

Kamika Winslet was working in alliance with the feds! There were numerous texts and e-mails between her and the agent's conversations in the documents. There were also pictures of her, and the man that I recognized to be one of the agents that came to the station to investigate her that day I'd properly introduced myself, but that wasn't even the bomb that rocked my world. Kamicka was cooperating to bring down an Assata Lamar—a Dunte 'Pain' Jackson—and a *Bennie 'Goose' Weatly.*

Each name had a picture attached to it, and all three men were assumed to be the heads of a murderous drug empire dubbed, '*The Kreek Boys.*' My eyes bore into the image of the last man—he was a lean, handsome man with dreadlocks and a contagious smile. Shock—disappointment—but even deeper, betrayal filled me up internally as a river clouded my vision. I used the back of my hand to wipe the unfallen tears away before they had the privilege of staining my beautiful face.

I wouldn't give him the pleasure of my tears. '*Why didn't he just keep it real? Why did I always have to miss out on love? Why—*' so many thoughts bounced in the walls of my head until one became so prominent, I placed my hand over my mouth to keep from crying out. '*Winslet's mystery man was the same man that not only was I possibly in love with but also the man the FBI claims was responsible for mass murder!*'

Renta

Chapter Thirteen
Wedding Bells

~Snow~
~Three Weeks Later~

My plans were almost complete—after I'd exposed that crooked DEA agent, I *personally* delivered a surprise to the Federal Agent Harrison. I wanted him to know that he wasn't inaccessible. My plans were simple—I *truly* ached to fuck Assata, my pussy dripped for the experience. I was gonna get Russia completely out of my hair and by the time the Bureau of Investigations could blink their lying eyes, I'd be somewhere on an erotic island getting my pussy sucked as I sipped Mai Tai's. I loved my newfound liberation. For once in my life, I was free to live without the reproach of a man. I loved the freedom of doing what the hell I wanted—when I wanted.

Goose was the only one that knew where I lived, and that's because we had unfinished business. I'd changed my entire appearance—I'd shaved my hair very low. I now sported an Amber Rose even all over and though my curvaceous body was still thick as ever, I'd recently gotten my ass reduced. I even went down a cup with my breasts to ensure that every precautionary measure was up to par with the description on my passport and new ID.

"Yep, still got it!" I whispered to myself before palming my tits as I admired my nakedness in the full-length mirror.

I turned sideways to get a good look at my ass. I made each ass cheek jiggle before deciding I'd better stop the bullshit and get dressed before I was late for my date. As I slipped into a thirty-one-hundred-dollar crystal embellished candy pantsuit, I fantasized of fucking Assata in every way imaginable. I laughed to myself as I decided to go panty-less and bra-less. After dabbing a tab bit of La Vie Belle perfume on my wrists, neck, and cleavage, I slid into the last accessories that would let whoever was taking notice know that there was more hood to me than simply my ass.

The cool grey Jordan's complimented the grey pantsuit as if they came as a unit, but I was sure that the bitches at the affair I was attending wasn't up on that candy shit. I smiled as I admired myself.

'*They may not be up on the three-thousand-dollar designer, but anyone would recognize the shoe game—even the snobbish bitches attending the classy affair.*' I thought as I snatched up the twenty-four-hundred-dollar Raffia handbag I'd recently purchased from the Salvatore Ferragamo Collection.

I inventoried the contents of my purse as I opened the door. I wanted to make sure I had everything I needed, but an icy voice froze my blood as my head snapped up in surprise.

"My dear, Pandora—it's such a pleasure to see you again—" Doctor V stood in the doorway brandishing a strange device in my direction.

'*How did they find me!*' I thought frantically.

"Going somewhere?" he asked in a sickeningly, excited tone, and just as I got a grip on the .25, I kept in my purse, his hand flexed on the device and a set of prongs shot out and into my skin. I crashed to the floor from the high voltage of the taser.

****

~Jazzy~

I sat perfectly still as Mama Smith put the finishing touches on my makeup. It was my big day—the day that I'd waited on my entire life, and everything was perfect, *everything* but the man I was set to stand before God with. For those last few months, I think I'd convinced myself that I could settle down with Shotta. I'd convinced myself that loving him was enough, but the truth of the matter was—love isn't enough to maintain a relationship, let alone a marriage. Love was a beautiful feeling, but beautiful wasn't enough to blindfold a woman to the ugly, my heart longed for a gangsta that I could feel in my spirit.

The lack of peace—the incompletion of his nature left me cold inside to know that I was the cause of his internal chaos. I missed him, I willed that thought of him—*needed* him to understand that my heart cried for his gangsterisms just as much as the animal within him roared for what only I could give him.

"There—all done!" Mama Smith exclaimed. She stood and admired her handiwork. "You're beautiful, Jazmina, my son doesn't—" Her words trailed off as her eyes searched mine as if she could see right through them to the turmoil that wrapped around my heart like a serpent constricting around its prey. "What's wrong, baby? You're gonna be walking down the aisle in less than ten minutes, and instead of looking like you're about to pledge your life to the man of your dreams, you're sitting here looking like there is a million places you'd rather be, but here." She took the seat in front of me and took my face in her hands. "Sweetie, I know my son isn't the best man he could be, but he loves you. Now, I won't try to convince you that you're making the best decision by walking down that aisle to him because every woman must learn how to walk in her own pair of heels, but baby—" she paused to wipe a lone tear from my right eye.

"Love is like a puzzle of a million pieces. You can work on the puzzle forever—only to finally get to the last piece and realize you've made a mistake, and you end up having to start all over in certain places—" She picked up the eyeliner and redid the portion I'd ruined. "—but, sometimes—sometimes, Jazmina, you find a partner to put the puzzle together with you, and no matter how many times you place the *right* pieces in the *wrong* places, the trial and error journey make the time invested worthwhile, and you know what?" Mama Smith asked as she stood and helped me out my seat—taking my hand.

She walked me over to a full-length mirror and stepped behind me to place my veil on my head, then she looked up at me through our reflections in the mirror. "After the two of you finally get it right, and the puzzle is complete—you realize that it was never about finishing the puzzle, but more of the love and experiences you made in creating it. In the end, you'll break that puzzle down, and try it all over again—that's what love is, Jazz. The trial and error that leads to forever."

****

~Snow~

When my eyes cracked open, a splitting headache caused me to wince in agony. For vital moments I couldn't figure out where I was or how I'd gotten there, but the sound of Doctor V's voice triggered something inside me that made it all come rushing back.

'What the hell has he done to me?' I thought frantically.

"Welcome back, dear Pandora. I thought I added too much juice in my little toy." He laughed as he fumbled with something that I couldn't see.

I cracked my eyes open again, and this time the light was a little more bearable. Without having to look, I knew my wrists and ankles were bound, yet I allowed my eyes to roam to get a better feel for my predicament. My wrists were bound to the corners of my headboard and my ankles were tied to the end bedposts. My limbs were splayed as if I were crucified with my legs open.

My vision was still clouded when I asked, "What did you give me, you, sick son of a bitch!"

The malicious fucker made a tsking sound with his teeth before responding, "Now, now, my beautiful slut, Pandora. You know how much I disdain foul language." He smiled brightly as he strolled over to me and plopped down on the edge of the bed right where he'd have a direct view of my pussy lips.

I lifted my head slightly, and that's when I noticed the scalpel gleaming in his hand, my heartbeat accelerated. *'Why did he need it, what was his plans?'* My thoughts clashed like waves running onto the shore.

"You know, Pandora, I truly enjoy your—how may I say tis—" He placed a single finger to his temple as if he was deep in thought before snapping his fingers and pointing at my pussy. "De way you entice with your—your lower lips." He laughed as he traced the outer folds of my treasure with the flat side of the blade. "But de boss has tired of your promiscuity." He shrugged as if the decision was out of his hands. "Pandora—you know, at times I wondered why your mother gave you such a name, but it's fitting," he said before crawling between my legs, and using his thumb and pointer finger to capture the right side of my cunt. "Pandora was the first woman bestowed upon mankind as punishment for Prometheus's theft of fire. She was trusted with a box containing all the ills that had the potential to plague people and out of curiosity the dumb bitch opened it."

Though whatever he'd drugged me with had me numb to the touch, the blade slicing into the soft flesh of my femininity caused me to scream out in despair. The blade sliced right through me as if my flesh was mere butter under the kiss of the blade.

"She released all the evils of human life when she opened that box, mi darling, and *I* was one of them," he said before popping the soft flesh of what made me a woman into his mouth.

****

~**Jazzy**~

A big smile was plastered on my face as my dad walked me down the aisle. Even with his shortcomings, the man always seemed to be around when it counted. The flashes from the camera's, the fawning over how beautiful I was—all the way down to the flower girl was like a fairytale. Up ahead, Shotta stood smiling at me as if he'd hit the lottery, and at that moment, I knew that he truly loved me. He was a very handsome man, the Armani inspired tux fitted him like someone had painted it on him. The sky blue, and white color scheme contrasted with his skin in a way that only a bright color would a black man. His dreads were freshly oiled and tied back. No one could deny that he was the most gorgeous brotha in the room.

The walk seemed to take forever to make it to him, but once there, my father kissed me before taking his seat. I stared up into the eyes of the man that I'd be spending the rest of my life with. He smiled at me as the preacher began.

"We are gathered here today to join these two in holy matrimony. What God has created let no other separate. This is a lifetime commitment, and it's rare for people of this era to make the righteous decision to stand before God and pledge their lives to each other. In the good book of Proverbs, chapter eighteen—verse twenty, brothas and sistas, it says, *he who finds a wife finds a good thing.* I am here to tell ya that the good book has never lied!" he shouted to the praises and Amen's of those in attendance.

I glanced back to where Charla sat next to her mom, she winked at me.

'*Was I overreacting? Wasn't my anxiety normal?*' I wondered as my eyes found Shotta's and I smiled as if I was the happiest woman in the world.

****

~Assata~

We pulled up to the house three SUVs deep, and before the truck could stop completely—I was out and headed for the front door with the Mac .90 in my palms. I didn't give a fuck what was on the inside of that house, Jazzy was comin' up out that mu'fucka or I planned to go up in there to see what the B-I was. I heard doors opening behind me and knew without looking back my hounds were backin' me with the typa heat that would heat up an Alaskan Winter.

I pressed my finger down on the buzzer and didn't let up until I heard someone say. "Hold the fuck up mu'fucka, I'm comin'. Stop ringing the *fuckin'* bell before I—" she was saying as the door swung open to reveal fifteen red-clad madmen, strapped up like the Unabomber.

The cigarette that dangling from her lips tumbled to the ground as her hands shot up in protest. "Wait—wait, don't kill me y'all! I got kids, a husband, *and* my granny on life support, please don't"—

"Chill, lil' mama—" I interrupted her as I lowered the monstrous gun. "We ain't coming for no static unless that's the only option. Where Jazzy at?" I inquired.

The shock on her face was ever present as her eyes left me and observed my niggaz who undoubtfully still had them burnas aimed in our direction. The silly girl was so shook she didn't realize that if they were to air that bitch out, I was only in the line of fire.

"Jazzy?" she questioned—her expression merged into one of confusion.

My patience was thin as she tried to figure out why fifteen gang members would show up strapped for one woman. She'd obviously never heard about Helen of Troy—for that one solid bitch, niggas would go to war! I was ready to get my baby and mash out. I knew those West Coast niggas were very territorial, and really wasn't feeling the third coast swag in terms of that gang shit. So, I was pressed for time—I didn't wanna litter those people's streets with blood stains and choppa bullets, but her next words told me that, that might have to be an option.

"Jazzy—Jazmina is down at the First Baptist. Today is her big day—she's getting married!" The lil' pretty woman spoke with a semi-smug look on her face.

Fire danced in my eyes as I reached out with the speed of a fired bullet and grabbed her by the throat. "Well, I guess you'll be coming with me, mama, cause I need directions. And the *only* way Jazmina is gonna stand in front of a preacher with anotha nigga is if a casket is involved," I spat before snatchin' her lil' ass up.

****

~Detective Harrison~

My life had turned into a James Patterson novel. The day that Pandora had hand-delivered me the package. I opened it, and pictures of my entire family and home were inside. There were also a dozen or so plastic snowflakes. I know Pandora's handle was 'Snow', so it was obvious she was thumbing her nose at me, and the FBI. She was letting me know that not only could she get up on me, but also was privy of my family. That day that she came to my office, I was called down to the first-floor restrooms where I was showed the artificial identification, and gel packs she'd used to make herself look pudgy. The woman was a true con woman. I knew that was only the manifestation of the late Bobby 'Brains' Ray.

"Sir, what did you say your name was?" the waiter brought me out of my reflections.

I blinked—it took me a second or two to remember I was at *Delarenta's*, a handsome restaurant in Downtown Dallas. I was taking my wife out to celebrate our tenth-year anniversary, and I planned to use it as a means to make up for the long nights invested at the job.

"Sorry—my name is, Harrison. I made reservations for two— my companion should have already arrived." I smiled as he looked down at his list.

His finger scrolled down the page until it paused. "Yes, Brian Harrison, table for two. Mrs. Harrison is here and has been seated already." He bowed and waved his hand in a dramatic sweep. "Shall we?"

****

~Back at the Office~

Agent Forrest rode the elevator up to Harrison's office. He was oblivious to the powers that be that was on to his scandalous ways, but even when one has one up on their opponent—they have to be aware of all possibilities. No one had enlightened Harrison's receptionist to the foul agent. So, when he arrived—it wasn't a red flag because the agent and Harrison were close pals, and there were times Harrison allowed the Drug Enforcement Agent to wait in his office until he got there. So, when he arrived and told her he was there to pick up a file that Harrison had left in his office, it didn't seem uncommon.

The door opened on Harrison's floor, and the rogue cop followed the highly polished floors to Harrison's office. He glanced around studiously before entering and headed straight for the file cabinet where Harrison kept all his cases and collected data. He began to search for the file on Russia, but it was missing. Frustrated—he figured the quickest way to obtain the info he needed was to get it off the laptop, he *knew* Harrison kept his back up data on. He powered the computer up, and as soon as the screen lit up, it read: *Enter Password.*

****

~Jazzy~

"Do you, Maurice Smith, take Jazmina McKennedy, to be your lawfully wedded wife—to have, and to hold—through sickness, and health—till death do you part?"

I heard the words as if they were far off. For some strange reason, my heartbeat was pounding against my chest, unexplained anger gave me hot flashes as I stared at Shotta.

He continued to smile before he said, "I do."

Tears converged in my eyes, *'Was I happy—disappointed? What was wrong with me?'* I thought.

I was confused about the sudden tidal wave of emotions stirring inside me like a hurricane. I knew that Assata's feeling affected me for reasons that only God could explain, but never had it been that powerful unless we were close. I shook my head slightly to clear it as the preacher turned to face me.

"Do you, Jazmina McKennedy, take this man Maurice Smith, to be your lawfully wedded husband—to have and to hold— through sickness, and health—till death do you part?" he asked.

I studied Shotta so long that his face contorted into a frown. "I do." The words slipped from my lips but seemed foreign to my own ears.

Shotta's face instantly brightened as the preacher raised his hand above us. "If anyone in attendance feels that these two beautiful people shouldn't be joined in holy matrimony—speak now or forever hold your—"

Boom!

A loud disturbance interrupted the ending rites and caused all eyes to fly to the back of the chapel. The doors flew apart as a stampede of men rushed the church. At first, I thought we'd all be killed because of Shotta's gang affiliation—those men wore red mechanic jumpsuits with blood-red or burgundy bandanas covering their heads and faces. Shotta's best man and homies jolted to the attention, but the monstrous artillery that the fifteen men had trained on *everybody* warned them that any false move would end fatally. Five of them had taken up the right side of the church while five of them secured the left, but it was the five that strolled up the center aisle that made my mouth drop to the floor, and my eyes to find those of the man that had *finally* climbed the mountains to find what we both knew was truly his.

****

~Agent Forrest~

He tried every password he thought Harrison would use, but all failed. He'd tried Caroline—his wife's name. Matt, and Susan—Harrison's son and daughters names. He'd even tried Harrison's wedding anniversary which was that day! None of them worked. Forrest leaned back in the seat exasperated.

'*What the fuck could it be*?' he thought.

Then—as if the heavens had shined down on him, his eyes fell to the open *Denton Record-Chronical* that laid on the desk. It was open to an article on David 'Ice-Berg' Swanson—the man

Harrison had been obsessing over for the past two years. On a hunch, Harrison typed in the words *David Swanson*, that didn't work. So, he tried *Ice-Berg*—bingo: *Access granted.*

****

~Assata~

Me, Goose, Pain, Spyda, and my dawg Thug took up the center aisle. The infrared emitting from the aims of their heat danced over the man that Jazzy stood beside. He had long dreads like Goose, but his pretty boy features made it hard to tell if he was 'bout that action. I didn't underestimate no man though—I knew that looks had nothing to do with the darkness of a man heart.

So, as I approached them, I kept my eyes trained on homie as my lips parted. "Preacher, I ain't tryin' to be disrespectful, my nigga, but I got a hunnid reason in this here drum why these two won't *eva* be happily married," I declared once I was a safe enough distance away, that if shit got funky, I'd still be able to work the Mac efficiently. I turned my vision to the only peace I'd ever known. Jazzy was beautiful in a powder blue wedding gown that had a train that trailed behind her about eight feet. Our eyes bore into each others. "Sup, ma, you wasn't gonna invite me to your wedding or what?" I asked with the big gun hanging loosely by my leg.

Queen's mouth opened and closed as if she wanted to speak, but her voice was failing her. He exotic grey eyes were lit with something-something that only *I* could recognize. It was the look of one that had given up on real love. The eyes of a woman that had settled. Jazzy had lost hope in me ever understanding her letter, but even the beast needed the beauty to help him turn back into a man.

"Say, Cuz, have you, niggas lost ya mu'fuckin minds? Fuck is you, Loc, you betta get the fuck up outta here!" the dread head roared.

Four red dots slowly crawled up his chest until they merged into one as my dawgs found their mark.

"Say, Rusta, you may wanna put a muzzle on yo' tongue before yo' face replace Jesus' on that cross up there on that pulpit," I hissed as my eyes met his.

From his stare, I could tell he wanted to test our nuts, but the dot in the center of his forehead had him look cross-eyed as his dumb ass attempted to swat it away.

Without taking my eyes off the fuck nigga, I spoke to my heart, "Jazz, I'll neva force myself on no woman, and I don't know if you love this sucka or not, but for this shit I hold in here for you—" I tapped my chest with a gloved fist. "I climbed the mountain for you. If you do love him, you may as well stay up there, and pledge your forevas to him. I don't think I'll ever be able to accept you loving anotha nigga, but the heart of a gangsta will always strangle his pride because his heart is his *strongest* weakness." I looked into her bright eyes and willed my gangsterisms to penetrate her. "I've fucked hundreds of bitches—touched a mill ticket and had threesomes with some of the baddest bitches in the land. As fucked up as that shit sounds—the truth is, none of that has filled the hole in my chest like you have."

I took a step closer, at the same time the dread head stepped forward, and pushed Jazzy behind him. I had to admit the boy was bold. Still—I gave it to shawty from the gut, "I ain't eva chased no female, but we know your heart beats for this shit right here." I tapped my chest with the butt of the .90. "It's time to come home, mama! You ain't happy with this clown." The dye was cast.

Her silence spoke volumes and I waited for her to run into my arms, but with each passing second of her silence, I knew that fairytales didn't always come true. '*Shy had lied to me—Lovey had as well.*' I held my head as I turned to walk away.

"I'm sorry—I'm so, so sorry," I heard her whisper at my back, but she could save her sympathy.

Real niggas accepted defeat just as well as they accepted victory, and I'd just been defeated by what shoulda neva been my opposition.

****

~Agent Forrest~

What I found shattered my world—picture after picture of me and Russia in lewd sexual positions, photos of private meetings, and a few at the Grand Hotel. I was so shocked that I sat there staring absently at the screen—initially, I'd been after the file to find out who the confidential informant was on the case, but what I'd found was a confidential case on *me*! Perspiration dotted my flesh as my mind raced at a suicidal pace.

'*How'd they get these photos—maybe they were on their way to arrest me right that minute!*' My thoughts morphed into a space of paranoia that caused me to bolt from the chair frantically.

Without turning the computer off, I rushed out of the room, and pulled my cell from my hip—I speed dialed a number as my head swiveled back, and forth in search of an ambush. Rather than take the elevator I took the stairs.

'*I have to get out of here, my days as a Drug Enforcement Agent are numbered,*' I thought as the line was picked up.

"Mr. Forrest is everything alright—I thought—"

"Shut the hell up and listen!" I cut him off in midsentence. "Get a jet fueled and prepare for the return—I'm speaking like yesterday," I demanded and disconnected the call right as I made it to the exit door.

The stairwell was dark as I peeked into the receptionist area, Angela was on the phone laughing at something whoever was on the other line had said. Everything seemed normal, but I knew the game the big boy played, so I waited a few more minutes before rushing out with my weapon drawn. The look on the receptionist's face was priceless as her eyes took in my disheveled appearance— her eyes dropped to the gun in my hand, and I thought about killing her, or maybe taking her hostage till I was safe.

"What the—are you, alright, Mr. Forrest?" she fumbled over her words fearfully.

I allowed my eyes to stay fixated on her. I was searching for the slightest indication that she was putting on a show so I could blow her fucking brains out. Certain that she wasn't putting on an act, I left her sitting there with her mouth agape.

****

~Jazzy~

"I'm sorry—so, so sorry." I murmured.

My heart shattered with each word, *'I'd just said I do to Shotta, I couldn't just walk away from the vow I'd just made in front of not only hundreds of people, but also God—could I?'* My heart answered as I repeated to myself. "I never meant to hurt you, I'm sorry—so sorry." I reached down to slide the heels off my feet, and without warning—I attempted to run toward Assata.

Shotta caught me by the back of the neck. "Bitch, where you think you're going?" he growled.

He must have thought the men from the south were pussy or something, but the sounds of gunshots cleared the air as his shoulder exploded, and blood splattered my dress. I broke free from his grasp.

"Assata!" I screamed from my soul, "Wait, baby!"

****

~Agent Harrison~

After a delicious dinner of lamb chops and a few glasses of Chateauneuf du Pape, full-bodied wine from the Southern Rhone River Valley. Me and my wife shared a chilled dessert of Panna Cotta. I sat quietly as she shared her needs and caught me up on the missed games—the growth of children. I felt like a complete ass as I realized that I barely knew my own family.

"Your son is growing up so fast, hon, and he's at the age where he needs the love of his father. I am his mother, I can teach him many things, but Matt needs you to be there to root him on at his baseball games. We miss you, babe," My wife whispered as I reached over and took her warm hand in mine.

I loved my family and knew that my job was taking a toll on them. So, I made a vow that I would stand on regardless as to what happened. "Caroline, I know I haven't been the best father or husband to you all, and I promise to do better. You and the kids are—" the sound of my phone gave me a pause as an irritated expression replaced the love she had just given me.

We both knew the ringtone belonged to the office, just as my receptionist knew not to disturb me unless it was absolutely necessary. I gave her an apologetic look as I held up a finger to ask for a *short* moment. My wife rolled her eyes at me.

"Hello?" I answered.

"Harrison, I think you need to check on Agent Forrest from the DEA," her words were panicked.

Confusion seeped into my senses. "What—I mean, why?" I asked as a nauseating feeling crept into my stomach.

Angela took a deep breath before her words ended my anniversary. "Well—he came into the office earlier to retrieve the file that you sent him to get, but—"

"What!" I raged.

I was already out of my seat and heading for the door, leaving my wife sitting at the table with tears running down her face.

"Tell me you didn't let him in my office, Angela," I pleaded even though there was nothing for him to find.

He didn't know the password to my computer, and he didn't know we were on to him, but I wasn't too fawn of him snooping around my office while I wasn't there.

"Well, yea—I thought you sent him, and—"

"Pack your things, Angela, you've done enough," I said before disconnecting the call.

I loved the woman like a sister, but her blunders were costly. The last thought I had before hopping behind the wheel and burning rubber out of the parking garage was, *"My marriage was over—that was the last straw.'* I *felt* it!

****

~Assata~

The gunfire and Jazzy screaming my name caused me to spin around with the tool ready to spit, but Jazzy caught me off guard as she flew into my arms and wrapped her arms around my neck.

She buried her face in my neck and bathe me in her tears. "Baby, forgive me—*please!*" she whispered. "He—just forgive me, Assata, I've never loved another man like I love you."

As she spoke, my eyes lifted to observe my surroundings—the dread head was clutching his shoulder tryin' to stop the bleeding as an older woman, and what looked to be her daughter kneeled to assess the damage. I knew it was time to get the hell up outta there before things got worse. The tension was thick as the best man, and a few otha cats fidgeted while screw facing us. I met each man's gaze before my eyes fell on Pain. He was clutchin' twin Glock sixteens and anticipating retribution for shootin' their potna.

"You boys got what you came for—she's made her choice. It's best y'all leave before the cops get here," The older woman spoke her peace.

Jazmina disentangled herself from me and turned to face her. "I'm sorry, mama, but this is where my heart is."

She stared expectantly, the older woman smiled a weak smile as she nodded her head in understanding. "Every woman has her own heels to walk in, sweetie, just keep in touch," she responded.

I didn't know who the woman was, but at the moment she'd won my respect. I took Jazzy's hand and led her out of the church as my niggas backed out with the business ends of them heatas still trained on the crowd. As the last one backed outta the church, I heard the dread head vow to find us, and repay the disrespect. I stored it in my head as we headed back to the Lone Star State.

Chapter Fourteen
Why You Lie

~Ice Berg~
~Two Weeks Later~

Darkness blankets this cold cell—the atmosphere was so silent that the drippin' of my leaking faucet sounded like rain splashing upon the surface of a body of water. It was three am and freezing cold as I sat in the darkness. I watched two small mice dart in and out of my cell in search of deserted crumbs that may or may not fill them up. It had been two weeks since I'd woken up out of surgery to find my wrists cuffed to the hospital bed and Agent Harrison sitting at my bedside with a smile so big it looked as if it hurt his face. Shit was fucked up for the kid, and at times I'd wished I'd died in the blast. I knew there was no way I'd escape from those white folks grasp, and after the dick sucka had read the thirty-five count indictment—I knew that if I didn't tuck my tail, and turn rat—the *least* they'd give me was foreva and a day in prison. I reflected on portions of me, and the agent's convo before I got transported to Florence.

"I won't bullshit you, Swanson I lost hope in ever finding you. It was like you just up and disappeared, but then we struck gold!" He smiled brightly as he laid down the paper, he was reading and stood up. "We found out about your surgeries, and your dynamic drug empire you forged with the MS-13. You've been a very busy man, Mr. Ice-Berg, and I've been just as busy trying to find you so the United States could stick a needle in your arm to get justice for all the lives you've destroyed," he spat. "Unless you might want to save yourself?" he proposed.

I laughed in his face—I knew that was comin'. So many niggas were turning rat that the laws thought every nigga was a rodent. "I'll take the needle, white boy, I ain't got shit to spit box 'bout unless my lawyer present." Those were the last words I'd spoken to the sucka the entire thirty minutes he threatened and taunted me.

Now as I sat lost in a cold cell, I sat as still as a statue. Shadows danced all around me, and loneliness was so thick that it was suffocating. Suddenly, a splash of sound tainted the silence—a raging voice filled with anger—malice—and hate. Somewhere down the long line of cells, a roar emitted from behind a locked door. Pain laced the tone as he screamed at whoever caused him to become unbalanced.

"Fuck you, you, sorry motherfucker, I'll kill you! You think I'm a hoe—huh?" he raved.

Then, there was deep silence again, a silence so thick it could drive one mad. I sat still—listening for the response from whoever he was beefin' with, but after two or three minutes without one—reality set in. There would be no response to the man's madness because whomever he was speaking to didn't exist! It was all mental. Still—I was unflinching with the darkness. I could feel the walls coming alive as my thoughts ran rapid. The cliché that people often used in jest became terrifying to me '*if these walls could talk.*' If people only knew that those walls could not only talk but also steal the sanity from some of the strongest men.

They reveal a reality so deep, and brazen that one that seeks an escape from their reality finds it through either taking a dull blade, and slashing their wrists, or simply finding a peaceful road within the walls of their mind, and venturing so far inside that self-created paradise that they forget the way back out. I sat inside that cold cell, the frigid air that entered from the broken windows licked my skin as the pressures of life, the abandonment of family, and the betrayed love caused grown men to muffle their cries. There were eight more hours before my first day of a speedy trial, and I knew the state was seeking the death penalty.

I thought back to the man that screamed just minutes ago. I wondered what drove him to that dark place? That's when reality stole my breath, and the hurricane inside me swirled vengefully. The storm cascaded down my face as two words blew through my mind as if blown by a gust of wind: *it's expected.* The mind of a maniac!

****

~Jazzy~

It had been a while since I'd been able to just relax, and vibe with my girls. When I'd moved out west, we had lost touch and I'd missed them. Charla was like a sista to me, and I wouldn't trade her for the world, but it was nothin' like being home. Me, Marcella, Shay, and some girl name Cleo lounged around at Shay's house that she'd recently bought. My girl had done well for herself—in my absence, she had gotten herself knocked up by her high school sweetheart Bobo. They were having twins, and I was so happy for my girl. Pregnancy agreed with her, and as we sat around taking shots of Ciroc, Shay sipped orange juice and told us of the names they'd come up with.

As she spoke, I couldn't help but notice how touchy Marcella and the girl Cleo were with each other. I had a strong feeling that they were a bit more than just friends, but who was I to judge. I was just glad to be back home.

"So, Ms. Thang, you have a lot to catch up on. Ya fast ass just up and disappeared on us. I won't even lie, I was fucked up with you! You left and didn't keep in touch with nobody but—" Shay began but became choked up at the thought of Tessa's name.

Our girl had been missing for months, but finally, they'd found her along with some other woman—their bodies bullet-ridden, and corroding from the weather, and animal life. Someone had done my girl dirty, and the hood had all fingers pointing to Twisted's crazy ass. Word 'round the way was that she'd been caught creeping on him, and he'd drove her out to the country, and did her dirty. The police couldn't even identify Tessa—they had to use dental records, and DNA analysis to confirm who she was.

Marcella shook her head in dismay. "That's crazy how they did sis, shit crazy out here—everybody dying and shit. Y'all heard what happened to, Armani?" she asked.

I shook my head—I didn't know too much about the girl, but I'd heard her, and my girls had gotten close. Marcella told us that the word on the street was a poisonous snake had gotten into Armani's apartment somehow. I noticed Shay was staring at her with a look that I couldn't quite put my finger on, it was borderline accusatory. I'd been knowing the two women my entire life and knew that when Shay had that look—she was on the verge of giving someone a piece or her mind.

"They say that Assata is the one that found her and her daughter—you know that was Assata lil' bitch while you were away. I tried to tell, Armani, it wasn't a good idea to mess with him cause you was our girl—"

My eyes shot to Marcella as her words stabbed me in the chest. It wasn't like I didn't know Assata was doing him while I was out of the picture, but *damn*. I'd thought he'd have more respect for me than to fuck with someone I knew. Even though I didn't know her, Armani was fuckin' with *my* hood bitches, and that made it a violation. I never understood how niggas and females ended up fucking with their ex's friends. There was no future in shit like that. It only revealed the snake shit that was in their veins out the gate.

"I don't even know why you fuck with that dirty ass nigga Assata, the nigga not right, bitch. He tried to fuck me, and I—"

"Bitch stop lying on that man!" Shay interrupted Marcella's rant. She rolled her eyes at Marcella. "You's a messy bitch, Mar, you ain't even have to air that man's business like that. We wasn't even cool with, Armani, *you* were!" She rubbed her belly as if the children inside her could feel their mother's irritation.

Marcella leaned back in the chair with a smug look on her face. "Shay, how would your sheltered ass know what the hell is going on in the hood? That nigga keeps you cooped up in this house so much you should have bed sores." She mocked before picking up her glass and downing the shot.

I followed suit and pasted a generic smile on my face. "Naw—it's cool, Shay, Assata already told me about his situation with, Armani," I lied to save face. No woman wanted to feel foolish, and a lot of times we'd lie for the same dawg ass nigga that had no respect for us. It wasn't that we were trying to protect the nigga, but more in the name of protecting ourselves from the '*I told you so's*'. "My question is, why did it take me comin' back for you to tell me that?" My eyes bore into Marcella's. "Real bitches don't keep those type of secrets, Mar, especially from their girls. If Assata was trying to fuck you—why you didn't lace my stilettos?" I asked as all eyes fell on Marcella.

I don't know if it was the liquor or if the shit had built up inside of me, and it was just that time to give it to her ass, but I did exactly that. "You know what, I've been wondering about your motives for a while—" I spoke as I reached down and refilled my glass. "—you knew I was running from my past—you knew how I feel about, Assata, Marcella, but you brought the enemy to my doorstep. That nigga Shotta beat my ass and forced me to move back to Cali, and I heard from you twice the entire time I was there," I spat.

Shay's mouth fell to the floor as she shook her head as if she couldn't believe what I'd just said.

Marcella shot up from her seat. "Oh—so you gonna gang up on me?" She was so dramatic. "Jazzy, you *know* I'll kick your ass. So, I don't know why you're over there talking all greasy. Bitch, I call myself pulling your skirt to the fact your triflin' ass nigga can't keep his dick in his pants, and you cap an attitude with *me*?" She rolled her neck sassy-like before turning her wrath to Shay. "And bitch, I'm the one that's been here with you making sure you make it to those doctor's appointments while that nigga has loved his job more than he loved you!" Marcella was on a roll as she placed her hand on her hip and let the alcohol reveal things she wouldn't have if she was sober. "But you're letting this bitch come up in here and—"

That was as far as she made it before I leaped from the spot I'd been sitting on the couch and hit the bitch with a left hook. I followed up with a right jab to her temple and dropped her to the floor.

"Bitch—I ain't gonna be too many more bitches!" I spazzed on her. "Now, get your ass up—you've been havin' this ass whooping coming for years. I'm not that docile, *yes girl* I was when we were sixteen." I was hyped as I bent down and tied my J's.

****

~Goose~

"Hey, baby!" Tonya blushed as the door swung open.

I pulled her juicy ass into my embrace. "Sup, Ms. Lady?" I asked her real smooth-like.

It had been almost two weeks since I'd last fucked with her, and if I was, to be honest with myself—I missed her. Within my forty-four years of living, I'd come to realize that it's *always* the relationship that wasn't supposed to last that ends up being the one that holds on to your heart the strongest. I released her, stepped back, and allowed my vision to take her in. Lil one was showing her ass. Tonya Johnson was a thick woman. Not as in fat, but more like one of those super thick women that if she ate *one* more cookie she'd be classified as such. Tonya's shit was tight though—she reminded me of a curvier Jill Scott. That night she wore a see-through teddy that had my dick stand at attention as I stared at her chocolate nipples through the fabric of the transparent material.

She had her hair fro'd out, but tied back by a black scarf, impulsively, my eyes fell to her feet—*check*! I smiled as I diverted my eyes from her pretty manicured toes, pass her recently shaven legs, on up to the juicy ass imprint of her paradise that was concealed behind black lace.

"Are you gonna come in or continue to stare until I catch pneumonia?" She smiled at me with chocolate lips.

Her fragrance made love to my senses as she took my hands and guided me into her warm abode. She locked the door behind me before reaching down to untie the gray and black Prada shoes that I wore—one by one she helped me out of them before walking me over to a red loveseat.

"Sit, baby—make yourself at home." She turned and headed toward the kitchen with a sway to her shapely hips. Her ass was oiled and glowing in the candlelit room. "What would you like to drink handsome?" she asked as she disappeared around the corner.

I got comfortable and took in the décor of her spot. White carpet—that told me she was a clean woman. No mu'fucka in their right mind would dare get a heaven white carpet installed in their *living room* if they were dirty or kept company over. The furniture consisted of red love seats that complimented a soft red velvet sofa. There was a framed portrait of Medgar Evers hanging above the fireplace—I stared into his still eyes, sadness was instant as I realized that death didn't give a fuck about what typa person you were. When God called your number, you had no choice but to answer. The Civil Rights worker was from Mississippi, and he'd been killed by a sniper after a broadcast of a pro-Civil Rights speech by President J.F. Kennedy. I shook my head at the irony of how my people had come so far, but still—still being killed for our desire for equality.

"What you got?" I inquired as my eyes took in the gold trimmed glass coffee table.

The glass was supported by a piece in the shape of Africa that was carved out of white marble. The sista was for the people, and I respected her taste.

"Um—I have Remy XO—let me see what else," Tonya called out after a brief moment. The aroma of whatever she'd cooked wafted into the room, and it smelt like freedom to a man that's been locked up for decades. "Okay—I have Smirnoff Lime, Kahlua, Wine, Kool-Aid, and water. Pick your poison, brotha."

The light from the three different size red candles flickered and cast dancing shadows around the room as I got up, walked over to her entertainment system and appraised her CD collection.

'Do people still buy CD's?' I wondered.

Queen had some good shit—*Dru Hill, Jagged Edge, Sade, Betty,* and even some *Miles Davis.* I chose *Jagged Edge J.E. Heartbreak* – *'What You Tryna Do'* was my shit.

"I'll take the Remy—neat!" I shouted mildly as J.E. set the tempo.

I turned to head back to my seat, but at that moment Tonya came out of the kitchen carrying my plate and requested drink to the dining room. I followed—the way that ass swallowed the string of that sexy ass nightie made me want to skip dinner and go straight to dessert. Shawty sat the plate and drink down before pulling out my chair.

"Dinner is served, Monsieur," she announced with a French dialect.

I laughed as I took my seat. Queen used a small knife and fork to cut the meat into bite-sized chunks, and with her free hand cupped under the fork to catch anything that fell she straddled me with a smile, with anticipating eyes, Tonya fed me.

"I cooked you smothered pork chops, cream corn, green beans, and mash potatoes. I hope you like it—are you a Muslim— I mean, it's too late, but—" she rambled nervously.

I could tell she wanted to please me, but I wasn't a Muslim and the perfectly seasoned meat and potatoes were fire. I swallowed my food before banishing her anxiety. "Naw—I ain't no Muslim, and you can thank whoever taught you how to burn in the kitchen, you're the gospel!" The tension in her body eased evidently. "I just hope desert is just as good," I added before she fed me a forkful of chops and green beans.

A panicked expression etched into her features. I had to contain my laughter as Tonya took a sip from my cup to cover her reaction.

"I didn't make any dessert, but I—"

"Shissh!" I hushed her with a finger to her succulent lips.

"What you tryna do for it—heard that you been lookin' for— good love, and I'm for sure that I know just what you came here for/ what you tryna do for it—I'll spend all my loot for it/ tell me,

baby, what you tryna do—" Jagged Edge serenaded the atmosphere as I looked lady in her eyes.

"You're my dessert, Queen."

****

~Ice Berg~

"Swanson—get ready for an attorney visit!" The guard came on the intercom. My eyes cracked open slightly—glancing over at the digital clock I'd gotten off the commissary, I wanted to pull the blanket back over my head and drift back to sleep, but— "Swanson—be ready in twenty minutes." My desire was crushed.

I sat up groggily—the chill in the cell caused me to shiver. I knew I'd never get used to not waking up in my own bed—nor wearing another man's clothes. It was six-fifty am, and those bitches were already trying to rush me to the guillotine.

"Yea—whateva, white boy," I whispered. I squeezed a bit of toothpaste on my toothbrush.

"They're gonna give you the needle, nigger, and when they do—I'll be sure to get a front row seat," The racist mu'fucka blurted before he laughed.

I shook my head slightly—they were eavesdropping on me— there was no privacy in jail.

"Say—say, youngsta, I heard what that white boy just said. Don't worry 'bout that cracka, stay focused, lil' brotha," an old school cat that was in the cell beside me whispered.

His name was Rodney K. and he'd been gone for two decades for a string of bank robberies. We'd met my second day on the compound. I wasn't tryin' to be on no friendly shit with none of those cats, but school put me up on all the rules of fed life. I was truly fucked up 'bout my fate, but it was the hand I was dealt. If I woulda stuck to the script and left the game I wouldn't have been in that predicament.

"Ain't shit, old head, I'm on all ten, my lil' brotha lost his life to this shit—I owe it to him to stay stiff," I responded as I got dressed.

The truth was, my heart was sick, there was no such thing as a man that was 'bout something in them streets, and he wasn't fucked up 'bout leaving the shit he bled, sweated, and killed for to anotha nigga. I neva understood how niggas could say, *'if you do this or that, and you get bammed—you can't be fucked up 'bout the consequences!'* It *had* to have been a nothin' ass nigga with no money that created that statement. If a nigga has something worth missin', he's gonna be fucked up 'bout fuckin' it off—it don't matter what the fuck he'd done.

"Say, school, what you think my odds are, fam?" There was a brief pause before homie said some shit that ended our brief association.

"Say, youngsta, I ain't gonna cut no corners with you, ya dig. I've been locked up in this cage for going on twenty-one years, and I've seen these white folks hang niggas for shit as petty as being a felon in possession. You're in for a helluva ride, but—as they say, you can't be fucked up 'bout something you did. Know what I'm sayin' youngin'?"

I stared at the wall as if I could see him through it. "Bitch ass nigga!" I whispered.

"You say something, youngsta?" he asked with a hint of uncertainty.

****

~Goose~

My toes curled as Tonya attempted to suck my soul from my dick. To keep from screaming out like a lil' bitch, I spread her juicy folds and buried my face in heaven. Capturing her clit with my lips—I applied gentle pressure as I allowed my spit to build up in my mouth. I'd heard that no one knows how to eat pussy better than anotha woman, but I begged to differ. All it took was for a man to pay attention to the signs—read her body with each lick—suck, and kiss and it would tell you what the business was. My point was proven as I reached up and placed my thumb against her asshole. I didn't insert it, just applied pressure to let her anticipate a darker side of euphoria.

We were in the sixty-nine position, and neither one of us could run from the other as a deep moan escaped from deep inside her. Her lips slid up my shaft until she had the head captured like a soldier on the wrong side of enemy lines. The black woman's tongue kissed my manhood and attempted to close her legs around my head, but with her on top—I wrapped my arms around her waist before making my tongue dance over the tip of her clit. Her body told me it wouldn't be long—but her head game had me on the edge of Mount Everest. If she didn't bust in the next few seconds, I was gonna commit blissful suicide.

Our bodies must have been in unison because just as I pushed the tip of my thumb inside her ass—my spirit turned into liquid and shot from me at the same time a thunderstorm poured from paradise. We rode the waves until the earthquake subsided, and after she'd composed herself—Tonya repositioned herself on top of me. Those titties swung in front of my face like a piece of meat dangled in front of a starved animal. It was instinctive to latch onto them. I sucked the right nipple as I rolled the left between my thumb and pointer finger. Tonya moaned as she massaged my length with her pussy lips causing me to swell beneath her. She lifted before reachin' down and inserting me inside her sacred place—fire dripped around me as juices escaped her.

She lifted until her lower lips held me by the tip, and without warning dropped down on me with an arch to her back. She did this a few times before leaning forward, stretching her body out on top of me and beginning to pop that pussy. I reached down and spread her ass cheeks apart as far as I could.

Just as my body tensed and a roar was crawling up my throat, Ms. Lady slowed her pace. "Shit—you're a mu'fucka," I growled as her tight lips squeezed me.

"No, Papi, I'm not ready for you to bust yet," she whispered softly as her eyes rolled over me.

Her lips were parted as her breathing came out in sexy short breaths with each rise and fall of her body. Tonya lifted and placed one hand on my chest as she bucked on top of me. I was on the verge of throwin' that dick back when the strangest thing happened—

"Um—um—um—ohh, God, daddy, you want to bust in this pussy—huh?" she cried as she quickened her pace. My nut was surging through my body as I felt her waterfall pour down upon me in a gush of sticky pleasure. "Ohh!" she screamed.

I tried to get that nut outta me, but she'd stopped fuckin' me. "Naw—keep going, baby, I'm almost there!" I growled.

But she merely stared down at me as I felt her hand slide from underneath the pillow. "Later for that, *Goose*," she spat in contempt.

My heart instantly froze. *'How the fuck she know my name?'* I thought as my mind lusted for the Glock .17, I had on the floor by my clothes, but the .40 aimed at my face made me disregard any rash decisions.

"So—what's next, you're gonna kill me or take me in, *Detective* Johnson?"

Surprise exploded over her face as she wondered how I found out what she hadn't revealed to me, but it only lasted a brief moment. "I guess we both have secrets, huh?" She smiled a sad smile. "The difference is, *Goose*—" she put emphasis on my street handle. "—the difference is that my secret doesn't have the FBI building a case on me for an 848 CCE and heading a murdering group of savages!" She'd dropped a bomb on me.

It was my time to be surprised. *'What the fuck?'* I wondered.

She must have found my facial expression comical because she laughed as if I was the most pitiful thing. "Oh—him didn't know him was on the big boy's radar?" She mocked in an animated child's voice. The bitch lifted off me—carefully. She kept the tool on me as she eased out of the bed. "Why though, Mark—" she paused before shaking her head as if to clear it of the name.

"I mean, Bennie—Goose—what the fuck ever your name is!" she screamed. A storm converged in her eyes. "Just tell me why-why lie to me?"

Renta

Chapter Fifteen
Snake Bitch

~Twisted~

I had the lil' pretty bitch bent ova the counter as I dug in that pussy like I owned it.

"Oh—Twisted, fuck—me!" she moaned in painful bliss.

I'd been fuckin' wit' lil' one for a few weeks. I always knew she wanted to give me the pussy, but since she was from the other side, I kept my distance. Yet, the girl was persistent! One day the treacherous bitch pulled up on me at the club and dropped a bomb on me. She said she had some info that would put me a step ahead of my enemies. I thought the slut was tryin to play me.

"Bitch fuck you mean Assata and Pain—Pain ain't amongst the living no more," I growled, but even with the lights being dimmed, I could see the confusion on her face.

"I don't understand—what you tryna say, nigga, I'm lying?" Marcella frowned.

The slut was either a great actress or she truly knew something I didn't, so I downed my shot and repeated what I'd said. Marcella took it all in before the snake bitch put me on to how she'd been at the house when Pain had gotten sown up and even when B.G. had sent shots in Lovey's spot. I thought the hoe had had one too many drinks when she let me, and Lil Ben take her to the tell. We blew the girl's back out before takin' turns bustin' on her titties and face. Afterward, she told me everything she knew 'bout them boys. She even put me on to how she and Pain fucked around every now and then. She told me that he had a tendency to spill his guts to her during pillow talk.

I laughed at the weenie ass nigga—I never understood why niggas got their dick wet and felt the need to tell a hoe their life story like the freak wasn't gonna meet anotha nigga with some good dick. Females talked the most in three situations—when they're emotional—at the beauty salon—or when they getting some good dick. When a boss all up in them guts, the hoe gonna repeat everything she'd been told!

I thought as the poisonous bitch gripped the counter with each stroke, I hit her wit. That monsta raged out of me as I pulled out and busted all ova Marcella's ass cheeks. Just like the slut she was, she spun around, dropped to her knees, and wrapped her lips around my deflating manhood. She sucked and pulled on that mu'fucka until she got every drop.

I had to fight the lady off my shit. "Damn, bitch—what you tryna do?" I asked as I pulled my pants up and got myself together.

Marcella stood and pulled her dress down from around her waist before wiping her mouth and smiling. "Nigga, you know I'm trying to make us official. What, you thought I'm fuckin' and suckin' cause I'm a nympho or sumthin'?" the silly bitch asked.

I laughed in her face before I turned and walked off without entertaining what she already knew. We were at the trap on Ruth Street—Lil Ben and Krazy were in the living room playing Call of Duty on the PS4. I shook my head in disappointment—the niggas were so entranced with the game that if the reaper showed up at that moment, everybody in the spot woulda had a first-class ticket to the cemetery.

I snatched the blunt from between Lil Ben's lips. "Damn, Loc, fuck you doing?" he demanded with a quick glance at me before turning his attention back to the game.

I laughed mildly, I *had* to be getting soft. The young cats of his era were fucked up, but I had the remedy—before anyone knew my intentions, I had the burna in my hands and aimed at the TV—*Boc! Boc!* I squeezed the trigga. The TV exploded as all three of them tensed. I heard rushed footsteps coming from the back room and just as my eyes found the startled expressions of Lil Ben and Krazy, my shoota Pac Man joined the party.

"You, niggas 'round here playin' games and getting high like this a mu'fuckin' party or somthin'!" I gritted. "The big homie fightin' for his life and our enemies after our head, but you, niggas rather kill niggas on a game!" I was on fire. All eyes were tuned in—fear, frustration, but most importantly, respect radiated from their stares. "Since you real good game playin' ass niggas wanna play Call of mu'fuckin' Duty—*I'm* callin' y'all to duty! This bitch Marcella makin' it official today. So, you niggas strap up and be ready!"

I turned to walk away, but just like the dumb hoe she was, Marcella had to tempt fate. "Damn, nigga, fuck you keep disrespectin' me like that?" she demanded with attitude in her stance.

I paused before turning to face her—tension was thick as I strode ova to her. She stared at me defiantly, but I could sense the fear just behind the tough girl act. I lifted my hand—she flinched. I smiled and ran the back of my hand down her soft cheek.

"Disrespect you?" I asked with a crooked grin. "Aren't you the same female that me and my nigga took turns fuckin' a few weeks ago?"

Shawty rolled her eyes before slapping my hand away. "Fuck you, Twisted, you're a hoe ass nigga!" she snapped.

I laughed in her face before turning and heading to the back room. Her words didn't faze me cause they were the gospel—my mama told me I'd be a hoe ass nigga the first time I stole a few dollars out her pocketbook when I was a lil' nigga. Since then, I made it big business to live up to that prediction, but even better— I had more pressing shit to tend to than tryin' to remind a hoe that she was, in fact, a hoe.

'*Even when a prostitute becomes a devout Christian, she still had to pray for that freak that resided just beyond that Bible,*' I laughed at the thought.

****

~Assata~

I stripped out of my clothes until my dick swung free, and the ink that tainted my flesh was on full display. Snatching a pair of Gucci briefs out of the drawer, I turned and headed to the bathroom, but a fleeting thought made me double back to take the black and brown .380 from under my pillow. I checked to ensure the clip was full, and one was in the head. I couldn't rationalize it, but I couldn't shake the nagging feeling that something fucked up was 'bout to happen. I didn't know when or what, but a man's gut is his navigational system, and I trusted mine with every beat of my heart.

I turned at the sound of Jazzy entering the room—she'd been on some other shit for the past few days. She wasn't fuckin' with me, and the attitude that radiated from her body language told me she had some beef on her chest. Three days ago, she'd come home with some scratches on her face, her knuckles bleeding, and a busted lip. It was evident that she'd been in a scuffle, but I'd neva been the typa nigga to press a female for details.

"A woman could be a man's realist confidant or his fakest ally—if she truly belonged to a particular man, she'd never keep secrets," Lovey once told me that a real woman kept her castle clean so there was no need for a maid.

She'll talk when she's ready,' I thought as Jazz huffed around the room *yearning* for a nigga to respond.

She was as naked as the day she was born—ass on fleek with a mouthful of titties that drooped just a bit to let a nigga know she had weight to 'em. A few stretch marks complimented her waist, and the shit turned me on. She'd recently gotten my name tattooed across her lower back to let it be known she belonged to the Boss, and as she made up the bed, I could tell she was flexin' on me by *dry* bending ova and shit. I flashed her a mouthful of diamonds before going 'bout my B-I, I had to tend to my shit. I'd been absent from the streets way too long, and though I trusted my niggas to make sure my portion of bread was righteous, I knew money had a way of tempting the most loyal of men.

I stepped into the steam filled bathroom, laid the tool down on the ledge, and stepped into the glass encased shower. The water was almost scolding, but that's how I rocked. I bowed my head under the shower nozzle—hot water poured over me in a cascade of streaming rain. My thoughts were everywhere as I reflected on everything that had transpired in the past six months. Lovey—I missed her with all my soul. I needed that advice—that love only a righteous black woman could give. As I wondered 'bout the vision I had of her and Shy in that meadow, I didn't know if it was the drugs I'd been exposed to or if there was a such thing as divine intervention.

Shy had said some shit that *still* didn't make sense, but for some reason, my thoughts carried me to Pain's call earlier that morning. He'd had me and Goose on three-way when he said he'd made plans to fuck with Marcella's trick ass. Fam told us he didn't feel right but didn't think the hoe would try any funny business when she *knew* his get down. Goose asked the nigga why he'd even entertain a bitch his gut warned him 'bout, but we both knew Pain and Marcella had been doin' them for years. Pain had a hunger for snake bitches that I never understood, and Marcella was as serpentine as they came.

I had the same gut feeling Pain had, so I made a mental note to pull up where she wanted to meet. She wanted to go see the Christmas Parade they were having Downtown Fort. Worth, even though it would be crawling with boys in blue—I didn't put nothin' pass a baby snake. They bit and didn't know the amount of venom to use to kill their prey—so they overkilled.

"So—you wanna fuck, Marcella, huh?" The glass door flew open.

I had to wipe the water out my face before my confused stare landed on Jazzy. She stood there fuming with her hair wild and curly. He gray eyes bore into mine as she bounced her left leg.

"Fuck you talmbout, fam?" I asked confused. '*I wouldn't fuck that bitch with an aids patient dick!*' I thought.

"Assata Lamar, answer my question—miss me with all the theatrics! That bitch threw it in my face how you was pushin' up on her—ugh, Marcella, Satta?" she teared up before rolling her eyes. "Out of all the hoes that would fuck you just to say they did—why my homegirl, huh? I don't deserve more respect than that?"

I picked up the towel and Gucci body wash, then squeezed a small mountain on the cloth. I began to lather up before lookin' back at the crazy woman. "First off, at this point—I don't know how much respect you deserve. You left me for a whole 'notha nigga, Jazmina, remember?" I punctured her pride.

I could tell my words cut deep as she dropped her head to hide the shame that swam in her pretty eyes.

'Fuck it, I can't let her think she Gucci just cause we're rockin again—that would open doors for her to think the shit was cooked, and she could fuck ova me and get away with it. Naw—naw, the next betrayal would cost everybody involved,' I thought before giving my Queen the peace she needed. "Secondly, *you know* I'm way too 'G' to run up in one of ya potnas, Jazzy."

Her eyes lifted to mine. "You promise, Satta, you promise?" she whispered.

I didn't even respond to that shit—my yes was my yes, and my no was my no. I reached out gently grabbed her wrist and pulled her closer. I placed the lathered towel in her hand before placing it on what was swingin' between my legs—she lifted my inches and cleaned my nuts.

"Jazzy, you have to know the nigga you commit yourself to without a shadow of a doubt, ma. There can never be longevity in a trustless relationship. When a man and his gal winning, even ya potna's will do hoe shit to rob you of what *should be* sucka proof."

She stared at me as she digested the diamonds, I was droppin' on her. The slow strokes she used to purge my dick of any evidence of the past was awakening the beast in me.

"Betrayal is suicide, ma, and shouldn't no otha nigga be able to game *mine*—push up—nor divide this shit. I ain't tried, nor want to fuck Marcella's punk ass, and if *that's* who you squabbled—you out of line, my nigga."

Heat instantly lit in her eyes as she stopped cleansing me. "*Why?* That bitch deserved that ass-whoopin'! What, you trying to protect the bitch, Assata?" she spat with a roll of her eyes. Dick on strong, I pulled her lil' ass inside the steaming shower and closed the glass. "Boy stop—I'm not tryin' to get my hair—" she was in the midst of sayin' before I slid my tongue in her mouth.

A soft moan replaced her words before I broke the kiss and spun her around. "Shut the fuck up, Jazz, you outta line cause when a nigga run his dick in the next bitch—it ain't *her* fault. It's no such thing as accidentally fuckin', just as a female can't force *yo'* nigga's dick in her." I slid deep inside shawty. She cried out as I grabbed a handful of her hair and pulled her head back with another thrust. "The same goes for a female, a bitch don't just fall on anotha nigga's dick—you know what that means?" I growled.

Jazzy's pussy lips kissed my nuts as I buried myself inside her. "Whaa—what, baby, what does it mean?" she cried out as her lower lips hugged me.

"It means this pussy mine, and betrayal is unacceptable—promise me I won't have to—shit—to damn, ma—" I was stroking that pussy feverishly. I released her hair and latched on to her waist as she left her prints on the fogged glass. She worked my dick like a boss bitch. "Promise I won't have to put yo brains on anotha nigga's pillow." I bit down on her shoulder as a demon shot from my soul and entered her heaven.

"On, Ellen, bae—no—this yo—your pussy!"

****

~Pain~

~Four Hours Later~

I pulled the Jag up to the curb—I was late to the parade, but I wasn't on nobody's time, but mine. All morning my stomach had knots, I couldn't quite put my finger on it, but I just wasn't feelin' that parade shit. I'd just made up my mind to smash off and text the hoe Marcella when a knock on my passenger window made me reach for the Glock .17. Marcella stood with an irritated look on her face, but I paid the hoe no mind as I finished the blunt and put the clip in the astray. I stepped out of the whip and inspected one of the twenty-six-inch big heads the truck was squattin' on. Through its reflection, I could see Marcella approaching from behind.

"Damn, Pain, why you always gotta be late to shit? You're thirty minutes late!" she spazzed as I stood and faced her.

I allowed my eyes to roam for any signs of fuck shit, but the sounds of Christmas carols and the sight of police eased my apprehension. My eyes took her in—the lady was the sexiest *reptile* I'd ever laid eyes on. Her long hair had been hot combed bone straight but feathered out her mocha toned face. I recognized the forest green wool Jeffery Dodd turtle neck dress I'd gotten her a year ago. It molested her curves until it opened and hid the knee-high snakeskin boots she wore. The Fleur du Mal trench coat she wore set the outfit perfectly.

"Some shit came up, Mami. What the bidness tho?" I allowed my eyes to tell her what she knew I wanted.

Marcella smiled a mischievous smile before grabbing my hand and leading me toward the long procession of joyful people singing Christmas carols. We were at the back of the spectators; we had a clear view of the parade, but we seemed to be in our own lil spot of seclusion. Downtown Fort. Worth was a contradicting contrast to the rest of the city. I knew that just beyond the outdated red brick building, neighborhoods such as the Bloody Stop Six, Eastwood, Poly, Riverside, Como, and the entire south side, were poverty-stricken and plagued by death, trap houses, and more death.

A noise from my left caused me to jump—I turned to investigate, but the bum dumpster diving for food or whatever he was looking for eased that gangsta shit in me. I eased my hand away from the Glock on my waist.

"Why yo' scary ass so jumpy today?" Marcella asked as her eyes studied me peculiarly. Her eyes turned to the dirty man digging in the trash—shaking her head sadly, Marcella returned her attention to me. "That's fucked up, I wonder—" her voice trailed off as my phone rung.

I looked at it and answered without taking my eyes off lil' one. "What's brackin', Bleed?" I barked at Assata. The nigga had his music so loud he couldn't hear me. '*I hate when he do that shit!*' I fumed.

I heard the volume drop before fam barked back. "What's toppin', Rusta, where the fuck that hoe got you? I'm just pullin' up, but it's too many mu'fuckas out here."

My spirit eased dramatically—my nigga was on deck, and I knew we'd die for each otha. I looked around to get a feel for where I was at, but Marcella's posture caught my attention. She seemed fidgety—nervous! She slightly perspired and that set off alarms in my head. My mind automatically took me back to the day Tessa tried to clip me—the way the ese bitch was actin'.

"Bitch, fuck you sweating for—it's forty degrees and windy!" I spazzed on Marcella.

Her eyes shot to me at the same time that a sharp pain hit my side. "Get the fuck out the way, bitch nigga!" A gruff voice spat as a group of young boys in white and baby blue North Carolina units passed by.

The cat that spoke was the one that elbowed me—he spun around and tossed up his set. "Fo'Tray on mines, cuz!" He did a backward crip walk and continued to twist his fingers into gang signs.

Even though I knew they had the ups on me, my next reaction was the only justification for disrespect. I reached under my hoodie and pulled the tool.

"Pacman, what it wuz, homie, who dat nigga?" A loud voice came from my right.

I turned my attention that way and I knew it was do or die for me. It was 'bout twelve more of those pussy boys approachin' fast. I made up my mind when the second group was about ten feet away. I *had* to draw first blood and use the bitch Marcella for a shield. Without much more thought, I aimed at the nigga that had elbowed me and let that led speak. As I fired, I backpedaled toward the parade—in an instant it was pandemonium.

After the first few shots shit got crazy—the parade turned into a stampede and I could hear someone screaming. *"Police—police!"*

That wasn't enough to stop the showdown that was taking place. I counted each shot I took, but the painful feeling of my stomach exploding made me double over. I don't know where the shot came from until I fell to my knee and glanced around. I clutched my stomach in agony as the bitch nigga that elbowed me headed in my direction. He must have thought he was bulletproof, but I gave him the answer when I fired his bitch ass up. The slug parted his high-top fade and I watched as his noodles painted the baby blue jacket he wore. I had no idea where the punk hoe Marcella had disappeared to, but I knew I had to get to one of those police officers. It was either hell or the cell for me and though neither was a choice I'd make under usual circumstances, shid, it was a choice I *needed* to make. I tried my best to slow the bleeding as I stumbled to my feet and through the panic mob of paraders.

"I see him, homie, there he is! Get that fuck nigga for the big homie!" I heard someone scream from behind.

I glanced back and spotted the fuck boy Lil Ben hot on my trail—I turned slightly, aimed and hit him up. A red stain appeared where his left shoulder used to be.

"Say, homie, you need to get help—you're hit!" A familiar voice stole my attention.

I was losing blood fast, but I spun to match the face with the voice. The bum that was just digging in the trash stood before me, but rather than leftover food—he aimed a big pistol at me. Twisted smiled at me from behind the dirt he'd smudged on his face.

"So, the hoe wasn't lyin', huh?" he asked.

I was confused as to what the fuck he meant, but there was no time for guessing games. I wasn't 'bout to die in a city I'd neva shed blood in.

I aimed at that boy the same time that someone yelled, "Fort Worth PD, drop your weapons—drop your weapons!"

Both of our eyes flew to the pudgy white cop but Twisted was a man with nothin' to lose. He smiled wickedly before doing what any madman would do—the power from whateva it was that he was firing at the officer had so much kick that his arm vibrated as he squeezed the trigger. I began to feel faint as I took aim and opened Twisted's chest up. Surprise registered on his face as he swung the burna on me and squeezed at the same time I blew his mu'fuckin' brains out!

Part Three
~I'm Dying~

I heard somewhere that real didn't exist no more—I laugh every time I hear that shit. Yea, homie, real still exist, it's just that fake people had duplicated a real mu'fuckas images so perfectly that one can't tell them apart until the fire melts the façade and exposes what's hidden behind the mask. No man wants to be viewed as a fuck boy, just as no woman want to be viewed as a fake bitch, but reality is—pressure makes diamonds and bust pipes with the exact amount of pressure. It's easy to profess loyalty to something you neva been placed in the position to betray.

Shit crazy—everybody wanna go to heaven, but nobody wanna die! Everybody wanna be solid, but don't wanna face off with the shit that is required of the life. That shit is as much of a contradiction as black people repping for the motherland—walking 'round in Africa's colors, wearing African beads with a big ass pendant in the shape of Africa, but failing to understand that 'most' Africans don't like or give a damn 'bout us. So much tumbles through my head, but the most powerful thought is—I'm dying!

Renta

Chapter Sixteen
Loose Ends

~Harrison~
~Two Weeks Later~

I'd just gotten off the phone with the Tarrant County Police Department. There had been a massacre out that way, and some casualties were some of Denton Underworlds Finest. '*The Christmas Parade Massacre,*' as the news was calling it had gotten coverage on over sixty major news stations. The White House had even flown some of their people up to the Dallas and Fort. Worth area. The area had once been the murder capital, and the mayor of the city wanted the culprits responsible standing trial like yesterday.

Earl 'Twisted' Goldsmith, Dunte 'Pain' Jackson, and a few pedestrians were killed in the shootout that was said to have sparked over gang involvement. I was just finishing up a few notes on the file I'd been given on Jackson when something in one of the photos caused me to pause. One of the photos—a photo of him and six guys set off something in my head. The man in the center was roughly five-eleven in height, dark-skinned, and had a distinctiveness in his posture. It was his eyes that rocketed my mind back to the video of the bank heist. As they say—*the eyes never lie*!

What gave credence to my hunch was the sixth man in the photo—he was a short lean man dressed in all black. His youthful features were dimmed by the cold stare of a young man that had lost his innocence way too early. His name was 'Tomorrow Kennedy' and he was one of the two slain men that we'd found at the Armor truck scene. My pulse quickened—impulsively, my eyes flew back to the man in the middle.

'*Who was he?*' My thoughts were loud as I picked up the phone and rung my new secretary.

"Yes, Mr. Harrison, what can I do for you?" Sarah Jane inquired.

I could hardly contain my excitement, I was sure I was on to something. "I need you to call down to evidence and get me the video footage on the bank robbery case; I think it's under 'exhibit x'!"

"Will do—anything else?" she responded.

I thought about it for a second or two. "Yes, if you see Agent Louding, send him to my office. I think I just solved the Denton County Bank Heist!"

****

~Detective Winslet~

"Girl, where your restroom at? Those drinks are working on my bladder!" Tonya stood and squeezed her legs together like a little girl.

We laughed at her antics, and once I gave her directions—I turned my attention back to the Scrabble board. We were having a girl's night at my house, and the only three women that knew where I lived were all in attendance. Tonya, my sister Jacqueline, and her girlfriend Jada.

"Pneumatology—" I spelt out the word with the little square pieces.

"Now, you know that's not a word, Kamicka. I think I'm gonna challenge it," Jacqueline stated as she reached out for the Scrabble Dictionary.

I gave her a challenging smirk—I'd played the game so much that I knew words that a lot of people wouldn't. I watched my sisters face change as she read the definition aloud.

"Doctrine or study of spiritual beings and phenomena. Ain't that a bitch!" she exclaimed as she slammed the book shut and slouched back in her seat. "I quit—you're too smart, Kamicka."

I laughed at her silliness. My sister had always been a poor sport. Ten minutes later I glanced at my watch, my eyes wandered to my dark hallway.

'What was taking Tonya so long—had she found the re-stroom? Was she taking number two in my shit!' I thought at the same time my sister verbalized my sentiments.

"You think she's okay—she's been gone a while?"

****

~Detective Tonya Johnson~

I had just finished the unthinkable. I had to calm my nerves before turning to head back to the others.

"What the hell are you doing in my room!" a shrill voice demanded.

My eyes shot to Kamicka Winslet—I'm sure I looked like a deer trapped in a speeding car's headlights, but I was a born actor.

In spite of my original reaction, I plastered a confused look on my face. "Wha—what?" I stammered in feigned ignorance. "I used the restroom! You have all the doors in the hall closed except this one, and I didn't want to be snooping around your place." I shrugged my shoulders as if my decision was harmless. "I figured there was a little girl's room in here—so I used it." I smiled at her. "Are you angry with me or something?" The look on my face was innocent. I could tell I'd disarmed her by the way her stance relaxed, but her eyes still held a hint of suspicion. I knew the sneaky bitch was on high alert—being a detective, I'd learned that when people did so much dirt, they were *always* suspicious of others.

'I guess that's what happens when you've fucked over so many people, it was just common sense that karma was near,' I thought as Winslet's body stiffened again.

Her eyes shot to my hands. "Why would you need gloves to use the restroom, Tonya?"

Her question made me smile brightly before reaching in my pocket and pulling out a pink and purple wrapper that I'd balled up. It was already torn open, so after reaching in and pulling out the soiled tampon, I held it up to show her the blood smears which were actually red dye. "It's that time of the month—" I revealed as I watched Winslet's facial expression melt into shame. "Am I missing something here, Kamicka, what were you think—" my voice trailed off as a wounded expression blossomed on my face. Kamicka dropped her head—embarrassed. I used that as my escape route. "Oh—you *assumed* I was up to something foul!" I shook my head—artificial disappointment radiated from my stare as she lifted her eyes to me.

"I'm sorry, T, I just—"

I stopped her midsentence with a raised palm. "Don't—just—don't. I don't know what you were thinking, and quite frankly—I don't give a damn. I've lived a long time, Kamicka, and I'm old enough to know when I'm not trusted," that was my last words to the bitch before I stormed passed her and her sister that had been standing in the hallway being nosey.

I gathered my things and left that house like it was on fire. The entire time I was thinking—*the crazy thing a woman does for some good dick and a little tender love and care.*

****

~Ice Berg~

I was escorted into a pure white room that was bare except for two chairs and a black table. I was chained when the door opened and a smooth—polished brotha strode in like he had the power to free me from my chains personally. I kept my eyes on him as he walked to the otha seat and laid his briefcase on the table.

He smiled at me before stretching his hand. "Mr. Swanson, my name is K. Sharp and I was hired to represent you in this case."

I stared up at the fool—it took him a second or two before his eyes fell to my shackled hands. His hand fell away as he took his seat. "My apologies—I wasn't expecting them to—"

"Who hired you, homie, I have a lawyer retained already," I interrupted him and got straight to the business.

He gave me a resigned smile—opened the briefcase and pulled out some papers as he spoke, "Your relative, Earl Goldsmith, retained me because he felt that you needed—how can I phrase this—" He laid the papers on the table before looking up. "—a man of color, that's a little more experienced in these kinds of cases," he said.

My chest filled with pride, my homie wanted me free. Most times greed was so thick in the circle that as soon as the head got bammed, the next hungriest soldier plotted against him rather than holding him down.

I nodded. "That's what's up, make sho' you tell Cuz I owe him one," I acknowledged.

The attorney gave me a look that was a mixture of surprises and fear. I was 'bout to inquire when he pulled a newspaper out of his briefcase and tossed it face up on the table. "I think you need to see this!"

We stared at each other before my eyes dropped to the paper. There—on the front page wore a collage of photos with the caption: *'Christmas Parade Massacre'* boldly printed across the top of them. Without moving, I allowed my eyes to digest what my heart refused to accept. The first row of pictures began with a few smiling white people, but the second set is what took my breath away—Pacman, Pain, Twisted's faces stared back at me. My eyes seemed frozen on Twisted's image—forever frozen in a moment past. Thoughts of him, Nutz and me zoomed through my mind like a movie played in fast forward.

"I'm sorry, Mr. Swanson, Mr. Goldsmith was slain in a gun battle right after I was hired."

****

~Assata~

I was still in shock as I sat outside the church house blowin' my brains out with the sour I was filling my lungs with. I sat slouched in the SS—blowin' and downin' an eighth of that purple shit out of a big gulp cup. The fam was burying my flesh, and the going away party was packed. My chest was empty—stomach filled with shit that had the potential to rock me to sleep foreva—but my head was somewhere dark. After each inhale of the blunt, a different piece of my soul fell from my eyes. First—Moose let that bitch nigga kill her—then Shy got whacked by the same nigga we came out the mud with. Lovey may as well have died by my own hands and I had to live wit' that shit till the dark angel came to get me.

Now—before the blood could dry off my heart for that loss—here Pain go! Through clouded vision, I rested my head against the headrest and allowed my mind to carry me back to that day a few weeks ago.

I'd arrived at the parade and parked the big body before hittin' Pain to see where he was at. Bro answered on the second ring.

"What's brackin', Bleed?" I turned down the knock in the whip.

I knew bro hated when I tried to talk over music. "What's toppin', Rusta, where the fuck that hoe got you—I'm just pullin' up, but it's too many mu'fuckas out here," I finally replied.

I could hear him flippin' out on Marcella's trick ass before the phone fell. I screamed his name ova and ova again as I bolted through the crowd in search of him. I could hear the crip nigga talk that talk and knowin' my brotha—I could already picture the scene as it unfolded. We were bred to shoot first to prevent from dying first, and Pain was the quickest to the draw out of our circle. Gunshots are unmistakable, and as they rung off—I dropped my phone and ran towards the direction people fled from. I was momentarily lost in the mob of people running for their lives and cradling crying children.

It was a madhouse of hysterical people searching for a safe haven from the devil's playground. By the time I made it free of the stampede, I ran straight into a wounded dude. He wore baby blue and white head to toe and the only contrast was the trail of blood spilling from his right shoulder. I didn't recognize the sucka, but the colors he wore was the reason I knocked his thoughts all over the street.

"Say—where all the shootin' coming from, Bleed?" I made my presence known.

Being that he was wounded and glancing behind for his attacker, he was surprised as he turned his head to come face to face with the Boogyman. I moved with the speed of light as I yanked him close to me as if I was embracing long lost family—homie was stunned. His shock prevented him from reacting the way a 'real' killa would in that moment of self-preservation. By the time he attempted to push me off him, I had the tool planted in his stomach and played with the trigga as if it was my bitches clit and I was determined to make her cum. The first shot stunned him—his face froze in a silent scream. His eyes pled with me as the second shot rocketed through his intestines and shattered his spinal column.

I released him and watched as he crumbled to the dirty street as shots rung off in the distance—through bloodthirsty eyes. I smiled at homie before painting the asphalt with his scalp. I took off in hot pursuit of my brotha.

Just as the crowd of people thinned out, I heard, "Police—Tarrant County PD; drop your weapons—drop your weapons!"

There—in the middle of the street stood Pain and some dirty man in raggedy clothes. I watched in horror as the bum took aim at the law and fired at the same time that Pain squeezed the trigga. My brotha clutched his stomach as he fired and the blood that leaked into his hands told its own tale. Led opened the bum's chest, but the bitch nigga wasn't leaving this earth without company—he swung the tool around and hit Pain up with two to the chest before his face was blown into a bloody mess. As my brotha fell to his death, the boys in blue were on their way. I took one more look at Pain's still form, to retain the pain in my chest. As I fled the scene, the only thing that was for sure was the thought of how the death toll was 'bout to rise in the metroplex.

****

~The Russian~

Russia and Agent Forrest sat down to eat in the suite of the luxury hotel. It was a beautiful day on the majestic island of Dubai. The sun reflected off the Azure waters—the curtains were open and allowed the sun to pour in through the tinted window.

"Brunch is served!" the personal waiter announced as he placed the last dish on the table.

Forrest smiled at Russia dotingly. Russia returned the gesture before taking a demure sip from his orange juice. He set his glass down before picking up a soft cloth to dab at the corners of his mouth.

"So—de focking government is on to us, hmm?" he asked as his radiant blue eyes found the agents. "I no understand *how* after all de discretion—de careful planning—*how* does something of tis sort happen?" he inquired in his thick tongue.

Agent Forrest shrugged before using a steak knife to cut a bite-sized piece of tenderloin—he popped it in his mouth and savored its flavor. The juicy seasons were like a burst of heaven in his mouth. "This tenderloin is the best I've tasted," he complimented the waiter that stood nearby. He nodded modestly; the compliment was well received.

"What's next—we can't—can't"—Forrest stammered with a confused look on his face. He perspired slightly as he reached for his glass of water. It had suddenly become hot in the room and his throat itched.

Russia smiled before taking his glass and sipping from it again. "Yes—that's the beauty of poison, it has many stages." He tilted his glass in Forrest direction. "Next will be asphyxiation—the constriction of your throat muscles that will close your throat preventing air in or out of your lungs—chu will be dead in seconds." He clapped his hands as Forrest scrambled to his feet.

He clawed at his throat—his eyes were the size of silver dollars, pleading—*why* was the question hidden within their depths. "It's an extract from the poisonous Bella Dona herb. I had it inbred with a secretion of poison from the Black Mamba snake—deadly concoction!" He pointed at Forrest as he crumbled to the ground. Foam spewed from Forrest's lips in a frosty mist of bubbles. "I mas tie all loose ends, my dear lover," Russia said as he stood and made eye contact with the waiter.

The waiter took the silent communication and walked over to the convulsing agent—pulling out his phone, he began snapping pictures from different angles. Russia cleaned his hands on the cloth before wiping his prints from the glass he'd drank from.

"Enough, Gergi, have the men clean up. It's time to move from 'tis place." He tossed the words over his shoulder as he headed for the door.

****

~Kamika Winslet~

I'd never seen anything like it—I didn't understand how folks felt comfortable placing their bandanas on that man's casket. I was appalled at how those men disrespected God's house by bringing their weapons in. It was a zoo in the church house—men without shirts stepped up to the casket and laid money and drugs inside as if the man could take them into the next life. I was sickened with my people as me and Goose made our way to view his fallen brother. I glanced over at Goose, wondering for the hundredth time if it was some kinda macho thing with him or if he merely wasn't the type of man to show emotions. Since I'd known the man, he'd lost the closest people to him and have yet to show any form of remorse.

He released my hand as he stared down at his brother's cold frame. Goose stared at him with an expressionless face as his hand traced the polished oak of the casket. His eyes closed and soft words escaped his lips that I couldn't hear, but I hoped he was also praying for himself. That night the FBI wanted to take him in, though we couldn't get him on the drug charges, it was a grand slam framing him with the murder of Detective Hunter. That funeral would be the last the murderer would see as a free man.

Renta

Chapter Seventeen
Indictments

~Ice Berg~
~Three Weeks Later~

"Ladies and gentlemen today is the day that we prove to the world justice is not just a word, but a declaration of the United States of America that we stand by. Today I will prove without a reasonable doubt that the accused is not only guilty of polluting our great state with drugs but also—he's a heartless killer that's taken the lives of over twenty-five men and women," she began.

The Federal Attorney stood from her seat, Catrina Keen was a tall, lean woman. She had a reputation of being relentless and very convincing in front of a jury. This day she wore a navy-blue pants suit that hugged her model-like frame. The heels she wore were cheap, but a compliment to the outfit. White as ivory with cropped blonde hair, the attorney commanded attention as she took a stack of pictures out of her briefcase before nodding to her assistant. The assistant was a young ambitious Latin man that aspired to follow in her footsteps.

Together they set up a stand with a portable lecture board attached to it. After it was in place, together they began tacking pictures onto it until it was filled in a pyramid pattern. It depicted scenes of compressed blocks of heroin and cocaine. Others of murder scenes littered with spent bullet casings—still, the most prominent photo was the top one. It was a photo of me having what looked to be a dinner of some sort with the infamous drug lord, Russia. The attorney still held four pictures in her hand when she strode over to the jury box and allowed her powerful green eyes to capture every man and woman that sat in those seats. Five men and seven women—*one* Uncle Tom lookin' nigga, I knew I was done for.

The white woman handed one of the photos to the foreperson of the jury. "This photo is a younger version of the man we're here to trial. It's him *before* the surgery he got to elude justice." She allowed the picture to be passed to each juror before passing a second one. "And this is him *after*."

I watched the mild facial expressions of the twelve people that were there to play God with my life. I wondered what the other two pictures were, but I didn't have to wait long.

"Now—the third picture I need you—the great people of this country to brace yourselves for. This picture not only depicts what this man is capable of but also the heartless savagery committed by his very hands!" she spoke matter factly.

As soon as the foreperson set eyes on the picture, I knew I was a dead man in tall grass. He cringed before passing the picture off and looking at me as if he hoped to be the executioner when they strapped me to the table. I was lost as to what the picture was until it got back to the federal bitch, and she held it up for the courtroom to see.

"This, ladies and gentlemen, is a result of David 'Ice-Berg' Swanson's heartless perspective on how to rid the world of law-abiding citizens."

The punk bitch strode closer to the spectators in the court-room—her assistant handed her anotha photo in the process. She glanced down at it before offering him a proud smile and raising it so that all could see—"This is a renowned arts agent—beautiful wife—daughter, and an active member in her community. This woman has never had so much as a speeding ticket! She's—" the attorney was setting the stage before I blocked her lame ass out.

I didn't know who the woman on the photo was, I never forgot a face, and I *neva* laid eyes on that woman before. I thought they were playing games that the feds play when they're thirsty for you, but I was about to get a front row seat to a lesson on the conspiracy of the 848 *CCE*. Continuing a Criminal Enterprise was a bad mu'fucka, and *everybody* that the feds had proof of you fuckin' with was open for indictment. The crazy part was, in the feds a mu'fucka could steal your life off testimony! Hearsay was just as powerful as physical evidence in the feds, and if you were the big willy in your squad—everything the next mu'fucka did fell on yo' head as well. My attorney stiffened beside me when the crooked bitch dropped a bomb on me that was enough to bury me alive.

"Her name is Destiny Kendricks, and she *was* the then leading attorney for the Federal Bureau of Investigations *wife!*"

She allowed the powerful statement to absorb the attention of the crowd before she held up the crime scene photographers photo of Destiny's brains splattered all over the passenger seat of my brother's car.

"Oh my God—she was all I had! *How could you—how—could—you!*"

Someone exploded from the back of the room. I turned to find an elder man clutching a hysterical woman to his chest. I was confused as I turned back to the attorney that handed the photos to her assistant.

"Destiny's parents, ladies, and gentlemen." She nodded to the embracing couple.

"Shit!" My lawyer hissed before bolting from his seat. "Objection, your Honor—the State is using evidence that wasn't in the discovery of evidence. I ask that those pictures be struck from the record!"

Judge McKalister stared at the federal attorney from over his square spectacles. "Is this so, Mrs. Keen?"

The attorney smiled wryly before nodding in acknowledgment. "My apologies your, Honor—it was last minute and—"

"Please strike this from the record, Mrs. Woods," he said to the stenographer who typed all that was said. "No more monkey business, counsel." He nodded as if bored.

Federal Attorney Catrina Keen strode over to her seat with an air of accomplishment before turning sharp eyes to me and my lawyer. "Nothing further your Honor."

****

~Winslet~

The night was silent as me and Goose found peace in the waters of our lovemaking. We'd just had some of the most mind-boggling sex I'd ever experienced, and my heart truly ached for what I had to do, but the government wanted heads to roll and I couldn't be one of them.

"What you thinking 'bout, Mika?" Goose broke the silence as his fingers traced the outline of my back.

We laid naked in the middle of his bed—a damp sheet half covering our flesh as I rested my head on his chest and played with his chest hairs. "Um—I'm thinking—" I paused to look up at him. Pushing a few stray dreads out of his face, I looked down at Goose, he was a handsome man. "I'm thinking that you are the perfect man and have so much potential," I told him as my breath caught in my chest. His pointer finger was tantalizing as he made slow—delicious circles around my left nipple. "You just—just have to *see* it, Bennie, you can be so much more than a—" my voice trailed off.

I could see his golden smile turn to darkness before he finished my sentence, "—a murderer—dopeboy—street?"

I placed my lips against his to quiet the truth of his words. At that moment, his phone saved me from having to elaborate. I reached over and retrieved it before handing it to him.

He glanced at the screen before answering. "Talk to me." He listened for all of two seconds before telling whomever it was that it was okay to come over. He disconnected the call before gently removing me from his chest and sliding from the bed. "Assata's on the way over—he's stressed over Pain's death. I'm 'bout to take a quick shower, Queen, I'll be out in a few. Why don't you get dressed and whip up a little late-night snack for a nigga? I'm hungry as a mu'fucka," he said as he headed for the bathroom.

I glanced at the clock on the nightstand – it was one thirty in the am and Assata's timing couldn't be any better. His name was on the indictment along with forty-five others, so this new turn of events would save me the trouble of having to find Assata when he'd heard his brother had been picked up. I crawled out of the bed and got my phone. I tip-toed through the hallway and paused at the closed bathroom door. I could hear Goose rapping along with some Jay-Z song as I rushed to the living room and made my call.

The phone was picked up on the first ring. "Now—it's done," I spoke to the one on the other end. Without a response, the line went dead.

****

~Assata~

I could see my breath cloud in front of me as I strapped the Friday the thirteenth mask on to my face and kneeled beside a blue Crown Vic I knew belonged to Crazy Loc's pussy ass. I rechecked the banana clip to ensure it was pregnant. There was another one upside down, and duck taped beside it to make it reversible.

"Sup, nigga, let's get this shit brackin'—it's cold as a—" Spyda began before I cut him short with a finger to my lips.

I looked up over the hood and peeled into the darkness. I knew my dawg Thug awaited the signal, but I wanted to lure those boys out to the spot before we put 'em to bed. I aimed the AK toward the street and let the red beam signal my nigga Lil K so he'd play his part. On cue, Heaven, Goose's all-white pit bull was like a white blur cutting through the darkness. She barked so loud I feared she'd wake the neighbors. I was surprised that the night crawlers weren't out—usually, even at two am the natives of Ruth Street were out lurking, but I assumed that the thirty and below winds made even the vampires of the street seek shelter.

Heaven stood in the middle of the yard barking and growling at the house as if it were a stranger attempting to approach her owner. I waited patiently—I knew my plot would pay off, and a few seconds later the porch light clicked on.

"What the fuck, cuz, whose dog is this?" Krazy Loc's first words split from his lips.

Heaven growled as she exposed her teeth to him. The white pit bull's eyes looked red under the glow of the moonlight and as she squatted back on her haunches, I knew her next move would be exactly what I needed.

"Take yo' ass back to where you belong, mutt, before I call the pound on you." Krazy Loc laughed before placing a cigarette to his lips and inhaling the cancerous smoke.

"Who dat, Loc, tell 'em to come in or close the door, homie, it's as cold as a polar bear's nuts out there!" someone yelled from inside the house.

Krazy turned his head to look back into the house, and that was the worst mistake he coulda made. "Nigga quit crying like a lil bitch—it just—" that's as far as he made it before Heaven was on him—viciously snapping her teeth. The bitch nigga fell back onto the porch as Heaven bit down into his arm. "Arrgh—get it off me—helppp—get the mu'fucka off me!" He was screaming and attempting to fight her off.

I knew there was no time to waste as I sprung to my feet and gave the signal. At that moment, a loud whistle cut through the air. "Heaven—here, girl, come!" I heard Lil K shout.

The dog shook Krazy Loc a few more times before releasing him and bolting off into the night—blood stained her white fur. At that moment, I could hear the block coming alive—whoeva was in that house were rushing to their potnas aid, but death had beat them to the sucka. Thug must have pulled the switch because all the lights went out in the spot and as soon as Krazy Loc lifted, he met eyes of the darker version of Michael Myers. I stood above him—head slightly tilted to the left with the Draco clutched in my hands.

I knew Thug had crept to the back of the house and by then, Spyda stood beside me with two tools in his hands. His eyes were bloodthirsty inside the ski mask he wore. Voices could be heard rushing toward the front door but it was too late.

"Please, Cuz, let me make it home. I don't know who you, niggas is, but y'all can have it all!" he cried.

"Say, loc, what the fuck going on?" A dark-skinned nigga I didn't recognize was the first to appear out the door.

His words got caught in his throat when he spotted me and Spyda with hunger in our stares that went beyond the station of food. We had a taste for blood, and I could feel the fear in the air as I let that pipe talk. Fire jumped from the short barrel of the Draco. I held it at an angle as I squeezed the trigga and bared witness to the maliciousness of what those bullets could do as chunks of Krazy Loc's body flew into the air with each shot. His chest was a bloody canvas when the sparks stopped, but Spyda wasn't satisfied. Though he'd hit his mark, and the dark-skinned cat was on his way to meet whoever awaited him on the other side, Spyda ran up on him with the burna aimed at his thinkin' cap.

"Ple—please—" the fallen soldier tried to speak through the blood bubbling out of his mouth and chest.

Spyda was in another zone when he squeezed the trigga on one of the burnas. The sparks from each shot lit up the darkness and caused momentary flashes of light to play over Spyda's ski-masked face. My nigga was on his killa shit as he screamed Boosie's lyrics until the gun clicked. *"Welcome to the mind of a maniac—street nigga—street nigga!"* he yelled before shots exploded from the darkness—straight in our direction.

****

~Harrison~

I stood over Winslet, she knew she'd blew it. I wasn't quite convinced that she didn't tip the perp off and allow him enough time to escape before making the call. One couldn't be too sure with rogue cops. If they'd break their oath, they'd made to protect their country, there was no telling what they were capable of. I stood there with my arms crossed over my chest when my next in command strode into the room with an evidence bag filled with a black substance.

"Heya, Harrison, looks like our boy shaved his locks off," he said before tossing me the bag.

I held it up and examined it—it was long strings of hair. Bennie Trice had cut his hair before disappearing out of the bathroom window. I was just about to respond when a short shapely woman was led into the room by a red-faced field officer. I stared at her peculiarly before she flashed me her credentials.

"Tonya Johnson—Division One Homicide," she acknowledged.

I offered her my hand before dismissing her. "Pleasure to meet you, Mrs. Johnson, but as you know this is a Federal Investigation. The city of Fort Worth nor the state has jurisdiction here." I glanced at the red face FBI agent that escorted her in. "Murry, please escort, Mrs.—"

Johnson cleared her throat before attempting to interrupt me, but Detective Winslet beat her to the punch. "It's okay, Harrison—she's one of mine," she whispered.

I looked from the shaken cop back to her pretty friend. I didn't give a damn who she was, she wasn't one of mine, and that was enough for *her* to be an acquaintance to the ruse. I was on the verge of saying just that when Detective Johnson smiled and handed me a warrant.

"I'm sorry, Mr. Harrison, but I'm afraid you've been outranked. Now, unless the Bureau has placed this woman under arrest, the City of Fort Worth and the State of Texas is placing her under arrest for the murder of Fort Worth's lead detective, Brian Hunter," the words tumbled out of her mouth before she turned to Winslet—she shook her head sadly. "You had us all fooled, Kamicka—you're nothin' but a manipulative—murdering rogue, and it's my pleasure to be the one to do the honors of placing cuffs on you. At one-thirty, a search warrant was issued for your home and the murder weapon you used to kill your partner was found between your mattress."

Kamicka Winslet was speechless as she turned to me for help. I looked down at the warrant and then back up at her; I couldn't help nor argue. Winslet must have seen it in my eyes because she sprung from the couch with tears in her eyes.

"This is absurd—I haven't killed anyone!" she shouted before her frantic eyes found mine. "Tell her, Harrison, tell her she can't do this—we had a deal—remember?" she pleaded.

I looked over at Louding, he seemed amused as he ate slices of an orange that he must have taken from those people's fridge.

"Get the boys to put out an all-points bulletin. Tell them we have a criminal on the loose in the Dallas, Fort Worth area, and he's armed and dangerous," I barked as Kamicka Winslet pled with her one-time good friend as she was being placed into handcuffs.

I couldn't worry about her—we had bigger fish to fry. It had been confirmed that the man, Assata Lamar was, in fact, the same man in the picture with the deceased Tomorrow Kennedy. Though the mask would make it a hard case to fight in court—the tattoo of a Lion's head that was on his neck would even the score.

"I'm sorry, Winslet, but you didn't hold up your end of the bargain," I responded as Kamicka Winslet was being led away.

Renta

Chapter Eighteen
The Devil Does Favors

~Ice Berg~
~Three Days Later~

"Mr. Simmons—you do know you're under oath, right?" K. Sharp, my lawyer questioned the rat ass nigga on the witness stand.

His name was Nick Simmons, but the streets knew him as Funk. He was a hustla from East Dallas that I knew through mutual associates, but we'd never associated exclusively. That's why I sat there shaking my head in confusion as he sat up there and fabricated a story of how I'd sold him ten bricks of heroin. It amazed me how niggas could spend their entire life portraying to be stand up guys, but when the time came for them to stand up—they placed their right hand on the Bible and told on every mu'fucka that was good to 'em.

I watched Funk nod his head in acknowledgment of the question. "Mr. Simmons, you must speak into the microphone so the lady that's typing can hear you clearly. Again—you do know you're under oath?" Sharp repeated the question.

Funk's eyes fell on me before he leaned closer to the mic and answered, "Yes—I know, I'm under oath."

I never broke my eye contact with the fuck boy. They say the eyes don't lie and as I gazed into his, a powerful reality drowned me within a sea of truth.

'The only reason the eyes don't lie is cause the eyes don't have a mouth. It's not the eyes that a nigga gotta worry about—it's the morality of a mufucka that has the power to change a life!' I thought before I was brought back to the present by the sound of my lawyer's voice.

"Good—good, now that that's established. I want to make sure we're clear here. You just told us that on the night of January fifth, you purchased ten kilos of heroin from my client. Is that correct?"

Funk sat up straight in his seat, before making eye contact with my lawyer. "Yea—that's the night I copped the work from dude," he confirmed.

Anger exploded within my internal—I couldn't understand how that bitch nigga could spit deceit from his lips. How he could try to fuck ova a man that he didn't even know. Funk was the eighth witness the state used to nail my casket closed. The eighth lying sum bitch that lied after placing their hand on the Bible.

"*Dude*—can you point at who *dude* is and place a name with the accusation? You do know his name, right? Especially since he trusted you well enough to sell you ten kilos," Sharp marked in a sarcastic tone.

Suppressed laughter could be heard around the room, but at that moment I found it hard to smile. "Yea—that's him, right there in the baby blue suit. That's Ice-Berg—he's the one I got the drugs from," Funk made being a rat official.

I gritted my teeth to keep from tellin' the snake to suck my dick. I turned my head to make sure my circle was hearin' that shit. My homie Big Compton put his fingers in the shape of the letter *C* and rubbed it over his chest to signify the love. Sharp strolled over to where I sat and shuffled through some papers on the defense table. Once he found what he was looking for, he began reading it to himself as he headed for the jury box. He nodded his head before handing the small stack of papers to the foreperson of the jury.

"This, ladies and gentlemen, is a copy of, Mr. Simmons report along with a copy of my client's whereabouts on the night of the witnesses arrest. If you look closely at the dates and times on both documents—you'll not only come to the conclusion that Mr. Simmons was nowhere near my client on the night of January fifth, but he's also guilty of perjury!" My lawyer shouted as he power-walked over to the witness stand.

He placed his hands on the edge of the highly polished wood and leaned forward in order to be eye to eye with the snake son of a bitch, Funk. "Mr. Simmons—how could you have gotten ten kilos of raw heroin from my client on the night of January fifth when he was laid up in a hospital bed suffering from a bomb blast? Could it be that the prosecution has coerced you into—"

"Objection—objection, your Honor, the defense is leading the witness. The witness isn't—"

"Enough—" the judge banged his gavel. "Now, Mrs. Keen, you heard the witness confession just as *I* did. As much as I didn't like it, the objection is overruled. It seems the prosecution is ill-prepared for this case. He interrupted her spiel. The judge's eyes strayed to, Sharp. "Counselor, you may proceed."

My lawyer nodded humbly but knew when to take his victories and run. "No further questions, your Honor," he said before smoothing his tie and heading back to take his seat.

****

~**Assata**~

Silence was thick in the confines of the rented Toyota. The only stain upon the tranquility was the sounds of Goose pushin' golden bullets into the thirty-round clip. I sat reclined in the passenger's seat—a thick cloud of potent Kush smoke swirled from my lips as I stared out the windshield. The Heavens were a canvas, a beautiful picture of tinted reds, purples, burnt oranges, and pinks. It was that time of morning where the sun was on the verge of kissing the horizon, but night seemed to want to wrestle.

"After this shit, I'm hanging the tools ups, lil' bruh. God has His ways of talkin' to every man and He's been talkin' to me for a while," Goose spoke before pushing the clip into its place and jackin' one in the head of the .40.

My eyes traveled to my flesh—I knew the grime of the streets had a way of stainin' a man's soul. The typa dirt that a nigga got exposed to while in the trenches, that shit seeped deep into the flesh and turned hearts black. I saluted my brother's need for change if a nigga's moves become counterproductive—he'd forever have a failure's story.

"Every man has to know his limits, Assata, the streets have an expiration date. Whether you believe it or not, homie, it's *something* up there in that sky. It's *something* that allows your insides—your brain, heart, guts—it's *something* that created that shit to operate in perfect union." Goose looked at me. "It's *something* that's given you more lives than a cat. Somebody got they hand on you, fam, and if you were smart, you'll seek that somebody before your number is called." Bro nodded his head at the little house we'd been camped outside of for the past four hours.

He had told me it was where the freak bitch Snow rested her head. We were there to get info on the Russians. Goose had laced me to what had gone down back at Lovey's spot. It was common sense that if the feds were at Goose's head—nine times out of ten, they were coming for mine as well. It was time to get out of the city before we were tossed inside a steel case. Goose was going back to San Antonio after this, and though I loved my nigga, I wanted to see the world. I was thinkin' somewhere like—like, Tobago Trinidad or something.

"You ready?" Goose disturbed my thoughts.

I reached down, took the FN off the floor and admired it. The gun was so pretty that I kissed it before I nodded my agreement.

****

~Ice Berg~

'I'm going home—I beat these white folks again!' That was my thoughts as my lawyer leaned in and whispered, "They have nothin' on you, Mr. Swanson, you are a lucky man."

I smiled, I knew shit wasn't sweet though. I knew how the feds worked. When they got you—they got you. There were ten more charges I had to beat, but none as big as this one. I was grateful.

"They seem to have one more witness," My lawyer spoke with a frown on his face. He looked confused as he studied the discovery packet.

That set off alarms with me. "What's up, Sharp, why you look so worried?"

He shook his head in confusion. "This—this witness they say his name is—"

"Does the State have anything else?" the judge interrupted him.

Both of our attention shot to the prosecutor. She stood with a smug look on her face. As the words slipped from her lips—my heart cracked. I was as baffled as ever by the name I didn't know if the devil did favors, but I needed a few. "Yes, Your Honor, we'd like to call our last witness to the stand, his name is *James Swanson.*"

****

~Goose~

We crept to the door of the quiet lil' house. We'd sat outside the spot for hours and there seemed to be no life inside. As soon as we pulled up to the door, we knew something was wrong. A purse and small gun were on the ground and what looked to be a single heel was strewn a few feet away. Me and Assata looked at each other with the same kinda expression on our face. *'What the fuck happened?'*

I shrugged at my brother before placing my ear to the door—silence. I checked the doorknob to see if it was locked and it turned with ease. I cracked it open before making sure my bro was ready. He clutched the FN with his gloved hand—his dark eyes hungry for blood. I pushed the door open and spun to the side just in case the reaper was sitting in wait. When no shots came our way—we threw caution to the wind and stepped passed the point of no return.

****

~Ice Berg~

"Can you state your name for the record?" the prosecutor asked.

I was in shock—so many memories ricochet through my mental. Us as lil' niggas—the sacrifices—the blood on our hands. At that moment, all that shit was in vain. A lot of times, the history between people is what strengthens the bond, but it's not enough to strengthen the loyalty. The Bible spoke on shit like that—the betrayal of my brother.

"My name is James Swanson," Nuts spoke in a whisper. My nigga couldn't even look at me—guilt and betrayal was the last stage of unforgiven sin.

"Mr. Swanson, can you tell us your relation to the defendant— who you are, and why you're here today?" DA Keen asked as she strode over to the jury box and handed the foreperson a packet similar to the one my lawyer had shown him.

"My name is James Swanson and I am the younger brother of David Swanson, also known as Ice-Berg," my younger brothers head was down as he spoke.

I took in his appearance—my little brother had lost a lot of weight. He was in a wheelchair and it was plain to see his confidence was shattered. My heart was a vessel of jagged pieces as I took in my family's condition.

'This is my flesh—the son of my T-Jones. I introduced him to the game and now look—he was trading not only his nuts but also my life for a chance at what I robbed him of, His life,' I thought before I was brought out of my thoughts by the sound of the voice I thought I'd never hear again.

"I'm here today to testify against my older brotha."

****

~**Assata**~

I'd just checked the last room and was on my way to find my brotha. We'd split up so we wouldn't be an easy target, but all I'd found was empty rooms and a vague pungent smell that only got stronger as I crept through the dim house. I made it to an open door at the far end of the house—the foul odor was thick there. Peepin' in, I was shot back to the day me and my uncle Brains stormed the Russian's house in search of the same woman that my brother now stood over. Snow was a bloody mess and the closer I came to the scene, the more I thought my mind was playing tricks on me. Her pussy looked mutilated! Snow's nipples were gone and there were various other parts of her that was missing.

Blood was everywhere—whoeva did her in was a lunatic. The foul odor wasn't the smell of death, but of loosening of bowels. Piss and secretion stained her blanket. The weird part was that whomeva did the deed to shawty wanted her to suffer. The soft rise and fall of her chest was the clear indication that the madman wanted her to bleed out. Torture was her companion and though I didn't know how she felt, I could only imagine how many times she'd prayed for death.

Goose leaned over her—he touched her arm and she jumped in agony. Her blue eyes cracked open and though death knocked at her door, the woman's soul just didn't seem ready to leave. Her eyes found Goose before they strayed to me, what seemed like shame—disgust—some sense of repulsion played over her features.

"Un—untie me," she croaked.

For the first time, I noticed that her wrists were bound to the headboard—her ankles to the end bedpost.

"The house clear?" Goose asked.

I nodded before using my free hand to undo her ankles. Goose freed her wrists. As soon as she was free, Snow attempted to close her legs, the room exploded with the agony of her pain.

"*Ohhh my, Goooddd*!" she screamed.

****

~Nutz~

"On the day of October sixteenth, me and a woman named Destiny Kendricks were stopped and surrounded by FBI agents. The car was filled with drugs and guns—there was no way we'd escape and there was no way to beat the odds. It turned out that not only was Destiny Kendricks an informant that had collected numerous wiretaps on me and my circle, but she was also the wife of former District Attorney, SaMage Kendricks," Nutz relived the moment that led to his current predicament.

I didn't know the specifics because during that time I was overseas. I watched my brother clutched the sides of the wheelchair. I knew him—spent my life teachin' him the ways of the gutta. Nutz spirit was broke—the love between us was too thick to ignore. I leaned over and whispered words to my lawyer that made his back stiffen and his eyes go back. We debated as my brotha spilt his guts to the same people that would attempt to slice both of our throats. My lawyer was heated with my decision, but what the fuck could he do. I turned my head so I could see the eyes of the woman that held both of us in her womb, and once our eyes collided—I knew I was makin' the right decision.

"Can you please tell us what happened after you were stopped, Mr. Swanson?" the bitch of an attorney asked Nutz.

He still hadn't raised his head—I hated that shit. "I—I killed her, I blew Destiny Kendricks brains out," he spat.

****

~**Assata**~

We sat and listened to the white woman tell her tale of how the crazed doctor had sliced her up and ate her bleeding flesh. I cringed at the thought of that shit—what kinda cat did that? It seemed as if Snow was avoiding eye contact with me. I didn't get it but didn't give a fuck. It was clear to anybody with a familiarity of death that she was 'bout to check out. She convulsed—cried out in between her words and the flow of blood from her many wounds allowed us a front row seat at the death place.

"I—I have information on how you can find the, Tiger. His home—his family here in the states," she whispered as she laid curled up in the fetal position.

My heartbeat quickened—revenge surged through me as I awaited her next words. "Where? You know we need that. Help us, and whateva you ask is done," Goose vowed.

He and Snow stared at each other for was seemed like a lifetime before she relented. "Kill me," she whispered with tears in her eyes.

Goose looked surprised, yet, I understood her request. A woman's lower lips—her physical attributes are what makes her a female. Snow knew that her time was up. Goose looked at me—he wasn't grasping her reasons, but *I* just wanted the Tiger.

I aimed the FN at her curled form. "You got our word—as soon as you give us what we came for, I'll honor your request."

Snow finally turned her cold blue eyes at me. The darkness in mine must have told her the truth of my promise. "In—in the closet. It's in the safe behind my clothes. The code is twelve-three-zero-twelve-sixteen-five," she revealed.

As soon as the words slipped from her lips, Goose bolted to the closet. Snow and I studied each other—her beauty was still evident even when smudged by tears and dried blood.

"Got it!" Goose shouted from the other room.

Snow nodded with a sad smile. "I wish I could have sucked your dick, but bad girls die young," she said.

I laughed at her brazenness before blowin' her mu'fuckin' brains all over the pillow.

****

~Ice Berg~

"I was hit fifteen times and assumed dead, but they detected a faint heartbeat. I woke up twenty-eight days later—chained to a hospital bed," Nutz had tears in his eyes as he spoke. He laughed bitterly. "They chained me to that bed without a reason. The doctors told me I was paralyzed from the waist down."

The prosecution had had enough of his life story—they now wanted what they brought him in for—me! "That's such a tragedy, Mr. Swanson, and I hope that you've learned something from all this," she said as she strolled over to the jury box and made eye contact with the twelve people that would determine my fate. "That packet is a discovery of evidence. It shows you the kilos of heroin, and pharmaceutical pills that was found in the hidden compartments of the car," she said before turning and walking over to where my brother sat. "Mr. Swanson, can you tell us where you came into possession of this quantity of drugs? From my understanding, those are uncut kilos of heroin that has the stamp of Los Zetas." She cast the bait.

For the first time since he'd been wheeled into the courtroom, Nutz looked up and straight into my eyes. An ocean covered within his—mine resembled the Great Lakes. Silence was as thick as rubber as we all awaited his admission. Slowly a lone tear dripped from his left eye before his eyes landed on our mom's.

"They set this up, they told me I'd walk—Berg didn't give me those drugs. The prosecutor told me I'd—"

"Objection your Honor—objection!" the prosecutor screamed over the chaos that erupted in the courtroom.

I neva took my eyes away from my brother as he cracked that diamond smile, he always gave me when he knew I'd be proud of him, but he didn't know I was about to make the ultimate sacrifice.

Chapter Nineteen
The Death Game

~Goose~

It had been a week since we obtained the info from Snow. That night I had found a writ envelope sealed by a string. I waited until me and my brother was safely away from the scene before opening it. It contained pictures of a woman that was clearly of Jewish descent. She looked to be in her mid-thirties, beautiful—innocent. Two kids that seemed loved, and well taken care of were captured leaving school, playing in their front yard and even leaving the church. Then, there was the man of the hour, the Tiger didn't look so much like a killa around his fam. The only contradiction that told the story of his insanity were the tattoos. As I studied a photo of him kissing the lady on the porch, I wondered if she knew her dude was a murderer.

"Sup, bruh, we gonna sit out here all morning or go put this work in?" Assata asked.

I knew time was of the essence, but I wanted to make sure we wouldn't be walkin' into a trap. This Russian fool wasn't like them lil' street punks we'd laid down, so we had to be 'bout or business when getting at him. I nodded my consent. We'd watched the house all night and morning but there was no sign of the Russian. I began to doubt the address we'd found in the envelope until seven that morning. The front door opened, and two small children ran out. A boy about six years old and another around eight raced to see who would get the front seat. The woman exited shortly after. I took a gentle gamble and assumed she was taking the kids to school. The Tiger didn't seem to be the type to let his woman work, so rather than follow her. I decided to wait for her return.

As we waited, we went over our plan and not even thirty minutes later my patience paid off, shawty returned. Assata slipped a hat on his head that read: '*Season of Bloom*'. It was a flower delivery hat that matched the delivery uniform that my brother hated. He grabbed the dozen roses off the back seat and got out of the car. I watched him walk up the driveway and up to the door. Once he rang the doorbell I pulled my infamous scalpel out of its cases. I watched the door open and the woman smiled at Assata—I had to pray that we didn't have to kill her. The woman had a beautiful smile.

****

~Assata~

"Good Morning, Ma'am, I'm looking for a Mrs. Cardova?" I use the name that was listed as the Tiger's wife. She had big dreamy eyes that first studied my features—the gold teeth, the storm that played inside my pupils. She looked skeptical until I broke the ice. "I know—I know, flower delivery doesn't usually look like this, but my employer is a friend of the family and took a chance at getting me out of the streets." I lifted a dozen roses up higher so she could see them. "If you don't take these, I may end up back at the burger joint." I smiled.

She took the bait—I guess it was better to have a black man delivering her flowers than making her food. She placed a hand over her mouth to stifle a giggle.

"I'm so sorry—I—I just didn't expect—um—" she fumbled over her words.

What she didn't expect was a gangsta with diamonds in his mouth delivering her a dozen roses. She took them before pulling them up to her nose and inhaling deeply.

"Who are they from?" she inquired.

I handed her the card and she did exactly what I thought she would—she opened the card and read the words *I'd* written.

They'll look beautiful on your grave.

First—confusion, then fear etched into her facial expression as her eyes slowly rose to mine. I had slipped the burna into my hand so swiftly that she hadn't noticed my movements. "Don't be stupid, ma, Jesus may have fucked with the Jews, but Hitler incinerated six million of 'em. I'm more like the latter."

****

~Agent Harrison~

I couldn't believe the nerve of the two wise guys. David Swanson, aka Ice-Berg, had literally beat the system *again*! The strange part was rather than walk, his lawyer had stepped over to the prosecutor's table and proposed the oddest thing ever known to the world—a life for a life. David Swanson was willing to not only plead guilty to all counts but also give up all that he knew on the Russian. All this for his brother to be able to walk free. I still couldn't believe it—talking about love! I was just about to call it a day when my desk phone rang. I hated when people waited to the last minute to chat.

"Yello?" I answered.

The noise on the other end of the phone let me know that my partner was on the chopper. "Heyya, Harrison, I have some good news for ya, bud. You need to burn ass to the nearest chopper and get to Denton, Texas. We have a tag on the Assata Lamar perp," He spoke over the wash of the chopper blades.

I wasted no time hanging up and running from my office—my marriage had ended because of those scum and it was time to return the favor.

****

~Assata~

"If you hurt her, I'll murder your entire bloodline." The icy voice spoke through the receiver. We'd tied the Tigers wife up and secured his spot. After we'd searched the entire house, I forced her to give me the number to reach him. She was loyal, but pain had a certain typa effect on people.

"Yea—yea—yea, dick sucka. You can speak all that gangsta shit you choose, but when you took Lovey, you took all that I loved." I used the tip of my tool to wipe his wife's tears. "Now I'm gonna return the favor—your life or your bitch. Either or, don't matter to me, homie." I smiled into the phone.

"Let me speak to her, you piece of shit nigger!" he spat.

The Tiger's accent was thick, I could tell he was beyond angry, but I also could hear the fear just beyond the surface. I looked down at the weeping woman—she looked even prettier with tears streamin' down her face.

I put the phone on speaker and stretched my hand toward her. "It's for you," I proposed.

Lil one's arms and hands were secured by a thick rope, so of course, she couldn't hold the phone. I laughed at my own sickness.

"Jacqueline—baby, have they hurt you—are you okay? Talk to me!" the Tiger screamed.

Through her tears, the woman revealed to us all that she had no idea what kind of husband she had.

"Joseph, wha—what is this? These people—who-who are they?" she asked between cries. "They say you're a—a killer, Joe, is this correct?" she cried but my soul was black—I think the loss of Pain was the last piece of good I had.

"Don't listen—they're liars, Jackie, I'll save you, baby," he vowed. "Where and what time, nigger!" he demanded.

I smiled in anticipation—death was in the air when I replied. "At your house, fuck boy, there's no place like home." I disconnected the call before I looked down at the tear-streaked face of the innocent—it was a fucked-up reality.

Casualties of war were the worst part of the game, yet, sometimes it took innocent blood to be shed in order to obtain the undivided attention of your enemy. Revenge was best served cold as I thought about how cold Lovey's grave was, I looked up at my older brother before looking back at shawty.

"Tell Lovey we're sending her some company," I spoke to the confused expression on her face. Before she could respond, Goose sawed so deep into her neck with his scalpel that her head almost swung free from her body. I had to look away—that shit didn't look that fucked up in the movies.

****

~Ice Berg~

"All rise for the Honorable Judge—" the bailiff announced.

It was two days after I'd confessed to all counts in my indictment. Two days since Nutz signed for fifteen years for the murder of Destiny Kendricks with a suspension of twelve of those years for my cooperation and guilty plea. Those white folks only cared about my guilty verdict. They didn't give a fuck about guilt or innocence—anyway, they could prove that they sentenced *somebody,* they were good wit' it. It was my sentencing and I already knew my destiny was bleak, but I could live with it. I was repayin' my brotha for givin' me a chance at life when he snatched up that DA's bitch. Plus—my lil' nigga deserved a chance at life. I knew niggas didn't respect me turnin' on the Russian's, but how I saw it—he was done either way. The fuck boy would neva be caught anyway—his bread was too long.

"All may be seated," The judge spoke before pushing his glasses up on his nose. "Does the jury have a verdict?" he looked to the jury box.

The foreperson stood. "We do Your Honor!"

I looked over at my moms—my niggas. Some shit just had to happen in order for life to operate in perfect order. I smiled as the white boy sealed my fate.

"We the jury find David Swanson—"

Boom!

The doors to the courtroom blew apart. Before anyone could react, Mexicans with tattoos covering their faces rushed the room brandishing big guns. One ran up the aisle and before they could take cover, he sprayed the jury box with bullets. The judge disappeared inside the judge's chambers, but the bailiff wasn't so lucky—MS-13 were in raw form when I was snatched up and rushed out the courtroom.

****

~Assata~

It was pitched black in the house when the door cracked open and the Russian rushed in with a pistol in his hand. I was surprised he'd come alone.

"Stop right there and toss the gun down," I spoke from the darkness.

The Tiger kicked the door closed and though I couldn't see him through the darkness, the soft thump of his metal hitting the carpet told me he'd complied. His shadow moved toward my voice—the man knew his house. The darkness didn't disturb his mission to save his wife, he made it to the den where I stood and reached to the wall for the light switch. As soon as light flooded the room, the Tigers eyes captured the horror movie that Goose had created with the sharp ass blade he'd become so surgical with.

Blood stains canvased the interior of the room—puddles of the sticky substance of his wife's life source congealed within the soft flooring. His wife Jacqueline was in so many pieces that the coroner wouldn't have a hard time finding the cause of death. The Tiger's first reaction was stunned silence as his eyes digested the slaughter—his wife's remains. What happened next was the type of shit out of a Jason Bourne Movie. Without warning, the Tiger's arm thrust forward—a flash of silver sliding from underneath the sleeve of the black trench coat he wore sliced through the air. I attempted to dive out of the way, but I wasn't quick enough—the sharp blade sliced through my flesh before lodging itself in my left shoulder blade.

Instinctively, the gun I'd held slipped from my grip as an animalistic roar escaped my lips. At the same time, the Tiger rushed in my direction midway to me, he leaped, spun around and kick into my chin. I crumbled to one knee, I was dazed, but when his right leg reared back for another kick that would have surely sent me to a dark place. I mustered every ounce of strength I could and lunged myself into his midsection. Wrapping my arms around his waist, I held on for dear life as we crushed into the wall so hard that his back crashed through it. Sheetrock and dust showered us—but that wasn't enough. The man was beyond himself with rage.

He brought his knee up fast—the impact of it caused air to explode from my lungs as I doubled over. He'd kneed me in the nuts and without hesitation, he used his hands like a sledgehammer and brought them down on the butt of the knife. The blade drove deeper into my flesh and bone. I howled in agony—I knew I was finished.

The Russian stood over me with a menacing stare. "You took her from me—my dear Jacqueline," he cried before reaching down and yanking the knife out of my shoulder.

A wicked smile curved his lips as he raised the serpentine blade high above his head, but before he could bring it down, my foot shot out and connected with his groin.

"Arrgh—" he blurted as he doubled over.

I crawled to my hands and knees—self-preservation raced through my nature as my fingers wrapped around the handle of my fallen pistol. As I rose to finish him off, the Tiger was regaining his composure. The only thing that stopped me from putting one in his melon was the torture my heart had incurred since he'd taken Lovey from me. I wanted to make him physically feel what he'd made me live with mentally. I brought the steel down across his nose—blood squirted a foot high as he stumbled backward. Surprise registered on his face when Goose's arm wrapped around his neck and pulled his head back to expose the soft flesh that hid his esophagus. Before the Tiger could react, a flash reflected within his pupils as the scalpel ran across his throat and left a smiley face in its wake.

Goose released him—the Tiger staggered before his hands shot to his throat in an attempt at stopping the blood flow. It wouldn't help though—his soul was spilling from the wound at an alarming speed. The man fell to his knees and stared up at me with hate in his eyes. I stumbled to my feet before placing the burna between the windows of his soul. Blood poured from him and seeped through his fingers as I stared back at him.

"Tell my, nigga, Shy that I sent you," I spat.

"Fuck you, nig—" Before he could get the word out, I molested the trigger.

His face exploded before the slug exited the back of his head. His body rocked slightly before tilting forward. The silence was thick when I looked over at my older brother.

"Fam—fuck took you so long!" I growled.

Goose shrugged before replying. "I wanted to see if you could still fight."

I stared at him with a puzzled expression on my face before laughter erupted from deep inside me. Once I stopped, I did the most logical thing a man that just escaped the fringes of death could do—I fainted.

Chapter Twenty
Who Shot Ya
~Marcella~

~Weeks Later~

"May—may I speak to, Jazmina?" I whispered into the receiver.

There was a long pause before the person on the other end answered, "Yes, this is she. May I ask who's speaking?" she responded.

Fear surged through me at the sound of her voice—not fear, uncertainty. I was second guessing myself. "Um—it's me, Marcella—" I paused to adjust the phone to my ear before continuing. "—we have a little misunderstanding and now you don't know the voice of your best friend? That's hurtful, Jazz."

Another pause greeted me, I thought she'd hung up until she exhaled a soft breath. "Uh—hi?" she responded skeptically. "How are you, Mar?" she whispered.

I could hear rustling and it sounded as if she'd gotten up before speaking again. She probably didn't want Assata's punk ass to know she was speaking to me.

"*Fake bitch,*" I whispered.

"Did you say something?" Jazz inquired.

"No!" I responded a little too loud. "No, I was commenting on this episode of Empire—Cookie can be such bitch sometimes." I laughed it off. "Um—listen, Jazz, I'm just calling to let you know that I'm sorry. I—I was wrong and—" I paused to be dramatic and gritted my teeth as I spoke again. "I miss my girls—" Another pause allowed silence to become uncomfortable. '*Maybe the damage was too deep to find our past within,*' I thought. "Jazz—you still there?" I inquired before looking at the screen to make sure the call was still connected.

"Yea—yea, I'm still here, Mar. I was just thinking, that's all," she whispered. "Listen, Mar, I've been knowing you since barbie dolls and our first period. You'll always be my girl but look— maybe we can talk tomorrow."

I had the impression that I'd interrupt something. I *hated* the thought of Assata fucking her, it made me sick to my stomach. I honestly couldn't explain why my emotions were so powerful for that man, but I knew he was supposed to be *mine*!

"Oh—okay, am I interrupting something?" I fished. I needed to know where she and Assata were.

"Oh—no!" she answered. "Well, not nothing too important, me and Assata are at the house about to go to the cemetery to visit Shy and Lovey before going to see that new, *Taraji P. Henson* movie."

'Bingo!' I thought. Women were so predictable. "Oh—okayyy!" I laughed. "Well, I won't hold you, I know you and your boo doing y'all. Just call me tomorrow, Mami, and we can do lunch," I proposed.

Jazmina accepted and we said our goodbyes before hanging up. As soon as she was off the line, I sent a text to someone.

//: Peoples Cemetery

****

~Jazzy~

I stepped back into the house after I'd gotten off the phone with Marcella. I sat on the couch before sliding my feet from the flip flops and tucking them underneath me. That call had rubbed me wrong for some odd reason. Marcella was a snake that felt like she was too big to apologize.

'She'd always been that way—so why now?' I wondered.

I pushed the thought to the back of my mind as I glanced at my watch. "Hurry up, baby, we gonna be late!" I whined.

It had been a few weeks since Assata had stumbled in bleeding all over the place. I didn't think he'd live through the night, but my baby was a souljah. They'd used some chic name Kristasia to patch him up and I'd been stuck to his side ever since. It was Thursday night and we were going to Lovey's resting place to celebrate her birthday. Afterward, we were making it a movie night.

We'd had a long talk and we both decided it was time for a change. Denton was too small, but even more—it was too much drama.

Assata's latest experience with the reaper had been his sign that there was no future in the streets. We'd discussed business opportunities, but there was something Assata wasn't telling me— something life altering. I wouldn't pry though, I also had a secret to share with him. We were pregnant and there was no question as to who the baby's father was. I glanced at the time again—impatience getting the best of me.

"Assata Lamar!" I called with a roll of my eyes.

"I'm on my way, ma, be easy," his slow ass shouted from somewhere at the back of the house.

I exhaled slowly as I prepared to wait, picking up the remote, I turned the plasma on, and channel searched until I found the news station. I liked to stay in tune with the craziness the world had going on, especially in Dallas/Fort. Worth. I don't know if it was a sign from Allah or if it was just a coincidence, but what I found on the screen stole my breath. There—on national television were mugshots of Assata and his entire circle.

My mouth hung open as the news reporter spoke, *"This is Anisha Danie with Channel Eight News of Dallas/Fort. Worth. I'm here at the home of Pandora Jacobs, the woman that allegedly murdered her sister in order to fake her own death. As you can see, officials have the area taped off and if you look behind me— you'll see the coroners wheeling what's said to be Ms. Jacobs remains,"* she announced as she and her camera crew focused on the techs rolling a stretcher with a zipped up body bag on it. *"As you know, this is also the woman that is assumed to have had ties to not only the Russian Black Mamba Cartel but Denton's own Kreek Boys. A powerful drug operation headed by an Assata Lamar, Dunte 'Pain' Jackson, Bennie 'Goose' Trice of San Antonio Texas, and an unnamed suspect. The FBI—"*

As she spoke my eyes tried to keep up with my brain. In the background, there were FBI Agents congregating with local law enforcement. I wasn't so naïve to the fact that I didn't know that the Federal Bureau didn't usually involve themselves in normal murder investigations. The screen proved me right when Assata's, Goose's, and numerous other faces flashed onto the screen once again. This time it was to warn the metroplex to be on the lookout for them because they were fugitives and were considered armed and dangerous. It was open season—and it wouldn't be long before the authorities connected the dots and linked me to Assata. My nerves became jumpy as the reporter stopped a tall white guy in a blue FBI jacket.

"Agent Louding, can I have a moment of your time—is it true that Ms. Jacobs was slain in her own home? It's speculated that Assata Lamar and another man was seen leaving her home?" she shot off question after question.

The tall man seemed reluctant, but he stopped and gave her his attention. "At this time we're just speculating, but Assata Lamar and his circle are prime suspects in numerous investigations. If anyone spots these men, we advise the public to contact the authorities immediately!" he spoke with a hint of authoritative urgency. "These men are armed and dangerous—" he was saying when Assata finally walked into the living room dressed to the nines.

"I'm ready, baby, you want—" his words trailed off once he noticed my eyes glued to the television, I was at a loss for words. "What the fuck!" Assata exclaimed before the vase of flowers he'd planned on placing on Lovey's grave fell to the floor and shattered into thousands of pieces. I guess there would be a change in plans.

****

~Goose~

Tonya had packed the last of her things. The detective was leaving her career—her life—all of it behind in order to go on the run wit' a nigga. That night we were leaving that small city behind. I knew I couldn't go back to The Tone—the *state* was ova with for me. Assata had just hit me to inform me that our faces were plastered all over the TV. I was as paranoid as a crack head after a powerful hit of some potent dope. Every lil' sound made me jump.

"Almost ready, baby? Let me get the teddy you like so much, and we can leave," Tonya said before kissing me and heading to the back room.

As soon as she rounded the corner, I got up and followed her. She was in the walk-in closet searching for the nightie when I snuck up behind her and wrapped an arm around her waist.

She jumped in surprise. "Baby, you surprised me!" She laughed and went back to her business.

She never noticed the tool in my hand—my heart ached as I eased it to the back of her head. Tonya tensed instantly, I hated what I had to do, but the odds were already against me and if shit got ugly, I didn't want to take the risk of her turning into a rat. Tonya's heartbeat could be felt through her back—it's drumbeat against my chest in a frantic melody.

"Bennie—what are you doing?" she asked without moving.

My eyes clouded. "I love you," I whispered as a solitary tear leaked from my left eye. I was surprised at how powerful I felt for lady as I tightened my grip on her and hugged her. Love was in my embrace. "I really do, Tonya."

As if the thought of dying had just sunk in, Tonya Johnson attempted to defy fate. I expected it—I held tight before applying pressure to the sensitive trigger. The back of her head exploded through her forehead, blood splashed against my face as her body crumbled towards the floor and I fell with her. On my knees—in the silence of my sins—I cried as I prayed over her body.

****

~Pursuer~

As Assata sped out of the driveway, he was so in a hurry to leave that he never noticed the grey mustang following him. I'd been following him for months and the man had yet to notice. He was clueless about the danger that stalked him. As I followed from a safe distance, Assata made a sharp turn onto Teasley Lane. The move was so unexpected that I had to wonder if he'd spotted me. At the last minute, I had to slam down on the brakes to keep from being killed in oncoming traffic. A silver pickup zoomed pass, but not before the driver honked his horn and gave me the bird.

Furious, I slammed both fists against the steering wheel, I was stuck at the red light. As I sat impatiently drumming my fingers against the steering wheel, my mind replayed my last day with him—the lovemaking. The truth in his stare, I'd followed him ever since our separation and just the thought of him and the exotic looking woman he'd been keeping time with caused jealousy to erupt like a volcano within me.

'I'd learned through the girl, Marcella I'd met, that the girl's name was, Jazzy. My introduction to Marcella was pure luck. I'd been stalking Jazzy's house because I'd found out that's where Assata had been laying his head. One morning I was on my stake-out vibe when I noticed the girl Jazzy leaving the house. I decided to follow her to find out a little more about her. She led me to a beautiful brick home on the outskirts of the city and right as I settled in for the wait, the front door opened and out stormed Marcella. From her disheveled look, I could tell that there'd been a shuffle. I watched as she stormed off to her car and burnt rubber out of there. I followed—keeping an eye on her as I juggled the pros and cons.

By the time she pulled into her parking spot at her apartment complex, I had decided to take the gamble. I approached her and just as I thought—a woman's emotions could make her a snake or a loyal lioness. In Marcella's case, she was a Queen Cobra!

I was snapped out of my reflections by the vibrations of my phone—a text message that read: *People's Cemetery.*

As I glanced down at the screen, a smile kissed my lips.

****

~Assata~

I pulled the SS into the cemetery—I was 'bout to leave the city behind. By the time the sunset, I planned on being somewhere safe and making plans to get to Jazzy's native homeland in Trinidad. I just had to give my farewells to my fam before I left that part of my life behind. The car was silent as I killed the lights. Jazzy and I sat within that silence no doubt trying to figure out how things would be so different now that I was a fugitive of the law. "You don't have to do this—you can get out the car and—" I began before Jazzy held up her hand and interrupted me.

"Look—I don't need you telling me what I can or can't do, Assata. I'm with you, Papi, and I'm not losing you again. Now go speak your peace to Lovey and Shy so we can get out of here, Papi, we have to get somewhere safe," she spoke before rubbing her stomach.

She'd been doing that a lot lately and I wondered if she was prego. I leaned in her direction and planted a soft kiss on her lips. "Give me a moment with the fam and we'll get in the wind. I'll give your love to, Shy—" I spoke over my shoulder as I opened the door and stepped out into the chilly night. I respected lil' one—she was trying to troop for me even though she knew shit was ugly for me.

I noticed the fear just behind the tough girl spiel. I took the burna off my waist—locked it and held it out to Queen. She gazed up at me skeptically.

I smiled my assurance. "Just in case," I whispered.

The night blew its frigid breath as I turned and headed for Lovey's final resting place. I couldn't shake the feeling that for some strange reason, that particular walk felt different from the many others I'd taken. Like—the night was watching me. I shook it off, but one thought was prominent, '*I shoulda brought more artillery.*'

****

~Agent Harrison~

The text from the girl Marcella had led us to the cemetery. "Alpha Two—take your positions. They just pulled into the cemetery. There's two people in the car—our man and what looks to be a woman," I spoke into the radio before signaling to the officer to my left. I pointed to the far left, indicating that he should cover that area. He nodded his understanding before taking off in a crouch. Tapping the wireless device in my ear I spoke, "Alpha Two—do you copy?"

There was a brief pause before a response came over the sounds of rolling thunder, "Alpha Two to Alpha One—ten-four, we copy. I think we have company sir, another car has joined the party from the opposite side of the grounds. It looks to be a woman as well and she just exited the vehicle and disappeared into the cemetery," the officer informed.

Lightening danced across the night sky and I glanced up at the heavens before responding, "On my call, we're taking the subject down. Don't bother about any pedestrians. We're here for, Assata Lamar." My blood was liquid fire in my veins. I loved being in the field and making the world a better place for good working citizens.

"Alpha One—do you have a visual on the perp?" the voice inquired.

I looked through the night vision goggles before responding, "Roger that, Alpha Two, the perp is in our sights." I didn't know what Assata was doing at the cemetery, but he was about to get the biggest surprise of his life.

We had twenty-seven agents surrounding the place. Some were sharpshooters, but *all* of us had the type of artillery that would guarantee no funny business. The Kreek Circle had come to its end!

****

~Assata~

I glanced up to the sky, it was about to rain. I turned my attention to the cold marble that served as my Queens headstone. "I had flowers—even strawberries, your favorite but I messed it all up, Mama. Look, Lovey, I'm just here to let you know, I love you with my entire soul. I know I didn't grow to be the type of nigga you wanted me to be, but I always wanted to be. I never meant for things to turn out this way, Mama, I—I—"

"You just couldn't help who you are! You're a murderous—heartless piece of shit!" a cold voice spat from behind me.

I tensed before attempting to turn and acknowledge the woman I *almost* fell for, but the sharp barrel of a pistol dug into my back. "No! Don't try anything slick, Assata. As Allah is my witness—I'll kill you where you stand!" she cautioned.

Confusion swept through me, though I didn't know why she was there, I knew exactly who the velvet voice belonged to. She nudged me with the weapon. "Walk!" she demanded.

I stood motionless for a second, I wanted to test that gangsta shit she was talkin', but shawty had the ups on me, from my past builds with her.

I knew she wasn't one to bluff—so, I began to walk. "What's all this, ma, when you get—"

"Shut the fuck up!" she cut me off.

My blood raced through my veins as she directed me down a long narrow row of headstones. '*Where the fuck is she takin' me?*' I thought.

At that moment I kicked myself in the ass for leaving my tool with Jazmina. After about three minutes or so we were in the heart of the grounds.

"Stop!" she demanded. "Now, turn around—slowly. Don't think I won't kill you, Satta, on my brother's soul I will!" she passionately vowed.

I turned to face her—slowly, as soon as our eyes met, I became even more conflicted. "Peace, God, how've you been?" she asked as if that was the most rational shit to say.

I never took my eyes off her as her name slipped from my lips, "Peace, Earth, I could be betta—" My eyes strayed to the gun she held steady. "—especially if you weren't aiming a gun in my direction. What's the bidness, Freedom?"

****

~**Jazzy**~

I absently rubbed my stomach—a soft smile curved my lips as I thought about the child that was forming inside me. I had found out that I was six weeks pregnant earlier in the week and had planned on telling Assata *that* night, but things changed when my baby's face was plastered all over the TV screen. I glanced around.

"Come on, baby, we gotta go," I whispered.

I gave him five more minutes, but impatience won out. I clutched the big pistol tightly in my small hands as I slid from the car. The night was cold and windy, but I had to brave it. My baby had been gone too long. I couldn't shake the feeling that something was wrong—*I could feel it*. Slowly, I made my way through the long rows of headstones—I wasn't sure where Lovey's was, but I remembered that it wasn't too far from Shy's. I shivered as I navigated through the night and once I made it to my brother's plot, I began to search for Lovey's headstone. I was on the verge of calling out to Assata when a woman's voice carried on the wind.

I paused when I heard the malice in her voice, "Look at it!" she spat.

My stomach twisted Assata was in trouble. I squeezed the handle on the gun before heading in the direction of their voices.

****

~**Assata**~

"Look at it!" she yelled.

She used the barrel of the gun to point at a neglected patch of earth. Unlike the many others, this one had no tombstone. The only indication that it was a grave there was the small square piece of metal and plastic that told of who rested there. I recognized it as one of the tags they placed on a grave when the dead's loved ones couldn't afford a headstone. I looked back up at Free with an uncertain expression on my face.

I didn't have shit to do with that person not being able to afford a proper burial. "Sup, ma, you want to buy a headstone or something?" I asked only half joking. I was lost—confused *and* pressed for time. *'Fuck was going on? When did she get back? How did she know I'd be at the cemetery? More importantly, why the hell was Freedom aimin' a gun at me?'* Question after question danced around in my head.

Lightning suddenly streaked the sky in a violent scar of light. It illuminated her facial features giving her a pale, demonic look. Her eyes were drowned in grief, Freedom was fighting demons that even a priest couldn't cast out. She seemed to be praying or maybe she was talking to herself, but by the time her words made any sense to me, the sky had begun to cry.

"I got him Ja'Ron—you can rest in peace now," she whispered.

'What the fuck—fuck was Ja'Ron'? I thought.

Free must have noticed the confusion on my face. "Ja'Ron, this is, Assata—Assata, this is my brother, Ja'Ron." She laughed as her eyes became submerged in water that had nothin' to do with the rain. "Get on your knees—now!" she shouted as we both became soaked.

I merely stared. She may have had the upper hand, but if I was 'bout to die, it wouldn't be on my knees. *'On gang!'* I thought.

"Oh—you think I'm playing with you!" Before I could respond fire shot from the barrel and knocked me backward.

My shoulder opened in a spray of blood. "Fuck wrong with you, you, dumb bitch!" I hissed as I clutched my shoulder. That shit was the worst feeling I'd ever felt. "Fuck!" I shouted. Murder bled into my pupils as I attempted to apply pressure to the wound.

"Next time you will be less arrogant," she hissed with a crooked smile. "Now get on your knees!" she sounded like death itself.

Pride is one of the most dangerous things that a man with everything to lose has. I fought beyond mine and fell to my knees in a puddle of muddy water.

A satisfied smirk exploded on Free's face. "Ja'Ron was my younger brother—he came to Texas to make a living. A dirty living, but that's all he knew. My baby brother was all I had—my baby brother was taken away from my life by a heartless—animal of a man," she whispered as lightning flashed again.

Free stepped closer, but her sudden moment wasn't what caught my eye. In the distance, a shadow moved toward us. Jazzy had come for me. I trained my eyes on Free so she wouldn't see the new found hope in my stare, but then her words were like a time machine that shot me back head first into a dark night.

"My brother's name was, *York,* and you took him from me!"

****

~Agent Harrison~

"Alpha Two to Alpha One—there was a shot fired. We have the subjects in our sights, and it seems that the woman has the Lamar guy held at gunpoint. He's bleeding from what looks like a wound to the shoulder," the agent's voice cracked over the radio

I crouched low as the rain pelted my face. I held a pair of night vision Leica Binoculars to my eyes. "Copy that, Alpha Two, move in with caution. Try to proceed with peace, but use force if needed," I spoke as I crept slowly toward the woman, who had just slipped from the car that Assata arrived in. I wanted to alert her of our presence but I didn't want to alert Assata. I could only pray that my judgment was the best decision.

****

~Assata~

"Fuck y'all, niggas! Y'all niggas gonna have to murk me up in here, son. I'm Queens, nigga. Go hard or go home, Duke!" Gusto laughed.

Phew! Phew!

The sweet sounds of fireballs being hushed by a silencer flooded the room. York crumbled to the floor right next to Mi'shay.

My mind was back in that room—the same room where Six had setup the nigga at the strip club. His name was York. My eyes cleared and focused on Freedom before my mind took me back to our first date.

"Where did the Queen Freedom come from? I mean, you popped out of nowhere. To top it off, the accent gives you away. What is it, East Coast?" I'd asked.

Free's eyes twinkled. "You're full of surprises, Mr. Lamar. Yes, I'm from New York—Queens to be exact," she stated boldly.

When my eyes focused again, Free was smiling down at me. "So, you've figured it out, huh?" she screamed. "That night, you and those savages murdered my baby brother for *nothing!*" she shouted.

I noticed how her hand had begun to tremble. Though she hated me—though she burned to avenge her brother, the woman wasn't a killa. A quick glance let me know Jazzy was only about ten feet away. She held the big pistol tight as if it would fly away. Freedom was a quick observer—I could see the alarm in her eyes. She'd noticed my sneakiness, alarmed, she attempted to see what had my attention and that was all the time I needed to act. I sprung to my feet and rushed her.

She heard me and as she spun back in my direction, surprise was born in her eyes, both fired at the same time. I collided with Freedom and pulled her to the ground. We hit the ground with a splash. Without thinking, I scrambled for Free's hands, but it was a frivolous quest. The gun had fallen from her hand when the bullet hit her. Free's face was contorted in a mask of agony—her eyes held mine as she coughed and gasp in an attempt at pulling air back into her lungs.

"I—I hate—hate you," she rasped.

I don't know if I was more hurt that she'd whispered those word or because of the guilt I began to feel for all the lives I'd destroyed. Either or, I couldn't mask it. I watched Freedom take her last breath before I closed her vacant eyes. I rolled away from her before crawling to the nearest headstone that I could find. I leaned against it and glanced down at the inscription engraved into the cold stone. I laughed before reaching down and rubbing my stomach, for some reason it hurt. Using my other hand, I reached down into my pocket and pulled out the bag of pre-rolled blunts I'd rolled earlier that day. I took one from the bag before tossing the rest into the night.

I retrieved the lighter from my pocket and shielded the flame from the rain until the blunt was lit. I clutched my stomach again before I glanced down at the headstone once more—I had to laugh at the irony of it all. I was back where I started from the beginning. A movement to my right caused me to look up, Jazzy stood above me—stunned by her first kill. I understood—taking someone's life could steal the sanity from some of the strongest men. A woman had it worse, without warning, Jazmina dropped the gun and rushed over to me. Queen needed solace—she needed to be reassured that she'd made the right decision.

"Baby, oh my, God—I killed her. I—I—" Her words was lost within soft cries as she wrapped her arms around my neck and held on for dear life. I winced in pain and she noticed. "Are you, okay?" she asked pullin' away from me.

I nodded my head in confirmation. I was good, but I was beginning to see spots. Water streaked down my dark skin and as Jazzy studied me, she was wise enough to know the difference between the rain and the tears of a gangsta. Confusion bled into her stare as her eyes trailed from my face and landed on my right hand that was soaked in my blood. Her pretty eyes shot up—shock—disbelief—all the worst of emotions filled her stare, but she was just as beautiful as she was the night we'd reunited.

Jazmina slowly reached down and took my bloodied hand in hers—the sky lit up as she pulled it away to reveal the hole that the bullet had punched into me. Jazzy's eyes found mine once again and only then did she see the truth of my story. I was dying and this time there would be no escaping the reaper's grasp.

"I'm—I'm 'bout to—to—" I coughed, and a spray of blood flew from my lips. "I'm dying, ma," I whispered.

Jazzy just kept shaking her head no—she wanted to convince herself that I'd live forever, but as I sat there fighting for another breath, I knew that every dawg had its day.

"No—no, you're not about to die, *Assata Lamar*! No, you can't!" she cried. Her hazel-gray eyes were overflowing lakes as we stared at each other.

I was weak—tired, but I feared that if I so much as blinked, I wouldn't open my eyes again. "I love you, Jazz. I—I need you to make—me—a promise," I rasped. There was no bright lights or flashes of the past, but I knew death was there for me and it was being impatient.

"No, I won't let you-you can't die on us, Assata. You—" I raised my hand and stroked her soft face. Blood smeared her skin as she grabbed my fingers and held them to her face. "—anything," she relented.

I smiled, she was my rida. '*I knew Jazmina would carry me with her until she died, yet, that's not what I wanted. I wanted her to live and be happy. Most men hated the thought of another man cutting the female that they loved, but I learned that love was universal. If one truly gave a fuck 'bout someone, they'd want 'em happy regardless as to what happiness entailed.*' After that last thought, Lovey's question popped into my thoughts.

She turned to me with a penetrating look and asked me a question that was so simple, yet so hard to answer. She placed both hands on either side of my face. "Assata—do you care if you live or die?"

As I stepped back into the present, I realized that the time when a person is supposed to change is the time they realize it's too late. There on my death bed, I was finally able to give Lovey her answer, "Yes…Lovey, I want to live," I whispered, but I knew my time had expired.

****

~Jazzy~

"Freeze—don't move! This is the FBI—freeze—get on the ground—don't move!" an onslaught of voices demanded in unison.

Impulsively, I spun in surprise, dark shadows appeared from the darkness. They aimed gigantic guns at me with flashlights attached to them. They'd found us. I turned back to Assata—my heart cried harder than my eyes as he stared absently into nothing. There was no life inside him. I cried for him, I cried for the child growing inside my womb, and when my eyes fell upon the headstone that Assata was leaning against, I cried for the man that was buried underneath the six feet of dirt I sat on top of. Somehow Assata died at Shy's grave. The same place where we'd reunited. With that thought, I smiled before laying down flat on the wet grass. I'd teach my child everything I knew about a gangsta.

The End

Submission Guideline

Submit the first three chapters of your completed manuscript to ldpsubmissions@gmail.com, subject line: Your book's title. The manuscript must be in a .doc file and sent as an attachment. Document should be in Times New Roman, double spaced and in size 12 font. Also, provide your synopsis and full contact information. If sending multiple submissions, they must each be in a separate email.

Have a story but no way to send it electronically? You can still submit to LDP/Ca$h Presents. Send in the first three chapters, written or typed, of your completed manuscript to:

LDP: Submissions Dept
Po Box 870494
Mesquite, Tx 75187

DO NOT send original manuscript. Must be a duplicate.

Provide your synopsis and a cover letter containing your full contact information.

Thanks for considering LDP and Ca$h Presents.

<u>Coming Soon from Lock Down Publications/Ca$h Presents</u>

BOW DOWN TO MY GANGSTA

By **Ca$h**

TORN BETWEEN TWO

By **Coffee**

BLOOD STAINS OF A SHOTTA **III**

By **Jamaica**

STEADY MOBBIN **III**

By **Marcellus Allen**

BLOOD OF A BOSS **VI**

By **Askari**

LOYAL TO THE GAME **IV**

LIFE OF SIN III

By **T.J. & Jelissa**

A DOPEBOY'S PRAYER **II**

By **Eddie "Wolf" Lee**

IF LOVING YOU IS WRONG… **III**

LOVE ME EVEN WHEN IT HURTS **III**

By **Jelissa**

TRUE SAVAGE **VII**

By **Chris Green**

BLAST FOR ME **III**

DUFFLE BAG CARTEL III

By **Ghost**

ADDICTIED TO THE DRAMA **III**

By **Jamila Mathis**

A HUSTLER'S DECEIT 3

KILL ZONE **II**

BAE BELONGS TO ME III

SOUL OF A MONSTER

By **Aryanna**

THE COST OF LOYALTY **III**

By **Kweli**

SHE FELL IN LOVE WITH A REAL ONE **II**

By **Tamara Butler**

RENEGADE BOYS **III**

By **Meesha**

CORRUPTED BY A GANGSTA **IV**

By **Destiny Skai**

A GANGSTER'S CODE **III**

By **J-Blunt**

KING OF NEW YORK V

RISE TO POWER III

COKE KINGS II

By **T.J. Edwards**

GORILLAZ IN THE BAY III

De'Kari

THE STREETS ARE CALLING II

Duquie Wilson

KINGPIN KILLAZ IV

STREET KINGS 2

PAID IN BLOOD 2

Hood Rich

SINS OF A HUSTLA II

ASAD

TRIGGADALE II

Elijah R. Freeman

MARRIED TO A BOSS III

By Destiny Skai & Chris Green

Renta

KINGS OF THE GAME III
Playa Ray

By **T.J. Edwards**

IF LOVING HIM IS WRONG…I & II

LOVE ME EVEN WHEN IT HURTS I II

By **Jelissa**

WHEN THE STREETS CLAP BACK I & II III

By **Jibril Williams**

A DISTINGUISHED THUG STOLE MY HEART I II & III

LOVE SHOULDN'T HURT I II III

RENEGADE BOYS I & II

By **Meesha**

A GANGSTER'S CODE I &, II III

By **J-Blunt**

PUSH IT TO THE LIMIT

By **Bre' Hayes**

BLOOD OF A BOSS **I, II, III, IV, V**

By **Askari**

THE STREETS BLEED MURDER **I, II & III**

THE HEART OF A GANGSTA I II& III

By **Jerry Jackson**

CUM FOR ME

CUM FOR ME 2

CUM FOR ME 3

CUM FOR ME 4

An **LDP Erotica Collaboration**

BRIDE OF A HUSTLA **I II & II**

THE FETTI GIRLS **I, II& III**

CORRUPTED BY A GANGSTA I, II & III

By **Destiny Skai**

WHEN A GOOD GIRL GOES BAD

By **Adrienne**

THE COST OF LOYALTY

By Kweli

A GANGSTER'S REVENGE **I II III & IV**

THE BOSS MAN'S DAUGHTERS

THE BOSS MAN'S DAUGHTERS II

THE BOSSMAN'S DAUGHTERS III

THE BOSSMAN'S DAUGHTERS IV

THE BOSS MAN'S DAUGHTERS **V**

A SAVAGE LOVE **I & II**

BAE BELONGS TO ME I II

A HUSTLER'S DECEIT I, II, III

WHAT BAD BITCHES DO I, II, III

By **Aryanna**

A KINGPIN'S AMBITON

A KINGPIN'S AMBITION **II**

I MURDER FOR THE DOUGH

By **Ambitious**

TRUE SAVAGE

TRUE SAVAGE II

TRUE SAVAGE **III**

TRUE SAVAGE **IV**

TRUE SAVAGE **V**

TRUE SAVAGE **VI**

By **Chris Green**

A DOPEBOY'S PRAYER

By **Eddie "Wolf" Lee**

THE KING CARTEL **I, II & III**

By **Frank Gresham**

THESE NIGGAS AIN'T LOYAL **I, II & III**

By **Nikki Tee**

GANGSTA SHYT **I II &III**

By **CATO**

THE ULTIMATE BETRAYAL

By **Phoenix**

BOSS'N UP **I , II & III**

By **Royal Nicole**

I LOVE YOU TO DEATH

By Destiny J

I RIDE FOR MY HITTA

I STILL RIDE FOR MY HITTA

By **Misty Holt**

LOVE & CHASIN' PAPER

By **Qay Crockett**

TO DIE IN VAIN

SINS OF A HUSTLA

By **ASAD**

BROOKLYN HUSTLAZ

By **Boogsy Morina**

BROOKLYN ON LOCK I & II

By **Sonovia**

GANGSTA CITY

By **Teddy Duke**

A DRUG KING AND HIS DIAMOND I & II III

A DOPEMAN'S RICHES

HER MAN, MINE'S TOO I, II

CASH MONEY HO'S

By Nicole Goosby

TRAPHOUSE KING **I II & III**

KINGPIN KILLAZ I II III

STREET KINGS

PAID IN BLOOD

By **Hood Rich**

LIPSTICK KILLAH **I, II, III**

CRIME OF PASSION I & II

By **Mimi**

STEADY MOBBN' **I, II, III**

By **Marcellus Allen**

WHO SHOT YA **I, II, III**

Renta

GORILLAZ IN THE BAY **I II**

DE'KARI

TRIGGADALE

Elijah R. Freeman

GOD BLESS THE TRAPPERS I, II, III

THESE SCANDALOUS STREETS I, II, III

FEAR MY GANGSTA I, II, III

THESE STREETS DON'T LOVE NOBODY I, II

BURY ME A G I, II, III, IV, V

A GANGSTA'S EMPIRE I, II, III

Tranay Adams

THE STREETS ARE CALLING

Duquie Wilson

MARRIED TO A BOSS... I II

By **Destiny Skai & Chris Green**

KINGS OF THE GAME I II

Playa Ray

<u>BOOKS BY LDP'S CEO, CA$H</u>

<u>TRUST IN NO MAN</u>

<u>TRUST IN NO MAN 2</u>

<u>TRUST IN NO MAN 3</u>

<u>BONDED BY BLOOD</u>

<u>SHORTY GOT A THUG</u>

<u>THUGS CRY</u>

<u>THUGS CRY 2</u>

<u>THUGS CRY 3</u>

<u>TRUST NO BITCH</u>

<u>TRUST NO BITCH 2</u>

<u>TRUST NO BITCH 3</u>

<u>TIL MY CASKET DROPS</u>

<u>RESTRAINING ORDER</u>

<u>RESTRAINING ORDER 2</u>

<u>IN LOVE WITH A CONVICT</u>

<u>Coming Soon</u>

BONDED BY BLOOD 2

BOW DOWN TO MY GANGSTA

Renta

CPSIA information can be obtained
at www.ICGtesting.com
Printed in the USA
LVHW041156030320
648828LV00004B/190

9 781951 081041